BONES AND BOURBON

Deadly Drinks #1

Dorian Graves

Dorian Graves Fiction

EUGENE, OR

Dorian Graves Fiction
3950 Goodpasture Loop
M 341
Eugene, OR 97401
www.doriangraves.com

Publisher's Note: This is a work of fiction. Names, characters, places, and incidents are a product of the author's imagination. Locales and public names are sometimes used for atmospheric purposes. Any resemblance to actual people, living or dead, or to businesses, companies, events, institutions, or locales is completely coincidental.

Book Layout © 2017 BookDesignTemplates.com
Cover designed by M. Brackett - https://mbrackett.art/

Bones and Bourbon/ Dorian Graves. – 2nd ed.
ISBN 978-1-7348960-0-8

To Mom

For raising a reader, inspiring a writer, and above all else,
loving a family.

1 - RETZ

I woke up when teeth clamped down on my arm. I cranked the wheel and almost rammed into a guardrail before I realized I was driving. Neither of these things surprised me. It wasn't the first time I'd woken up just in time to feel the hurt for whatever I'd done while unconscious.

What did surprise me was the identity of my attacker: a lone unicorn head. No body, just flaring nostrils, bloodshot eyes, and two rows of long, sharp teeth that wouldn't have looked out of place on a shark.

I did the stupid thing and kept driving while shaking the unicorn head off my arm. Why? Because I'm Retz Gallows, and I'd learned that even if I had no idea what I was doing when I woke up, I needed to get the job done first and ask what the fuck happened later.

I focused on the teeth that had broken through my skin (and my favorite shirt to boot) and were piercing my arm bones. My first order of business was strengthening my skeleton so the unicorn's jaw couldn't snap anything in half. It took a few seconds for my bones to fortify, heavier but sturdy as stone. The unicorn gnawed my arm as if it were a chew toy. It snorted in confusion, both because of the sudden change and since there were no blood or muscles, only empty space between skin and bones.

In case such wasn't obvious, I'm not human. Well, not all the way. My father was a man of flesh, blood, and too many weapons hidden on him at any given time. But my mother was a huldra; her body was hollow, but she could still punch hard enough to stop a truck in its tracks. I'd seen her do it before too, though sadly, I hadn't inherited nearly the same strength. My brother had, and he got a tail too instead of the hollow body, so he got to be flesh and blood like a normal human, unless something had changed in the ten years since I'd last seen him. Not me, a man at face-value until you dug past the skin and found nothing there but bones. But my bizarre biology wasn't the reason why waking up to random assailants was a semi-frequent occurance.

I imagined how nice it'd be if the unicorn's teeth were fragile enough to crumble. As I did, they fell apart, leaving bits of teeth buried in my arm. The unicorn's head fell unceremoniously into the passenger seat, dripping blood where it landed.

No, I hadn't inherited the ability to control bones, though sensing them was as natural to me as seeing and hearing. It's a power my family wishes I'd never been given. But since I was pretty sure the unicorn head was no longer a threat, I decided it was time to ask the source of my powers what was going on.

I thought, *"Nalem, you'd better not be asleep. Mind telling me where the hell we are?"*

A deep, smooth voice purred an answer in my head, *"If you had bothered to look at the sign we just passed, you'd realize we're in Oregon."*

"In case you didn't notice, I was a bit preoccupied."

A chuckle reverberated in my skull, and I felt the false sensation of my arms stretching, the ghost of Nalem's actions. He didn't have a physical form—not one other than me—but he liked to leave false impressions of one kicking around my bones when mere words and insults wouldn't suffice. *"Of course I did. I can tell when you're borrowing my powers—and besides, who do you think left the head in here in the first place?"*

I rounded another corner as the aforementioned head tried to headbutt my arm, horn-first. I realized I couldn't affect the horn with my powers—it wasn't bone, but something magical that slipped away from my senses whenever I tried. I hardened my bones again and ignored the attack as I took in the scenery. True enough, we were on a half-paved road in the middle of nowhere, surrounded by evergreens trying to block out the bright blue sky. It was late July, so deep into summer that not even Oregon's predilection for rain kept the heat away. My windows were rolled down, seeing as the AC in my ancient Buick had died long ago.

"Two questions, then. Where are we going, and why do we have a unicorn head with us?"

"The same answer to both: We are traveling to visit...let us call her an old friend of mine. Her dwelling is hidden deep in these woods. And she's the sort of woman you always remember to bring a gift for."

I didn't understand what kind of gift a unicorn head was, but Nalem had strange ideas involving etiquette, at least when it was or wasn't appropriate to warp someone's skeleton. I'll be honest, I had no real idea what Nalem was. He had powers over bones, claimed to be old enough that he'd witnessed the rise and fall of Babylon, and my family hated him for more than just his tendency to take my body out on dangerous joyrides. He'd been with me for as long as I could remember, yelling at me to shut up when I cried, reluctantly calming me down when I wouldn't stop crying, and giving me advice with varying degrees of dubious morality. He was like an imaginary friend that settled for a neverending sleepover in my head. Except he wasn't made-up. Imaginary things didn't take over bodies or twist skeletons on a whim.

Which brings us back to the unicorn head. It seemed to have realized my bones wouldn't break. While I now sported some holes in my skin, the wounds were already knitting themselves back together with huldra-inherited speed. The head snorted and launched itself from the passenger seat with a whinny that'd make a shrieking banshee proud. The horn was aimed straight for my eye, so I ducked. The unicorn head sailed over me and out the window, leaving a trail of blood in its wake as it hit the road and rolled away.

Even as I sped up, I strained my powers to feel for the unicorn's bones. There was subtle static from the skeletons of the still-living birds and rodents flitting around the woods, and the oddly comforting presence of bones lost to the undergrowth or strewn along the side of the road. However, the unicorn head rolled to a stop and tried to right itself, snapping its broken teeth. There was no way for me to affect it from such a distance. I could only change the bones of the living if I had direct contact with the body, though I didn't have that limit with dead bones. Which only made me wonder how the unicorn kept moving without a body. I mean, *I* didn't need a heart or other organs to survive, but didn't unicorns?

"Actually, the horns are what keep them alive. So long as the horn is attached to the head, a unicorn could be in a thousand pieces and still strive to hunt you down." Nalem sighed and leaned back against my skull, false impressions in my body being his main form of self-expression when I was in control. At least, I'm fairly certain he didn't have a tiny

body trotting around in my head, but unlike a unicorn, I would die if I popped off my head and cracked it open to check. *The horns are also powerful purifying agents, which might have come in use if you weren't such a coward. But we do not have the time to turn back, and luckily for you, I brought a backup gift in case this exact scenario occurred.*

Translation: That had been a test in disguise, and I'd flunked. I tried to push the thought out of my mind and focus on what a nice day it was. But my curiosity got the better of me, so I pulled my senses away from my surroundings before the static of the living gave me a headache, and checked the rest of the car to figure out what Nalem's idea of a backup gift was.

"...Is that a dead goat in the trunk? What kind of lady would want a goat in the first place, much less a dead one?"

Instead of responding with words, Nalem answered with flashes of memories. I caught a brief glimpse of a gorgeous blonde surrounded by velvet and lace. Following that was a giant snake head adorned in golden scales, fangs bared as she lunged. A few other images spilled into each other, so fast I barely made out details. A city on fire, scales rising from ocean waves, the blonde dressed in mourning blacks under a cloudy sky. The styles were antiquated and the memories patchy; whoever this woman was, she had been around for at least a few centuries. And she could turn into a giant snake.

"Can't we deal with something normal for once?" I asked. My phone rang from somewhere in the car, so I opened compartments to figure out where Nalem had hidden it. *"Something like, I dunno...humans? Crazy cults or secret government groups, same as all the movies?"* The question was rhetorical, of course: most humans couldn't comprehend the supernatural. Whether I used my powers on dissected frogs or accidentally revealed the huldra-inherited hole in my back while swimming, unnatural sights always rearranged themselves in human memories to something that made sense. Even the rare exceptions, like my father, had difficulty believing some of the things they'd seen.

Nalem shook his head—at my question or at me calling movies normal, I'm not sure which—and directed my gaze to the glove compartment. *"The day an actual human becomes a threat to me, without any supernatural influence, will be the day I've lost all glory. Not that such a day will ever happen, little one."*

I ignored his cryptic comments as well as all the candy wrappers that fell out of my glove compartment when I grabbed my phone. I'd already had enough of Nalem's bullshit for one day.

"Hey, Retz here. What's up?"

"I've been trying to call you for hours!" That would be Mom, her already thick German accent even stronger than normal with relief and exasperation With all the chopping and bubbling in the background of what must've been our bustling kitchen back home, she'd taken to stress-cooking to cope, as usual. "There's a note here from Nalem that you left, but he didn't say where. Or why."

"What did he say?"

"Ahem. Erika, taking your son for a joyride. Do not expect to see us for a while. If you need Retz beforehand, suck it up. XO, XO, Nalem."

I glanced outside. To be honest, I had no idea exactly where we were or even what time it was. "Sorry, Mom. I just woke up, and somehow, I'm in Oregon. I'm guessing a few hours out from home, unless Nalem drives like you do."

Mom chuckled, though she still sounded ready to tear her tail out from worry, or would've if she still had one. As a huldra, Mom looked and sounded as human as anyone else, but back in the day when she had lived in Germany, she was a woodland seductress who could crack a man's skull with her bare hands. She was also one of the only people Nalem seemed to fear. Maybe it was because of the time when I was five and she'd chased him through the house with a soup ladle. He was silent a whole week after that. The fact that huldra didn't have bones for Nalem to break or internal organs to otherwise maim also bothered him more than he'd ever admit.

Mom clicked her tongue. "I should not be surprised. I already called the salon and told them you were sick."

Take these before you burn us up." She returned her attention to us while he dry-swallowed the pills. "No clue what the lamia came here for, but they have a heated castle and everything, hidden up in the mountains a few hours away."

"I'd hate to see their bills," Farris muttered. He eyed the bottle of pills. I followed his gaze and noticed that part of the cap was melted. "And you, you're not doing so hot. By which I mean you're too hot. Fever?"

"Poison." Isamu tugged the hem of his shirt down, revealing two puncture marks between his collarbone and shoulder. The skin around it was black with flecks of red and orange where veins should be. "We burned our way out, and I got bit. But I'm fine. We just need a bodyguard to get us out safely."

"You stop that." Aimi prodded her brother's arm again with a mock-punch. "You set our last hiding place on fire the other night. There's no use getting out of here if you die and explode everyone to smithereens."

With the furaribi bickering, the temperature rose. The tips of Isamu's fingertips were catching fire, and Aimi's eyes shared her brother's glow.

I stood and said with my best impression of Alexander, "Both of you, quiet. There's no time for fighting. Our first priority is to get rid of this poison, and then we can work on getting out of here."

Aimi's expression brightened, even as the fire in her eyes died down. Isamu pulled his knees to his chest again, muttering to himself.

Aimi shushed him, answering in what I assume was Japanese, then said to me, "I've got an idea on how to take care of the first part. But we have to act fast—part of the reason why it's an emergency. Either of you fought a unicorn before?"

"Unicorns are real?" Farris asked with wide eyes and an excited grin.

I didn't need to guess what he was imagining; I'd once thought the same thing. I nodded and tightened my grip on the notepad. I had fought unicorns before, once with Alexander and once alone. Neither were experiences I wanted to repeat.

"We sensed a herd wandering into the area last night," Aimi explained, waving toward some of the nearby woods. "And their horns cure toxins, right? Snap one off, bring it back here, and we can blow this joint without, well, blowing up ourselves."

A whole herd. I would've rather beat my head against the supports of the bridge. "I'm guessing you've never fought a unicorn before, either. Or were hunted by one."

Aimi and Farris both stared at me, bewildered.

Isamu murmured, "Hunted? Aren't they just magic horses?"

I tried so hard not to laugh.

Even after I explained to Farris the many dangers of unicorns, including their carnivore-sharp teeth, high speeds, and their inability to die until their horn was removed, he still said he wanted to ride one. I told him he was an idiot and would he please set the sword down, but he did not listen.

We were doing a quick run through town for gear before chasing unicorns. I stocked up on ammunition and found a bulletproof vest for Farris, which would at least protect him from taking a unicorn horn to the gut. Yet he still refused to even hold a gun, which was why we ended up checking out melee weapons. Most of them were for show, tucked in a small corner of a store that sold everything from fantastical statues to kitschy bumper stickers.

"Okay, I think I get how dangerous unicorns are," Farris said as he tested a rapier, taking a few swings and jabs before realizing how flimsy it was. His movements were rigid; I wasn't sure if from lack of practice, or because he had other things on his mind. "I'll find out all about that in an hour or two, if things go right. Right now, what I'm dying to hear is, how dangerous you are, babe?"

I was looking through packs of incense, seeing if any of them would be at all useful for exorcisms or other alchemical uses. "What do you mean?" I did not meet Farris's gaze.

"Well, you never told me what you and your family are, and here our clients have you pegged with one look. Makes me feel left out."

"There's not much to tell."

"Then it'll be easy to say, right?" Farris tried another sword, this one sturdier. He swung it with flourish, ending the strokes with it pointing at me. "Look, I've been with you for this long. I've figured out you're weird, your old man's even weirder, and that unicorns would eat me up like a Thanksgiving turkey."

"But you needed to know all that."

The look Farris gave me was dark, something I wasn't used to in his eyes.

I set the incense aside. "Hulderkind just means one of my parents was a huldra. It means I'm a bit stronger than other humans, and I have a tail hidden under my jacket. You found that out when we first met." No need to discuss the other drawbacks, ones I wouldn't let come up.

Farris moved the sword away from me, now examining the blade itself. "This brother I just learned about. Is he the same? I mean, I saw you pretty much break a wall once, so I'm asking in case he doesn't have the same taboos against punching people that you do."

"He doesn't punch. And no tail. Retz just heals fast like I do, and—"

"Wait, his name is Retz?" Farris raised an eyebrow. "What kind of a name is that?"

"Town in Austria. Erika named us after places there, where she and Alexander traveled. My birth name was from the region they were married in. So...if you ever meet any of my family, and they call me something other than Jarrod, that's why. I left home shortly after I changed it."

The darkness in Farris's eyes slipped, and he ruffled my hair. "I can punch anyone who slips, if you want. Like your brother, if we find him like your old man asked."

I imagined it. Retz would cringe. Then Nalem would decide on payback. I shook my head. "No. Bad idea. He'd break your hand, at the very least."

"I thought you said—"

"It's not because he's a hulderkind." I tapped the side of my head, right where Alexander would. "He's possessed by this...thing. Calls itself Nalem, sometimes takes him over. And they can control bones." Farris shuddered once he realized the implications. "Exactly. No punching."

"Right, and when were you going to tell me this?" When I didn't answer, Farris rolled his eyes and gave the sword a few more swings. His strokes were looser with this blade, far more fluid. He looked almost professional, and he noticed this as well. "When I remember where I learned this from, I'm so not telling you."

"You're being passive-aggressive."

"And you are being a secretive little shit. We're even." Farris sighed, another uncommon thing. "Look, haven't I been here for you ever since we met?"

I nodded. "It marks you as considerably more reckless than most."

"I'm a masochist who needs stubborn assholes like you in my life, I guess. But that's beside the point." Farris leaned over and tapped the side of my jaw, nudging me to look at him face-to-face. "Look, babe, you've gotta start trusting me with these things. We're partners, and that means we're together in everything. And I'm obviously the clueless fool here, so you need to keep me in the loop."

I wanted to say I would. The words just wouldn't come out of my mouth. Alexander's reminders echoed in my head that only my weapons would last me, nothing else, not even him. And that had turned out true so far.

I reached up and tugged a strand of Farris's hair, pulling it taut before letting it spring back up. "If the unicorns and my brother don't scare you off, I'll consider it."

I could tell by his face that it wasn't the answer Farris wanted, but the one he expected. He planted a quick kiss on my nose before standing up straight again. "Right. Well, I think this sword's the one for me, so let's check out and blow this joint." He grabbed my hand and pulled me toward the counter. "So wait, when it comes to unicorns, is the virgin myth true? If they mistook me for a virgin, could I ride one?"

I had to remind him that it wasn't true, and even if it was, he hadn't been a virgin for years and riding a unicorn was still a stupid idea. There was so much more I should have said, but I had no idea how to say sorry and mean it.

The main reason humanity has lost belief in supernatural beings is that those creatures have learned how to hide. Methods range from taking a human form as the furaribi do to living so far from civilization that they won't be bothered. The latter is easier than one would think, particularly since humans are so loud. It's easy for any creature to hear and hide before they can be spotted. Such was probably the modus operandi of the unicorn. The secret to encountering them, then, was being as silent as possible.

I crept through the woods in the vague direction Aimi had indicated. It would have been easier if I had ever learned to sense other supernaturals, but it was a skill I should've asked Erika to teach me before leaving home. The forest floor was covered in dried-out undergrowth and pine needles; almost all of the trees were pines, save for the occasional maple or oak.

Farris attempted to follow my quiet lead, but he hadn't spent ten years training under Alexander. Branches snapped under his shoes, and he kept walking right into the low-hanging branches. His makeshift scabbard nearly fell off his belt.

"So, should we be looking for unicorn tracks?" he asked, brushing a few stray twigs out of his hair. "Funny-shaped bite marks or sparkling rainbow shit or something?"

"That's the thing. Unicorns don't actually have horse hooves. More like deer feet, so it's easier to confuse their tracks with something else." I ducked under a low-hanging branch, pointing it out for Farris to avoid. "However, point out if you do see any weird teeth marks. Especially in any corpses."

My plan was to search around the closest ponds and lakes in the area. Contrary to popular belief, unicorns are actually related to the water-dwelling kelpies, with similarities such as a fondness for large expanses of water and a taste for blood. Unicorns, however, do have a purification agent in their horns in order to cleanse their favorite liquids—tainted lakes or poisoned blood, for example—so it serves as an effective antivenom. The problems, of course, are finding a unicorn and removing its horn in the first place. Their usual methods for dealing with opponents tend toward gore and eat first, ask questions never.

The rain increased as we wandered, skies darkening with the coming of night. I kept looking back to make sure Farris was behind me and not lost. The one time he wasn't there, I heard him off to the left, crashing through the brush before calling me over. I followed suit, but stopped before I reached him. He'd done what I'd asked and found a body. It had been a bear in life, but in death, it was just a husk. The side of its body was ripped apart, as if blades had ruptured it from the inside. It had no skeleton.

Farris turned to me. "If unicorns can do that to a body, I don't think I want to ride one anymore."

"That's not a unicorn's work." I willed myself to take a step closer. My heart raced, and I ran my tongue across my teeth even though they hadn't been melded together in years. Funny, how Alexander had brought up Nalem last night, and now...but there was no mistaking what lay before me. No one else could mutilate a body in such a way. "Remember what I said my brother could do?"

Farris gripped the hilt of his sword, teeth bared in disgust. "Great. Didn't realize your old man was sending us on a suicide mission." Confusion settled onto his face. "But what's he doing here? He's not in the same line of work as you, is he?"

I shook my head. It was a strange coincidence; I'd just heard from Alexander, and already, Retz was near. Did my father plan for this? Or worse, did Nalem?

I got to my feet. There weren't any nearby footprints. Either I'd have to search for Retz later, or he'd sense my familiar skeleton and come to me. I wasn't sure I was ready for either option; I'd assumed I had at least a few days to finish this new case before facing this reunion.

I resumed our search, grabbing Farris by the sleeve to make sure he followed. "Another warning. If Retz looks shy, he's fine to approach. If not, keep away. And he can only control your bones if he touches you. Dead bones are always fair game."

Farris was quiet for a moment. His knuckles were white as he clutched the hilt of his sword. "He wouldn't actually hurt us, or at least you. Would he?"

"Quite the opposite. I'm his favorite toy." Just remembering Nalem and his idea of fun made me want to turn tail and run. But with him was Retz, and I hadn't been fighting this long to give up on him just yet.

A shout rang out in the distance. It was followed by a low roar that, if I strained my ears, might be mistaken for neighing. Farris and I exchanged glances, realizing what had to be the source of the noise.

For the first time in over a decade, I ran toward my brother's aid.

I was there when my brother was born. It was not in a hospital, but in the woods, the same woods I was born in. It was night and a group of women I didn't remember seeing before escorted my mother into the shadows of the trees. They all had hollow backs with only darkness inside and tails peeking out from under their skirts and dresses. My mother was the exception, for she was the only one there who'd successfully married a human.

Alexander and I had to wait on the outskirts of that forest. The other huldra wanted me with them, saying that all women had to be present, but Alexander argued that I was too young. I was secretly thankful to be kept back, not just because being called a girl didn't sit quite right with me even then. I heard Erika screaming from that forest. I didn't want to see my mother—or anyone—in such pain.

I was swathed in an oversized jacket and playing with fallen branches. It was an exercise in not breaking things that my father ordered me to do. A grown huldra can straighten a horseshoe with bare hands and no effort; I had only a fraction of that strength as a child, but I still had to keep my power in check. Huldra were never shining examples of self-control, and I was to be an exception to the norm.

While I was aware that I wasn't a pure human, it had yet to hit me that such was strange. We all looked normal, after all. Mother worked hard to keep up appearances, but it seemed that a lot of folks tried hard to be perfect people. How often I broke things was attributed to childhood clumsiness. And from a young age, Alexander reminded me that we were normal. Do not discuss Mom's hollow friends or the strange creatures that sometimes visited our house. The most important rule, however, was to never hurt someone else, especially not other people, even if other humans did.

But in that moment, I was a normal girl, in an abnormal situation, who was excited to meet her baby sibling. I wasn't yet burdened by who he'd grow up to be; I hadn't even learned that I was getting a baby brother as opposed to a sister.

It took hours in the cool September air for my mother to return, the entourage of her sisters-in-spirit behind her and a small bundle in her arms. I was filled with awe and confusion. I hadn't expected the baby to be so small.

"How is it?" Alexander asked as he got to his feet. "What is it?"

"He is well. The birth went just fine." Though obviously tired, sweat dripping down her skin, my mother smiled. She was dressed in a white cotton dress, the same color as the blanket the baby was swathed in. "His name is Retz. That's where we were married, remember? I think it's a fitting name."

"I don't think he looks like a Retz," I piped up. I hadn't learned to hold my tongue yet. Alexander shook his head, but mother smiled and tilted the baby so I could get a better look at him.

"What do you think he looks like, then?"

My face scrunched up in thought. I finally responded, "A potato."

Mom chuckled softly, looking at the boy in her arms. "I suppose he does look a bit like a potato. But he's just been born. He'll look more normal once he grows a bit."

Alexander ran a finger across the wisps of black hair on my little brother's head. The baby yawned, clenching its tiny fists. My father's face bore too many emotions to name.

"Is this one human?" he asked.

I realized the implication, even if only subconsciously. I was not human, not the way my father was. I was something else. And judging by the sound of his voice, something wrong. Something not normal at all. Unsure of how to deal with this information, I returned to my pile of sticks and snapped them. All I had to do was pinch them in the middle for the wood to splinter and crack between my little fingers.

Shaking her head, Mom pulled down part of the blankets wrapped around the baby. I didn't see what they were looking at, didn't hear them whisper that no, my brother was even less normal than me. I was still wrestling with the budding concept of my inhumanity and the potential of being stuck with a brother that resembled a potato for the rest of my life.

I would later learn that those were the least of my worries. Before Retz even reached his first birthday, we would meet Nalem.

It was the same night that my brother first died.

5 - RETZ

It was getting dark by the time I reached the town where I sensed the furaribi, and with a herd of log trucks blocking the view of the road, I barely caught the sign informing me that I'd arrived in Cottage Grove. I hadn't decided if I should follow the bones and track down the furaribi, or focus more on finding a hotel.

If Nalem had been awake, I would've asked him which option he'd suggest, but as it was, he'd fallen back asleep. Waking him up would be less than beneficial to my health and the peace of many buried corpses, so I kept quiet. Instead, I figured I'd drive by and see if I could find where the furaribi were staying. My Buick sputtered in protest, but it protested everything I did.

I found myself driving along a river, which the summer had dried into a bare trickle, brightly colored rafts and lawn chairs abandoned on the banks. The streets were empty—no, there was one person hurrying along, short brown hair illuminated by the orange glow of the streetlamps turning on. She clutched a large paper bag to her chest. I watched from behind as she tripped on a cracked piece of sidewalk in her haste, sending the bag's contents flying.

I pulled over and rolled down the window, calling, "Need a hand, miss?"

"That'd be awfully nice of you!" The girl—she looked a bit younger than me, but not by much, was on her knees and trying to return the fallen supplies to the bag, which was tearing. I reached into the back of my car and found a few old fast-food bags, which I figured would be better than nothing, then hopped out and tossed things in. The items were mostly canned foods, tissues, and a bottle of fever reducer.

"Thanks," the girl said as I handed her what I'd saved, her warm skin a deep enough brown that mine was cold marble in comparison. She looked up at me with eyes that seemed to glow. "Oh! I didn't realize there were more of you."

I raised an eyebrow as I helped her to her feet. "What d'you mean by that?"

"Your brother didn't mention you'd be coming. They should already be off in the woods, but I can't sense that far to be sure." She brushed off her skirt before looking at me again. "My name's Aimi. I assume you're the...older Gallows brother?"

I admit, I stood there for a moment without saying anything. What was Jarrod doing out here, why would this girl hire him, and did we really look that similar? And again, seriously, he'd been gone for ten years and the day I make a deal for help, he reappears out of thin air? This had to be a trick, right?

Instead of dumping my sudden mental freakout on this gal, I forced a smile and said, "Younger, actually. What gave me away?"

"Finding a half-huldra's rare enough as is," Aimi said, "And you two look kinda alike. You've got the same nose." She glanced at the car, then up at me with the sweetest smile. "I'd hate to be a bother, but could you help and drive me back to my brother? The sooner I can get his medicine to him, the better." I wasn't used to such blunt requests with Nalem around, so I couldn't find words. "Please?" Aimi added, mistaking my pause for hesitation.

"Sure, I guess. Saves me a bit more time before trekking into the boonies, after all." I opened the door to the passenger seat for her. I apologized for the mess at the same time she apologized about distracting me from my job. We stared at each other for a moment, before she giggled and thanked me again.

As I sat down, I sensed for the furaribi. It was like a hook, starting from the toe bones in my pocket, reaching out into the world until they sank into something and pulled me in. Except this time, one tug was from farther away, but the other right next to me. I glanced at Aimi again. She looked human—but Lady Delight did say the furaribi had a human disguise.

At least Nalem wasn't awake to berate me for not paying attention. Then again, finding both my target and a lead on my brother in the span of five minutes? Maybe his paranoia could help me figure out who was throwing me for a loop and how. Unless he'd set this up, and was poised to knock it all down the minute I let myself relax. Who knew how busy he'd been during his last joyride?

Aimi instructed me on where to drive, but I already had a good sense using my powers. I parked next to an old covered bridge and helped Aimi carry her groceries underneath to the other furaribi, who was wrapped up in blankets and pressed against the iron supports of the bridge. His skin looked like wax and his eyes were dimmed candles, but just getting near him reminded me of the lamia's overheated castle.

"I'm back!" Aimi chirped. "And I found more help! Turns out, our brave little warrior forgot to mention his brother." She turned to me and introduced us. "Isamu, this is...the younger Mr. Gallows?" She cast a sheepish smile at me for having forgotten to ask my name.

"You guys can call me Retz," I said. The furaribi stared at me for a moment, as if waiting for me to explain the joke behind my strange name. "Mom apparently thought naming me after an obscure village was a great idea. But hey, 'least it's easy to remember."

"Right. Pleasure to meet you," Isamu murmured, obviously feeling it was anything but. His eyes shifted from a dim orange to a bright gold as he stared at me. "This one seems different from the other."

"Well, duh. What'd you expect, identical twins? Clones?" Aimi reached into the bag I was holding and pulled out the bottle of fever reducer. "I got a stronger kind. Don't spit 'em up this time."

He took the bottle with a wary glance. The sides of the bottle melted in his fingertips, filling the air with a rank scent of burning plastic. "How'd you afford these?"

"Tell a good-hearted churchgoer how hard life is but how much faith you have that it'll all turn out okay, and they'll do anything for their 'mutual' god." Aimi giggled, though it didn't quite reach her eyes. "Helps that I'm irresistibly cute."

"Keep dreaming." Isamu returned his attention to me as he fumbled with the bottle. "Are you okay? You feel poisonous." He furrowed his eyebrows, shook his head. "No. That's not it. Sorry, I just..."

"It's all right, I get what you mean. But I'm here to help you guys." Even if it meant recapturing them first. "I would've come with my bro, but I had to get the car fixed."

Isamu craned his head over to look at my parked Buick. He recoiled as if I'd shown him a mauled kitten. "That's your idea of fixed? What'd you use, duct tape and spit?"

"Sam, play nice." Aimi nudged her brother with her foot; he grumbled and opened the bottle to take his medicine. Aimi said to me, "So, gonna check with the guys? If they're in the woods already, their cell phones won't work, 'cause there's no service in the mountains."

"I, ah, figured that. Don't worry. I'm pretty good at tracking them down." I wiped my sopping hair out of my face. Guys, as in not just Jarrod? She mentioned Jarrod but no Dad, which seemed odd since she'd talked about how similar we all looked. But who else would Jarrod work with? Hell, I hadn't seen him in years. He could've met a lot of people in that time. "So, remind me what they're up to? They didn't bother to fill me in, just told me to check on you guys after I was done with the car." The lies were so natural, it was like Nalem was controlling my face and whispering in my ear. I wasn't sure if I should be proud or sickened.

"Little Miss Optimist here thought making them chase down unicorns for their horns was a good idea," Isamu grumbled. The tips of his cropped brown hair glowed a faint orange. "Doubt you can do much to keep 'em from being trampled."

I was so thankful that Nalem was asleep; he'd cackle so much over the fact that I'd had a unicorn horn and just let it sail out my car window. "You'd be surprised. I'm not what you'd call a fighter, but I've got tricks up my sleeves."

"That would explain a few vibes."

"You're getting fussy. Enough out of you." Aimi set down her bag and took me by the arm, escorting me back to the Buick. Her cheerful demeanor slipped with each step. "Sorry. He's...gotten worse, since your brother came through. Not weaker, but...he's burning up. Not a good thing, when you're made of fire." She sighed, and the air around us ticked up a few degrees. . "Think you and your brother can hurry up with that unicorn?"

"Of course. You'll see us again soon." I got back in the car, and Aimi waved me goodbye. She returned to her brother as I drove off, and as soon as she was out of sight, I sighed and released the false confidence I'd held. That had been close, and, quite frankly, I was scared. I had to worry about betraying not just the furaribi now, but also my brother. Which only raised more questions, the biggest one being where Dad was, if he wasn't with Jarrod. Or what Jarrod was doing here in the first place. Believe me, I wanted to see my brother again more than anything, but not like this. Not in the middle of Nalem's schemes. What if Jarrod got in the way, and Nalem hurt him like we were kids again?

Or worse, what if Jarrod found out what I was doing, and decided all the time he'd spent trying to save me was worthless?

And yet, the absence of Nalem's snide commentary made the situation all the more distressing. I prodded him in the back of my mind; he groaned and induced a migraine until I stopped. While I let the ache die away, I pulled over again and tried to sense Jarrod's location. It had been years since I'd felt his skeleton, but I figured it'd feel the same, just a little more worn.

I reached out, brushing against the whole town in my search. The bones of the living were static, which only served to worsen my headache. But there, just a few miles out of town, was a familiar sensation. I only sensed part of him, mostly the head and torso; the rest was obscured despite my best efforts. Deciding to ask Nalem why that was later, I got back on the road and followed.

I sometimes wonder what would happen if I had a time machine. In my darker moods, I imagine using it to find the first people who perpetuated the myth of unicorns being sweet and innocent creatures, and turn their spines into corkscrews. But I'm getting ahead of myself.

The closer I got to Jarrod, the harder it was to get a sense of his body. There was weird static coming from his limbs and neck, so trying to follow his path for more than a few seconds gave me a splitting headache. The man with him, who wasn't our dad or anyone I recognized, had a similar but less severe effect across his whole body. So instead of following them, I tracked down my other target: the unicorn. It was the same size as the one I'd dealt with earlier, with large healed-over cracks in one of its legs. Its head was bent, but it wasn't chewing anything; I guessed it was drinking water at a lake.

I stumbled through the woods, armed with only the light of my cell phone to keep the darkness at bay. The plants around me were dried out from the summer heat, crunching under my shoes despite my efforts to keep quiet. I used my powers to keep tabs on my targets; the unicorn stayed where it was, unfazed, while my brother and his companion meandered here and there the few times I risked a migraine to check on their progress. My powers also gave me glimpses of all the other wildlife nearby, every bird soaring over the trees or squirrel racing along branches. Even clearer were the corpses. Baby larks that never flew right, a fallen deer, and close to where I was, a bear. It must've been sick, because nothing felt either broken or old. I took a quick detour to reach it.

It had been dead a few days. Its body was bloated and starting to rot. Something had taken large bites out of its side. The bones were all intact, though. It was almost beautiful, how strong and sturdy they were.

"Take them with you."

I nearly jumped in my skin. *"Fuck! When did you wake up?"*

"Just now. Can't help but appreciate art." A groan echoed through my head as Nalem stirred. *"You're preparing to fight something, correct? I am still catching up, but that's the gist I'm getting."* Even as I spoke, I felt him sifting through

my recent memories. He did that whenever he wanted, and I had yet to figure out how to do the same to him without his permission.

"Searching for my brother and a unicorn horn. They're both nearby."

As I'd expected, Nalem cackled at the mention of the unicorn. He sat right up, the irony stronger than any shot of caffeine. *"Oh, and such a horn would have already been yours, if only you weren't such a coward! Now we have your brother on top of that... Yes, bring those bones along. The unicorn will try to kill you, and considering how long he's lived the hunter's life with your father, your brother might try to join in."*

I didn't want to believe him. He was just trying to unnerve me, but the words crept under my skin anyway. My chest constricted, and the smell of death wafted around me. I thought I'd left it behind at Lady Delight's, but it found me here.

"Point taken. Got any advice?"

"Sharpen that rib to tear it from the skin easier. Or turn back now. Have you already forgotten how poorly you handled your last encounter with a unicorn?"

No way I was turning back. I was going to find my brother, and I was going to help those furaribi before I dragged them through hell again. I followed Nalem's advice and sharpened the bones, helping them rip out of the layers of muscles, organs, and fur. Once removed, I held the complete skeleton there for a moment, standing in front of me as if alive once again. I reached out and stroked its skull from forehead to snout, marvelling at the design. Nalem was right; it really was art. My fingers came away slick with blood.

I pulled it along with my powers as I continued my trek. Keeping the bones in formation taxed my focus, so I let them drift, making sure they stayed close to me. I sharpened the limbs and paws until they seemed more blade than bone, and wished for some of that Pacific Northwest rain to clean my new weapons for me. I was getting closer to the unicorn, and Jarrod was now somewhere behind me. I wondered what he would think if he found me with what he was looking for. And would we be able to talk, or would his old fear of Nalem resurface?

"Oh, he'll fear me either way. It's no less than he deserves. The real question is whether he's strong enough to get over it." Nalem pretended to crack his knuckles, filling my thoughts with slow, sickening pops. *"I guess I'll stay awake for this brawl. Someone will need to save your hide."*

"Who says I need to be saved?"

"Trust me, you will."

I thought I knew what I was in for, having already fought a unicorn, but this one wasn't in pieces. I'd assumed earlier it was drinking. It was, but not from a lake. Blood from a buck it had gored dripped from the tip of its horn, droplets sliding down its white face. Even so, it seemed serene as its pure white coat reflected the pale light of my phone. The image was marred by its fiery red mane, a jagged scar along one leg, and rows of too-sharp teeth that rivaled those of my bear.

It turned toward me, lowering its head to charge. I pulled the thickest bones from the dead bear in front of me, fusing them into a shield as I backed away with my makeshift blades. The unicorn's horn shattered through my defenses. I screamed as I scrambled out of the way, tripping and falling onto my ass. The unicorn passed me without enough room to turn around. With a low whinny that I'm sure was actually a demonic laugh, it skidded to a stop. I was still trying to get to my feet.

Time for a different approach. I took the remaining bones I had and fused them into two thick blades. I stood in the unicorn's way, the skinniest matador with no one to cheer on his probable demise. The unicorn's horn was centered on my chest as it charged. I sent the blades forward, right at its knees, and jumped out of the way into the bushes. I wasn't quite fast enough; I hit it, but its body clipped my right side as it hurtled to a stop. The bone-swords were embedded in its front legs, but it kicked them off. The joke that unicorn blood is rainbow colored is a lie—they bleed just as red as what they eat.

I tried to get up but fell in pain instead. I had a few broken ribs and a fracture along my shoulder and shin. It was an easy fix with my powers, and at least I didn't have to worry about internal organs getting punctured. I never understood myself what energy fueled huldras and let us talk or think without organs, but at least it was intangible. Then the unicorn stared me dead in the eye as it snapped a bone-sword in half with its teeth. Even if I didn't have organs, I wouldn't be immune to decapitation if a unicorn decided to play vampire and chomp through my neck. Nalem swore and took over our powers, patching up my bones while I struggled to my feet. The unicorn whinnied, ready to charge again, and there was no way I'd get up fast enough.

My ears rang with the song of a shotgun blast.

The unicorn's side bled in torrents. Another shot rang out, tearing through its neck. The wielder of the gun stood between me and the beast. I recognized my father's old leather duster, and, hard as it was to believe, the man now wearing it. He fired a third time, and that shot tore off part of the unicorn's face, revealing its teeth in a morbid smile. Another guy ran in with a sword, but I stared up at the man with the shotgun instead as Nalem knit my bones back together.

"Jarrod?"

Without looking, he offered me a hand. I pulled myself to my feet, bones fixed but body still reeling from the pain. He didn't quite reach my shoulders; puberty hadn't blessed him like it had me in that department, though he'd finally grown a beard, and he looked strong enough to take out the unicorn with his bare hands if he had to.

After all, he'd inherited the strength from Mom's side of the family. As it was, the other guy, a well-dressed man with his wavy-brown hair tied back, had almost severed the unicorn's head with his sword. It had fallen over, but was still trying to bite him despite the blood loss.

I stumbled forward and stepped on the unicorn's neck near the wound. Nalem severed the vertebrae of the neck. I tried to make the head float up to me, but it wouldn't budge with my will—Nalem reminded me that unicorns lived so long as their horn was intact, no matter how many pieces they were in.

Before I figured out how to remove said horn, the other man picked up the head, glancing at my brother as he did. "Imagine this mounted on someone's wall."

"That's disgusting. We just need the horn." Jarrod strode up and snapped the horn off; the unicorn, both head and body, stilled. Jarrod turned the horn in his hand while the other dropped the head into the mud and kicked it for good measure. Jarrod then glanced up at me. "Hey."

"Hey yourself." I managed an awkward smile and wave. Jarrod didn't look like he wanted to fight me, but I was still on edge. When Jarrod left home ten years ago, he hadn't been so dangerous or worn. Reminded me of Dad, but smaller. Especially the way he held his shotgun. "Thanks for the save. I thought I was done for there."

"Told you that you'd need help," Nalem grumbled. I felt my body numb and realized that Nalem was taking our body's pain on himself, at least for the time being. *"A reward for not completely fucking up. You get it back once we find shelter."*

Meanwhile, Jarrod placed the horn in a pocket and returned the shotgun to a makeshift holster inside the coat. He was dressed in all black, including the oversized leather duster—the exception was a scarf, green as the plants around us would be once the rains hit.

"You're welcome," he told me. He didn't meet my gaze. "Nice to see you again, Retz. Didn't expect to find you here."

"Same. Funny, the way coincidences work." With a mental twitch, I added, "Nalem says hi too, along with a couple choice insults. Feel free to imagine those yourself."

"Right back at that predictable cretin. My words entirely." Jarrod took the unicorn horn back out of his pocket and turned it in his hands. Through the dried blood, it was almost translucent. I bet it'd look beautiful if raised to sunlight, but the night was still young. "Don't suppose you two are taunting unicorns for fun."

I shook my head. "Nah. I was in the area and gave a nice girl a ride. She happened to be your client, and recognized me as your brother, so she told me where you guys went. I figured a reunion might be nice after all this time, considering you and Dad dropped off the face of the earth." I turned toward the other man. "And you are?"

"Farris O'Reilly, at your service." He bowed with a mocking grin. "I'm your brother's assistant. Just learned that you exist and all, but it's a pleasure anyway."

"Yeah, likewise. Assistant? Thought that was your job, Jarrod."

Jarrod still didn't meet my eyes, but he nodded.

"Dad's not around at the moment, then?"

Another nod.

I assumed the worst, and the only thing to distract me was the unicorn corpse, gross and bloody. "This really isn't the place to play catch-up, is it? Look, I've got a car to drive us back to town. You can drop the horn off, and we can figure things out from there."

Jarrod and Farris shared a look. Farris nodded toward me and smiled. Jarrod sighed and finally looked at me. His face was way more tired than it should have been, but he still had Mom's eyes—they refused to settle on blue or gray.

"That would be smart," he said. "We should get out of here before the rest of the herd arrives. Mind leading us?"

"Not at all. This way, gentlemen." I waved them over. I'd left the bag with the furaribi toes in my glove compartment so I could find my car, not that I'd tell them that. The darkness settled in, and Farris and I tripped over everything in and out of sight. Jarrod had to haul us to our feet. Aside from a few reactions to Farris's quips, my brother and I didn't speak.

Jarrod finally asked. "This where you and Erika call home?" There was a nervous tone to his voice when he added, "Alexander and I had to lie low for a while. When we checked later, you and Erika had moved."

"Mom, you mean. We ended up in Washington. And we tried to call, but it said your number didn't exist."

"We were far off the grid." Jarrod sighed. "So then, what brings you to this neck of the woods?"

I thought a moment on what lie to spin. I decided to go with a twisted truth. "One of Nalem's old allies contacted him. We were heading down south to meet up with her, but I thought I felt something familiar here, and it was getting dark, so I decided to stop for the night. Then a cute girl with a hot skeletal structure—literally—asks for a ride, and who would I be if I said no?"

"Heh. Fate works in weird ways, doesn't it?" Farris strode ahead of me as we spoke, when the road came into view. "Say, look at that piece of shit."

"That's my piece of shit." I shone my phone at the Buick for a better view. It looked even more rusted and broken down in my phone's sterile light.

Farris made a painful noise, and Jarrod said nothing.

"It isn't pretty," I said, "but it'll get us to town and all that. Sorry in advance that there's so much clutter."

"The whole car is clutter," Farris muttered as he got in the back. He smiled as he backtracked and added, "But hey, better than a lot of things I've driven. It's lived-in, yeah?"

Jarrod sat in the back with Farris, and I wondered how he could sit so still with a shotgun digging into his side. I turned the ignition, and it took a few tries to finally awaken the Buick. It slid onto the road with crackling radio static as the headlights flickered in the night.

"You guys got a hotel room yet?" I asked as I switched the radio off.

"Haven't looked," Jarrod responded, arms crossed and eyes focused outside, not that there was anything to see but the vague silhouettes of trees against the sky.

Farris put an arm around Jarrod's shoulder. He said, "We should. Sleeping under the stars is nice and all, but we've been at it a couple weeks now. I could stand to stare aimlessly at a ceiling for a bit."

Jarrod snorted in response, and I thought I saw the ghost of a smile. I'd expected Jarrod to shove Farris away, but he surprised me by relaxing into the contact instead.

Farris must've caught me glancing at them in the mirror, because he said, "Sorry, didn't finish introducing myself. I'm dating your brother."

"Are you now? Jarrod, I didn't take you for the romantic type." Well, I hadn't taken him for any sort of type—I'd never been able to imagine him with anyone else, but when we'd last seen each other, I was ten and he'd only just become a teenager.

Jarrod sighed. "Farris, is this really the best time?"

"I prefer not to leave explanations for the last minute." There was something sharp to his voice that made Nalem stir, but we didn't say anything. "But yeah, we're a thing. Have been for, what, two years now?"

Cottage Grove was dark and desolate by the time we made it back, being the sort of town that closed its doors early. It seemed the only lights in the town were the neon signs of the sparse 24-hour fast-food chains, the vigils of their bored waiters only occasionally interrupted by a trucker taking a break from their travels.

"That's not bad. Longer than I've ever held a relationship." Well, I'd never actually had a girlfriend. Or boyfriend. Or anyone, for that matter. Nalem scared everyone who tried to get close, even friends. "Did Dad find out?"

"He...yes. Seemed to approve." Before I could ask what he meant, Jarrod straightened. "Shit. Retz, step on it."

"Why?" I asked. In response, Jarrod pointed out the window. There was a bright orange glow, which I realized wasn't from a neon sign. The gray smoke from a fire trailed into the sky like the stars along the Mikly Way had gone dark. I sensed the link from the toes in my glove compartment. "Well, isn't that lovely? Don't suppose you can shoot that to smithereens."

"Seeing as that's one of my clients, it'd be unwise." Jarrod was already removing his shotgun and setting it under the seat. "The sooner we can get the unicorn horn to them, the better. I don't suppose you can stop him from moving?"

The memory of how Jarrod learned that particular trick of mine lodged itself in my throat. It took me a moment to find the right words. "No, still haven't learned how to do that without physical contact. Or killing him. Say, got a fire extinguisher in that coat of yours?"

"No." Jarrod removed two pistols from their holsters on his belt. I recognized them as the same kind Dad used. "Farris, promise me that if any fire trucks show up, you won't actually hijack one unless strictly necessary."

"Oh, how you love to ruin my fun. Fine, I'll be good this time." Judging from the reluctance in Farris's voice and the fact that the statement was needed in the first place, Jarrod had a less than morally upstanding boyfriend. Oddly enough, I wasn't surprised.

We reached the covered bridge the furaribi had been under, and found it completely charred, burned boards littering the rocks and waters below. The trees were also burned, though not on fire, and the grass was scorched. The fire was farther along the road, heading toward the nearby high school. And there was a fire truck in the middle of the road, but it was completely melted in the middle.

"Guys? I don't think a truck's going to be enough."

6 - JARROD

It is a sad fact of life that neither humans nor huldra are fireproof. In a world of furaribi and other flammable creatures, immunity to fire would've made my job a lot more tolerable. As it was, a rampaging being hot enough to melt metal was close at hand, and I had nothing to stop it with. Such was my luck.

I assessed the situation as we got out of the car. One melted but not-yet-combusted fire truck, its occupants on the side of the road hiding and calling for backup. One nearby school, dark, hopefully empty. Lots of dry plants from the long summer, and only a river for water nearby. My estranged brother, my boyfriend, and myself, in possession of one car, three guns, and a sword, all of which would be useless against the flames. And bones, if we let Retz terrify the general populace.

And finally, two furaribi, one of which was racing around, screaming and clawing at his burning flesh. Their human skin was replaced by volcanic rock with bright veins of lava blood, and they had patches of flame along their extremities and replacing their eyes and hair. With arms warped by flames to resemble wings and talons instead of feet, I could see the distant connection to a phoenix—or a harpy born from a volcano. Other than their difference in size, Isamu being taller and lankier than his sister, the only way I could tell them apart was that Isamu was leaking blue flame. Aimi kept trying to grab her brother and hold him back, but he whirled out of the way whenever she got close. I guessed the pain from the poison was driving Isamu mad.

"All right. I've got an idea." I cracked my knuckles, first turning to Retz. I reached into my pocket, pulled out the unicorn horn, and handed it to him. "It's harder to burn bone than most common metals. You can still make bones fly through the air, right? Try to pierce Isamu with this. Pointy end first."

"I thought you were Mr. Marksman now, not me." Nevertheless, Retz took the horn from me, gripping it tightly in a hand with too-long fingers and knobby joints. "Besides, I can't control this. It's too...magic-y." I shot him an incredulous look. "Unicorns are freaks, man."

I decided it best not to argue. "That...doesn't explain anything, but fine. Any bones nearby you can summon? Tie it to a corpse and use that. There's bound to be a bone somewhere around here you can use." That taken care of, I turned to Farris. "Go talk to the firefighters. Find out what happened during their encounter, and make sure they don't try to call in cops or anything. We don't want the furaribi dead."

"Sure thing, babe," Farris answered with a mock salute. "But what about you?"

"I'm getting him to the river." Before either of them had a chance to protest, I ran. I had the speed and stamina they lacked, and the leather duster dealt with fire better than anything they wore. If they weren't idiots, they'd stick to the jobs I'd given them instead of getting themselves hurt.

I didn't even have to shout to get the furaribi's attention. Isamu saw me coming, his flames flaring as he screeched. The shriek was louder than my guns, nearly tearing out my eardrums. He charged, and I was reminded of the unicorn that tried to impale my brother. Aimi screamed at me to run. I waited until Isamu's smoke burned my nostrils and I felt the heat wafting off his skin, then ran, switching directions without warning. Zigzagging, a technique some animals use to get predators off their trail. It worked. Isamu wove behind me, the unpredictable changes in direction confusing enough to slow him down.

I didn't recognize the words when he shouted again, but the meaning in his voice was clear—pain. Sparks of blue fire leaked from his mouth and nose. His voice was going hoarse, flames dimming.

"Don't fail me now," I muttered, even though he couldn't hear me. "We're almost there." We reached the bank of the river, serene in comparison as it lulled past the outcrops of rock. The mad furaribi was right on my tail. I hit the edge of the bank and jumped. Years of practice ensured a landing on the rocks in the middle of the river, but keeping my footing on the uneven surface proved a harder challenge. I looked over my shoulder. Not expecting me to jump and hot on my trail, Isamu should've crashed into the water, dousing the flames. Then I'd dive back in when he was human again. But he wasn't there, and there were no trails of steam from the river to indicate he'd fallen in.

Confused, looked up and realized the wings replacing his arms actually worked. He dove toward me.

I jumped out of the way, arms out as I tried to keep balance on the rocks. Dried-out moss crackled under Isamu's talons as he landed. Heat wafted off of him. He took a step forward, and where he'd just stood was charred black. I reached for my pistols on instinct, even though they wouldn't have done any good.

His glare focused on me. "If you want to take me back," he said, voice cracking as he spoke, "then you're going down with me."

"I'm trying to help you," I reminded him. "I'd never turn you in."

His laugh was more of a bark. "Of course you'd say that!" His fists flared up, and he came at me once more.

With nothing to defend myself, I had to avoid his blows, cowed farther and farther along the length of the outcrop. Escaping into the river wasn't an option, because then Isamu would fly off and back into trouble. The possibility of being burned meant nothing if it kept others safe. Isamu's blows came close, grazing my duster, blistering deep holes in it but never breaking through. I refused to use my strength to hurt others, and Alexander trained me to dodge. Until Retz finished preparing the unicorn horn, that's all I needed to do.

It arrived once I was at the highest edge of the rocks. The horn sped through the air, tied with metal wire to a dead, half-rotten, and devoured duck. It might've looked morbidly comical, had I not had a furaribi screaming and trying to swat me into the river and its jagged rocks below. The duck hesitated in the air; I cursed how long Retz took to aim, and Isamu for not holding still. I took one last step back and realized I was out of rock. Only the very edge supported my foot, and it was going to give way if I shifted any more weight onto it.

With no other choice, I grabbed Isamu by the shoulders to hold him still. The flames flared again in a cacophony of orange and blue, and I smelled my gloves and skin burning. The furaribi tried to pull away, but I didn't need to hold him forever. The duck froze in the air before diving in, the unicorn horn burrowing into the furaribi's back. Everything screamed, even me. I stumbled backward, unable to keep my balance. We fell together.

I crashed into the river, only realizing how deep it really was once water rushed into my lungs. Every time I tried to break the surface, Isamu pulled me back down, determined to take me out with him even as his flames died down. And unlike other huldras, Retz and my mother included, I had internal organs, including lungs that were ready to burst.

It wouldn't be the first time I nearly drowned.

I didn't remember passing out, only waking up on the grass, soaked and heaving water out of my lungs. Collective sighs of relief surrounded me as I opened my eyes again. Half the world was blurry, but Farris crouched next to me. A few firefighters stood nearby.

"Done pretending to be a mermaid?" Farris asked. He was also soaked, and the concern he attempted to mask by the joke was still apparent.

My mouth felt waterlogged, so I nodded instead.

"Good. I hope that wasn't part of your plan."

I finished coughing up water as a firefighter knelt to treat my hands. My gloves were burned to the point of uselessness, and my skin was blistered red and peeling. Wielding my guns would be a bitch for a while.

Instead of dwelling on this, I answered, "It wasn't exactly what I planned, no. But what matters is that it worked."

Farris snickered, sitting down next to me, his leg pressed against mine. The contact was more comforting than I wanted to admit. "It did, but stupid stunts are supposed to be my job."

"I'm aware. Did you drag me out? Is everyone all right?"

The medic put something on my hands that made them sting even more. I tried not to wince.

My boyfriend smiled. "Yeah, I got to play the hero and save you. You're welcome." Farris ruffled my hair before continuing. "Isamu's passed out, so Retz is driving him and his sis somewhere they can stay for the night. Seeing as they burned down the last bridge they stayed under."

"Got it. And you're my hero. Happy?" I closed my eyes. My immediate worries dealt with, I resigned myself to being patched up. I already had a feeling this fight wouldn't be the worst of it—after all, there was the matter of my brother to deal with. I had Retz for the time, but Nalem couldn't resist trying to pick another fight for old time's sake. If I was lucky, that would be all he'd try. Luck and I never got along too well.

At least the rain finally eased up, and I allowed myself a minute to pretend that everything was going to be okay.

Farris and I got a hotel room at the same place Retz did, which was the cheapest place in town. It reeked of cigarette smoke, and a family of flies had taken up residence in our room. It was better than sleeping in the rain or in another bus. The hour was late, and Retz agreed that it'd be best for all of us to get some sleep before talking more.

I still wasn't sure what to make of my brother's sudden appearance. Yes, he'd helped me twice already, by finding the unicorn and stopping the rampaging furaribi. But running into him so quickly after my meeting with Alexander seemed too good to be true. Things never went so easily for me.

"It's just too great of a coincidence," I said as I checked my bandages again before trying to sleep. "I swear someone's playing us, and I'm not sure who."

"As I said, Fate works in strange ways." Farris watched me from his perch on the edge of the bed. "Supernatural things seem to attract one another, right? Makes sense to me."

"This might not be a coincidence, Farris, but I don't believe it's Fate, either. That doesn't exist. No, someone's playing us. Nalem or Alexander, not sure which, but one of them is."

Farris frowned, crossing his arms over his knees. "Fate does too exist, but fuck it for now. Whatever it is, why question things? You got your brother back, and we delivered that unicorn horn. That's good, right?"

I lay down next to him on the bed. "Maybe. Ask me when I've figured out what's going on." My vision swam, and it wasn't just from my lack of glasses—I had a spare pair, but I didn't wear them to bed. No, I knew what this was. "I think Alexander's calling again."

"Can't you take a message and get back to him?" Farris ran his fingers through my hair, his skin smelling of river water, smoke, and the pizza we'd nabbed for dinner. I pressed my head into his hand as my chest constricted. "Seriously, he just called last night. Or was it morning?"

"He's got no sense of time. The dead never do." I yawned, feeling myself on the edge of both sleep and consciousness. "Say, he's encountered more supernatural things than me. I'll ask if he's heard anything about Fate for you, okay?" This was not the first time Farris had brought it up, after all. Perhaps the concept held a clue to his past.

Before my boyfriend answered, I passed out for the third time in twenty-four hours.

I woke up again in Alexander's glade. Everything was coated in dried blood, and I feared it was my father's. But Alexander loomed over me, claws on my back bringing me to my feet. His body seemed more torn than the night before, his vines and already-ragged clothes bearing new gashes and bloodstains. The latter was strange; I was fairly sure he didn't have organs anymore, and they didn't work if he did.

"I'm guessing we've both had a rough time of it," I said, showing him my hands.

He clicked his tongue in obvious distaste.

"Yeah, I panicked when I did it. Dumb move. But I've got good news. Retz is with me."

Alexander's vines writhed around his body and face. He tapped the side of my head with one claw.

"What do I think? Well, sir, I'm not sure. It happened pretty quickly after you made your order, after all this time. I was working on another mission nearby, not actively searching for him."

I expected to be reprimand for my priorities. Instead, Alexander shook his head. He tapped my head twice, then traced something against my skull; two straight lines connected by a diagonal, the letter N.

"He hasn't shown up yet. Mocked me when he said hello through Retz, but hasn't exerted any influence beyond that." Unwilling to look into my father's eyes, I stared at my burned and bandaged hands as I cracked my knuckles. The pain felt distant there, though the pops echoed through the clearing. "I shouldn't have found Retz so quickly. Did you plan this somehow, or was it Nalem? Is he up to something?"

Alexander tilted his head up diagonally, a simultaneous yes and no. He made a few signs indicating that he had some sort of effect, but the motions he made weren't clear. I got the gist that he'd cut ties with something but wasn't sure how literally he meant it.

"I see. I think. So, what's next? Am I still bringing Retz here to you?"

Shaking his head, Alexander pointed to himself, mimed a scurrying motion with two claws, then pointed to me before gesturing to our surroundings.

"We just need to reach Arcadia, then, and you'll find us." A nod. My stomach lurched and twisted at the thought.

Arcadia is not our world but connected to it. My best guess was that it was an alternate dimension of some sorts. I didn't understand it, except that what I'd seen was overgrown with both plants and a strange energy. Alexander and I had first found it by accident during a case gone wrong, and it was there that he died. But he didn't stay dead; the plants themselves seemed to consume him, crowding over his corpse until he emerged the being before me. Even as we discussed finding Retz, I was not entirely sure this really was my father and not some simulacrum born from the union of Arcadia and my father's body.

For the time being, I had to believe it was Alexander. "Makes sense, sir. Your area does seem a bit too...bloodied to entertain guests."

Alexander shrugged.

"I felt a weird power the last time I was here. Did it cause this?"

Another nod, followed by a flurry of motions and signs too fast for me to read.

"Right. Er, is it dead?"

Another yes-and-no.

"Going to come back, you think?"

A shrug. In such moments, I wished he would speak, no matter how much trouble it might cause.

I tried to ask more questions, but he refused to answer. Instead of being thrown out of the vision like the night before, Alexander instead eased me out of it, letting the world slowly fade.

As he disappeared, I remembered to ask, "Sir, Farris and I were wondering...does Fate exist?"

The last image I had before waking up in the hotel room was my father's body shaking with laughter, but he didn't make a sound. His tongue was a rotting worm.

I couldn't see anything in the hotel, due to darkness and me not currently wearing my glasses. The bed was warm, at least, and Farris was curled up against my side.

I was worried that I'd woken him up, but then I heard him say, "About time. You weren't looking so hot."

"Confused is all. I didn't understand all of what Alexander said. Still not telling me what's going on."

"Runs in the family, hmm?"

I turned to face Farris, even though I could barely see him. He was shirtless, which revealed his freckled skin and the intricate crescent-shaped tattoo on his shoulder. As with everything else from his past, he had no idea where it came from.

"I explain things when they're important, Farris. If I don't, they're not worth worrying over. Can we drop this argument now?"

He grumbled, sitting up to wrap an arm around my shoulder and hold me against his chest. "You and your trust issues. I swear, it ain't good for you. Your head'll explode or something."

"If heads exploded from secrets, there'd be a lot less people in the world." I tried to pull away. "I need to go for a walk."

"We're out of booze, and you had two big fights in one day. Rest, you idiot."

I was strong enough to escape if I really wanted to. But I didn't want to hurt Farris, which would've been all too easy. It wasn't him I wanted to leave, just the argument.

I settled into his embrace. "Fine. But you can't tell me you wouldn't do the same if you wanted to keep someone safe from your past."

"I'd tell you if I had a family or wasn't a full-on human before we'd hit four years, and that's not nothing." Instead of continuing the argument, he held me tighter. "Once I do remember things, we'll figure out who I am together, good and bad. Promise."

I shuddered. "You don't understand how dangerous promises are."

"Everything's dangerous, if you think on it hard enough. You just have to decide what to trust in."

He made it sound easy. I wrestled with the idea the rest of the night until I gave in to sleep. My dreams were filled with fire and silent laughter.

It wore Retz's face, but as soon as I opened the hotel door to check on my little brother, I was sure he wasn't there. The smile he wore was too close to a sneer, his posture too open. I stood in the doorway as Nalem got to his feet. Old waves of fear resurfaced.

"I stopped by to see if Retz was awake, but it seems I've got you instead."

"Indeed. It's been awhile, Jarrod. You've grown up." Nalem rocked onto his heels, a habit he and Retz now shared. "Haven't grown in any good ways, far as I can tell, but I suppose you deserve credit for still being alive."

"Cut the shit." I refused to let myself get riled up by him. I was done letting him worm his way under my skin. "We're going to check on the furaribi soon. Retz better be in control when we head out in half an hour. Got it?"

"Is that a threat? Because you should remember how I react to attempted intimidation." He strode up to me. I backed away, not wanting to let him get so close. Something slammed against my heel, causing me to stumble. Nalem grabbed my forearm. The bone he'd struck me with, a small animal skull, floated over his shoulder and back into the hotel room. "What game should we play this time? See how long you can last with a broken arm or leg, maybe? Fuse your teeth together? Oooh, maybe I'll start decaying a bone and only stop when you've figured out which one it is. That'd be fun, wouldn't it?"

I clenched my fists. The pain from my burns flared. "We don't have time for this."

"You don't. Nor should you, after what you've done. But me? I have all the time in the world. Even when this vessel is gone, I'll keep going." His grin faltered. He tilted his head as if I was a curious toy while his hold on my arm tightened. "Now, whatever happened to your limbs? They feel...tainted."

I didn't have time to react. Nalem controlled my skeleton to enter the room and closed the door behind me. It was boiling hot inside. Stopping my bones to keep me from moving of my own accord, he pulled up the sleeves of my shirt and duster. My skin was covered with interlaced green runes, crisscrossing from my shoulder to my wrist. Nalem touched the skin and must have realized it wasn't human flesh at all.

"I've heard of sewing magic into a body, but never with plants." I couldn't tell if he was disturbed or intrigued at first. Then I understood it was both, and I'd somehow unnerved our family's nightmare. "I assume these are also on your legs and neck. The bones have the same feeling to them."

"You assume correctly." A pause spread. He knew what I wanted to ask, and I didn't want to give in to it, but curiosity got the better of me. "You recognize this?"

"A binding curse. I've seen it before, but I cannot read the language." Standing up straight and releasing me, Nalem added with a note of wistfulness, "Magic doesn't naturally occur in this world. It tends to rest beyond, but this here...definitely from Arcadia."

"Can you tell me how to remove it?"

"I wouldn't even if I did, but that's a moot point. I cannot even hope to understand this without my old notes. Pity what happened to those, isn't it?" He pulled his fingers back to crack them, far enough that the tips touched his wrist. Would've broken the hands of anyone else, but not my brother. He couldn't stay broken. "The irony that what was destroyed might've saved you...it's almost worth it. Almost."

Nalem paced away from me, his movements brimming with the confidence Retz never had. "Usually, the magic is performed with thread or yarn, and it's a simple—if painful—matter of ripping the spell out. However, not only do curses dig deep, but you also have thorns and vines. Perhaps even roots. They seem to have melded into your very bones." He spat the words with a grimace. "Ripping them out would leave you paralyzed from the neck down, at best. What's the curse, and how did you get it?"

I pulled my sleeve over my arm and backed away toward the door. "I'd rather not say. I appreciate the advice, but I should be going—"

"Ah. Something that'd be to my advantage to uncover, then?" He spun to face me, balancing on one foot like a puppet. I imagined Nalem playing with invisible strings on my brother's body. "Come on, you can tell your dear, sweet brother. Remember what your little lover said about trusting others, after all?"

I grabbed the doorknob. "You were listening."

"Not my fault the walls are so thin. My brain is now forever scarred by the sound of your stupid conversations and banal intercourse." His face twitched, and he stood on both feet again. "Your brother is awakening, and my hold is fragile. I figured I'd be nice by advising you on your curse and offering a warning, but I guess I'll refrain."

He wasn't making such offers out of the kindness of his heart. He was nothing if not predictable. "I'll pass. Get Retz out here. Twenty minutes." I opened the door behind me and began to leave.

"Fine. Ignore my help. I guess I'll have to show my charity with cruelty instead for you to believe me in the future." He sat on the edge of his bed, grinning again. "Too scared of pain from me to save yourself from other sources of agony. Now that's irony I can appreciate."

I bit back a retort and slammed the door behind me. I wasn't a coward. When I returned to my room, Farris glanced at me as he finished dressing. His gaze caught mine, and I realized that Nalem's comments about the thin walls were true. He'd overheard.

"He really hates you, huh?" There was an edge of worry in my boyfriend's voice. "Is he that way with everyone?"

I shook my head. "He has no problem hurting others, no, but he holds a grudge against me in particular."

Farris' stare asked the question he didn't voice.

"I destroyed something dear to him, long ago. Since he was hurting my brother. I was young enough that I hadn't quite shaken that eye-for-an-eye huldra logic yet."

Farris raised an eyebrow, and I realized I'd said too much. He crossed his arms, looking braced for an argument, but he surprised me by instead saying, "That's not fair. I mean, kids do stupid shit all the time. I'm sure even I did."

"Nalem isn't the most forgiving person, in case you can't tell. But that's a story for another time." I cracked my knuckles and readjusted the scarf around my neck. "Look, don't tell him anything, even if he tries to play nice. All right?"

Nalem was right; I was cursed. Farris knew the gist of it, but not how deep it ran. And Alexander...

Well, there's a reason he stopped speaking. The curse came from him, after all.

I woke up in the middle of pouring coffee and nearly spilled it all over myself as I came to consciousness. I was dressed in slacks, socks, and a button-up shirt, thermostat cranked up so high that most folks would be drenched in sweat. My hair was combed, but poorly enough that it resembled a molding haystack. I ached everywhere, even in places I didn't think could hurt.

Yup, Nalem had woken up first. It surprised me, remembering how tired he'd been, but I'd worn myself out too. Usually the most physical activity I got was working at the salon, which sometimes left me sore from having to hunch over people to cut and color their hair all day. Then I went and had three fights in one day. Nalem was quiet, but he'd pipe up again soon, so I drank the hotel's bitter coffee and fixed my hair.

Five minutes later, the door sounded like it was taking the brunt of a machine gun's wrath. I nearly tripped as I ran over, still trying to tame my hair as I opened the door.

Jarrod stood there, hands in his pockets and a new pair of glasses perched on his nose, with Farris next to him, ready to pound on the door again. Weariness lined their faces. The sky was already turning a vibrant blue, the town bustling with birds and truck drivers who'd awoken with the sun.

"Morning, guys. Sorry, I just woke up." I waved the hairbrush as if it would somehow explain everything. "Jarrod, how're your hands doing?"

"Serviceable." His eyes narrowed. "You're Retz again, right?"

Of course Nalem had been up to torment them. When we were kids, Nalem had only occasionally bothered Jarrod—my brother was more of a toy to be broken than anything. But then Jarrod had fought back, hard enough to wind up on Nalem's eternal shit list. So Nalem waking up early to continue his slow revenge was no shock, sad as that is to say.

"Yeah, I'm me. No idea what's going on, though, sorry. What's up?"

Jarrod's body relaxed when he realized it wasn't Nalem in control anymore. Or maybe it was alcohol, because I smelled it on his breath when he spoke. I was reminded of Dad during the last few years he'd lived with us; I'm not sure how to describe the pang of emotion which hit me with that thought.

"We're going to meet up with the furaribi. They hired us to escort them to safety after dealing with the unicorn."

Instead of confessing what I'd been hired to do, I asked, "You sure they're ready to travel yet? I mean, that unicorn horn isn't instantaneous, is it?"

"If any medicine was, I wouldn't hate their commercials so much," Farris answered, gaze focused at the wallet he juggled. Whose wallet? No clue. "But if there is an actual gang of lamia chasing them, they probably don't have the luxury of sick days."

"Our current predicament is," Jarrod cut in, "we need transportation and preferably a legal driver. You have a car and can defend yourself. Would you come with us?"

Would I? Good question, and one I didn't have an answer to. "Give me a moment. I need to get my shoes on." I closed the door, hoping they didn't mind waiting outside while I thought. I mentally prodded Nalem while I searched for my shoes.

"Here to attempt to chide me for talking to your brother? You jealous thing, you."

"It's not that. Jarrod wants me to join him and help the furaribi. I'm not sure what to do."

Nalem shrugged, the phantom sensation of his actions disconcerting against my own still bones. *"We must get those furaribi either way. You didn't tell him what we're doing, did you?"*

I shook my head.

"I'm impressed at your ability to keep your loose lips shut. But can you betray your brother's trust to do what you must?"

Shoes in hand, I sat on the bed, slipped them on, and laced the strings. *"Maybe if I explain things, he'll understand."*

"He takes after your father. Not one for our particular shades of moral gray." Nalem paced around the confines of my head. Pressure points made slow, measured progress through my head, accompanied by hallucinated clacks of bone on bone.. *"You've seen the looks he gives you. He doesn't trust you. He's a man dedicated to his cause—I've seen the type before. Doesn't matter if you're family, or if you explain how noble goals result from an ignoble journey."*

I finished the first shoe, the end knot tied into a noose. *"Then what do I do? Is completing this mission really so important?"*

"It will further my goals, and then we'll stop Lady Delight and free her creatures. My promise, scout's honor, needles in eyes and all that jazz." He tapped his fingers against his wrists, the clacking noise echoing in my ears. *"Go with them for now. Play nice like the lying little weasel you are. I'll contact Lady Delight once we have a destination, and you make sure we get there."*

The plan was a lump settling in my throat. I swallowed, feeling the pressure against my skin as I choked it down. *"And if Jarrod does turn against me?"* He wasn't the kid I'd grown up with, after all, and ten years was a long time to nurse a vendetta.

With a softness in his voice I wasn't used to, Nalem said, *"Then I'll deal with him for you, so you don't have to. It's such a sad thing when family turns on you, after all."*

My fingers fumbled with the laces of the other shoe. The heat of the room was getting to me, and my tongue felt dry. *"But they hate me because of you."*

"In part, but also because you're a freak." He spun on one heel, reversing the direction of his walk. *"Let's face it. You're the closest thing most mortals have seen to a necromancer, and you have a part of you—me—who disregards their morals. You hurt those close to you, and you don't act the same way they do. They don't understand you, which leads to fear and, in turn, hate."*

Second noose finished. I placed a pinkie in, as if it were a neck to snap, and tightened. He had a point, after all—he always did. *"I guess. You think she'll hate me too?"*

"She...?" Nalem stopped and tilted his head.

I reviewed a memory for him, of right after the fight when I drove the furaribi away. Aimi had watched me from the back seat, brother unconscious with his head in her lap. She'd thanked me, again and again, and said that she'd see me tomorrow once I dropped them off.

Nalem watched the snatches of kindness over and over again. *"She's a fool who's unaware what you're planning. Think she won't burn you once she finds out?"*

I pulled my hand away from my noose-knot, letting the laces scratch against my fingers, and lay back on the bed. The ceiling was covered in white stucco and old spiderwebs. *"I don't want to do this. I don't want to hurt them and make them hate me."*

"You can't avoid hurting and hating, little one. It's our nature."

A comforting pressure pushed into my hands, like they were being held by someone close to me.

"Now, go with them. Enjoy a chance to play the good guy before we fuck things up."

I took a deep breath and counted to ten, almost brave enough to argue. But I didn't have a choice, and I knew it. Might as well follow his advice and scrounge a little enjoyment out of this. I got to my feet, turned down the thermostat, and shrugged a coat on before going outside. Jarrod and Farris were still out there, muttering to each other, but they stopped when I came out.

"We can take my car," I said, pulling the keys out of my coat pocket. I smiled when I spoke, false as it felt. "I'm driving, and I get dibs on what music plays. Deal?"

"It's better than a bus," Jarrod said. He tried to steel himself to say something else as he looked up at me, but instead settled on "Thank you."

"No problem. Can't just ditch you for another ten years, now can I?" I didn't give them a chance to answer my biting joke. I led them to my car, keys in hand, and wondered if this was how animals felt when walking up to a slaughterhouse.

Since Isamu and Aimi no longer had a place to stay, but weren't in danger of burning anything else up since Isamu got the poison out of his system, I'd checked the furaribi into another hotel. It was nicer than the one we'd stayed in and on the other side of town. Well, I say checked them in, but really, I simply sensed which rooms were empty and snuck the siblings into one of them. We'd even found a sign to keep the maid service out, so no one checked in when they weren't supposed to. Seeing as the hotel was still intact—a crisp wooden "village" with plenty of gardens instead of a pile of ashes—I figured the unicorn horn had worked its magic.

The furaribi looked a lot better than the day before— amazing what a warm roof, a shower, and being stabbed with a horn from a carnivorous horse can do for a person. Isamu even had some color to his face, though he was wrapped up in as many blankets as he could find in the room. Aimi was dressed in a blue and white dress, which looked like it had once been fashionable before doing time on a thrft store rack. It wasn't as if they'd gotten away with pockets full of cash; after all, they'd barely escaped with their lives.

We briefly spoke—good morning, how are you feeling, congrats on not turning the hotel into an incinerator, and so on—while we positioned ourselves in the small hotel room. The room itself was spotless; the furaribi mentioned they'd cleaned rooms at a hotel for a while to get by, and old habits were hard to shake. Aimi sat next to Isamu on the bed, and he shed a few layers of blankets. Jarrod leaned against one wall, keeping all windows and doors in sight. Farris took a nearby chair and sat in it backward, using the back of it as an armrest. I grabbed a chair next to the door, in case anything went wrong and I had to either run or stop someone from coming in. Everyone kept glancing suspiciously at everyone else; at least their eyes weren't on me alone.

Once we settled, Farris surprised everyone by being the first to speak. "Right, so, escort mission, sounds good. I run away from shit all the time. It's great." He clapped his hands together and said, "But what I'm wondering is, why are you guys running anyway? First you tell us there's lamia involved, and now we've killed off a unicorn. What gives?" Jarrod opened his mouth to say something, but Farris interrupted, "Hon, I know it ain't your job to question your clients. That's why you keep me around."

Aimi stuttered a protest, but nothing intelligible came out.

Isamu sighed, sitting up a little straighter in his blanket nest. "Well, only fair of us to tell you what you're getting into. Any of you heard of Lady Delight?"

Jarrod and Farris admitted that no, they hadn't, and then everyone stared at me. I listened to Nalem's advice on what to say. "I heard she's a lamia, which I'm pretty sure is some kinda' snake person, right? Mom mentioned her once, I think. Old story that she was a guest at Queen Victoria's funeral or something."

Aimi nodded, swinging her legs over the edge of the bed. "Wouldn't put that past her. Yeah, she's a lamia. They're either half human and half snake, or way too much snake all at once. She's rich, powerful, and loves to collect things."

"A trait common to most lamia, from what I've read," Jarrod added with a nod. He had one hand over the hilt of one pistol and the other held a flask. An emotional twinge rocked me—what had he gone through with Dad to get him drinking before the bars even opened?

"Yeah, well, most lamia don't collect other nonhumans," Isamu grumbled. "She's got collectors and traders all around the world. She chased me and my mother through Japan, so we tried to lose them in Brazil. We didn't, but we found Aimi there. Then Mother gave her life to give us a chance to escape, but you see how well that turned out."

"Finding me actually might've made things worse," Aimi muttered. "Furaribi are only found in Japan—until me. If your mom hadn't brought me along—"

"Our mother," Isamu cut in sternly. "Biologic or not, we're all family, and that means we don't leave each other behind. Besides, Lady Delight would've been after you no matter where you came from. We're such rare commodities, after all. Exotic."

Jarrod and I exchanged glances, all too familiar with the feeling. Huldra were a bit more well-known than furaribi, but stories of seductresses with inhuman strength, hollow backs, and cow tails weren't exactly common either. I remembered the huldra I'd seen in the menagerie and wondered again what we'd do if that was our mother in her place. Or if being hulderkind meant my brother and I would be even rarer and more exciting pets to keep in cages.

Family doesn't leave each other behind, huh? Poor furaribi; that's what defines the Gallows nowadays.

"Depending on how you look at it, it wasn't a bad gig," Aimi continued, speaking quickly to change the subject. She tried to distract herself with folding more blankets, but that didn't get rid of the tenseness in her bones, the way her eyes kept to the floor. Neither of the siblings were catching fire, but the room smelled faintly of smoke. Her voice got quieter as she spoke. "We had a nice room—er, cage. Always able to eat and sleep. Lots of admirers. We were sorta' celebrities there."

"But you weren't free or anything, that it?" Farris guessed, slumped over enough to rest his chin on the back of the chair. "I mean, even princesses get sick of castles."

"Sure, lack of freedom, that was a thing." Isamu rolled his shoulders, though the rest of his body tensed. "And lack of privacy. People always watching. Expecting us to perform for them." He looked at each of us in turn, expression blank. "You got a sister?"

Farris hummed as he thought. "No clue. I might. I mean, not feeling a big no from that, so—"

"Ever get asked to fuck her?"

Farris went bright red, almost purple, and stammered out that of course he hadn't. Nalem made the most disgusted noise I had heard out of him and stabbed his fingers into my skull. This was followed by flashes of memories too fast for me to focus on. All I caught was the smile of a woman with dark hair, a brief moment imagining skeletal fingers around brown wrists, and a wave of revulsion at the very idea. I made a concentrated effort not to think and not to look at Jarrod, though I felt him stiffen as his fingers tightened around the neck of his bottle.

"We never actually had to go through with it," Aimi interjected, waving her hands as if she could expel the idea. "Lady Delight moved them along beforehand. Even she had standards." Aimi paused and added, with disgust, "Or she didn't want me pregnant. Which can't happen, not how our kind work, but who knows how much she learned about our kind beyond how rare we are."

"Point stands. When you're captive, people think they have power over you. Can make you do things." Isamu's gaze drifted out the window, as if it was his cage and those gawkers were right outside. "And with that kind of power, no morals. Any idea what it's like to be stuck in that?"

My skin felt tight as he spoke. Didn't help that Nalem said, *Fits you to the letter, doesn't it? Captive in your own body and mind.* If he was still shaken by Isamu's question, he hid it behind sharp insults.

Noting the tension in the room, Jarrod cleared his throat. "We get the picture. You got sick of it and burned your way out but were poisoned in the process. Made you feverish, possibly delusional. That's over now." He took a drink from his flask. "I'm impressed you managed to make it this far."

"We may or may not have stolen a car when we first escaped," Aimi admitted with a sly edge to her voice. "I mean, I did get my license right before we got captured. But Sammy here blew the car up."

Isamu huffed. "Hey, I would've done it even if I weren't sick. Harder to track and all." He turned to Jarrod. "We're planning to escape into California. Lose ourselves in the crowds, lay low, find a way to eventually get back to Japan and the rest of our family. But as you already figured out, we've used most of our energy escaping. And, well, last night. If we were found by the lamia now, we couldn't defend ourselves."

"We don't have money right now, but we'll get some!" Aimi chirped. "Whatever the price, you name it!"

While Jarrod protested that they didn't need to pay, I asked Nalem, *"Would that actually work for them? Hiding out in a city like that?"*

"The ability to sense nonmortals is, I've heard, quite similar to our bone sense. Have too many people around, too much static, and it's hard to tell which way is up." Nalem stopped clawing the inside of my skull, though my head still ached. *"If they made it to a populated city—say, San Francisco—finding them would be a bitch, even for a half-supernatural such as yourself."*

"Makes sense to me." I briefly listened to the others confirming distances and plans, piping up long enough to confirm that my car could make the trip. *"You've said before that you can't do it yourself. Why is that?"*

I felt Nalem's smile tug at my lips. *"Believe it or not, I was born human. And depending on your definition, I still am one."*

"Well, what are you by your definition?"

I wasn't sure if the pause was meant to be dramatic or if he actually thought before answering, *"I prefer to think of myself as a god."*

I came back into the others' conversation as it stretched into silence. Everyone was fidgeting. Jarrod drained the rest of his bottle. Isamu joined Aimi in folding the blankets he was no longer using.

"Just to be clear," Isamu muttered, "I wanted to apologize for what happened. I just...snapped. Got scared. Lost it. Shouldn't happen again." He squinted at the three of us in turn, and then asked Aimi, "I didn't hurt anyone, did I?"

"No humans," Aimi told him. "I've got a few bruises, and you burned Jarrod's hands."

My brother waved one to show this, angry red skin peeking out under his bandages.

"I guess he's hulderkind enough that we didn't risk a Harvester sighting or anything," she added.

I chose this moment to go ahead and stick my foot in my mouth. "What's a Harvester?" The lamia had mentioned it too, though of course I didn't say that.

All eyes were on me, mostly confused. An unusual glee bubbled in the back of my head, Nalem trying to hold in his amusement at my apparent stupidity.

I wondered what I'd said wrong until Farris said, "Man, even I know what the Harvester is. Or that it exists, at least."

"Ever wonder why humans don't believe we exist?" Aimi chirped, swinging her legs off the side of the bed again. "They can't remember us for long, most of the time. I'm sure you've noticed that. The newspapers are already saying that Isamu was some druggie accidentally torching himself, if you can believe that." She elbowed her brother in the side, and Isamu just rolled his eyes.

Her face turned serious again when she continued, "But sometimes, supernaturals think this means they can get away with attacking humans, thinking it won't be remembered. And that's where the Harvester comes in."

"It's some kinda supernatural boogeyman," Farris chimed in. "I've never seen him, but he sounds pretty freaky. Hooded and carrying a scythe, like the ol' grim reaper, but not a skeleton like all the art shows."

"It's covered in eyes."

All of us looked at Jarrod this time. His voice was so quiet, we almost didn't hear him. I felt him grinding his teeth together, fingers tightening again around the bottle neck. With the cracking glass of his bottle biting into his burns, it must've hurt, but he didn't stop.

Isamu asked, "You've seen it?"

Jarrod nodded, a curt motion. "The Harvester shows up at human deaths as well. It's not always easy to spot. Moves too fast. But it's there. Collects what looks like their eyes. Not their real ones. Not sure what they really are." A reluctant pause. "Eats them. Most of the time."

His gaze drifted to me, but Nalem took my body in a flash of numbness. I had to watch as I doubled over with mad laughter. The others shied away, but Jarrod braced to react to whatever Nalem was doing. Even I wasn't sure what that was.

"Oh, forgive me. You all just make him sound so mysterious and strange." Nalem stood up straighter, stretching my arms with loud pops. "The Harvester is simply a being who clings to the ever-expanding past. Nothing more, nothing less." Nalem tilted his head. Even through the numbness, I felt a strain from the unnatural angle that my neck was bending at. "But you remember seeing him, don't you, Jarrod? You were, what, five?"

Jarrod dropped the bottle, hands going to his holsters. "I've seen it a few times, in passing."

"No, wait. I want to hear this." Farris sat up straighter in his chair, even as the furaribi slunk farther from me and closer to the wall. "If the Harvester's such a freaky thing, there's a reason why you ran into it when you were a kid, ain't there, babe?"

"Of course there is," Nalem answered. And I tried for the life of me to remember why, but I had no clue. If Jarrod had only been five at the time, that would've left me at a year old, maybe even less. But that meant—

"You were five years old. Just a little *girl*." Nalem spat the word with glee. "I first saw you in blood-splattered pajamas. You met the Harvester when he came for your baby brother. Remember?" Nalem stepped forward.

Jarrod clenched his fists and teeth, tail swishing with nerves.

"And you were there when, despite all of Mommy's pleading because she was oh so scared, your daddy made a deal. Because what kind of a good parent lets their son die before he's had a chance to live? Am I right?"

I should have felt something, but my mind was so jumbled with thoughts, it was as numb as my body. With an aching sluggishness, I pieced the words together. I died. But I wasn't dead now. That meant...

"Dad's deal was...you?"

"So that's what you are." Aimi was still backed up against the wall, eyes wide with wonder even as the skin along her knuckles cracked and revealed the magma underneath.

Beside her, her brother was completely pale.

"The bones and the weird aura...you're Nalem, aren't you?"

"My reputation precedes me, I see." Nalem swooped into a low bow. "Yes, I am Nalem, savior of this pathetic host for almost twenty years running. I needed a vessel, and the Harvester, well, he owed me. Still does. It's a perpetual sort of thing." Nalem rocked onto the balls of my feet as he stood up, standing on tiptoe to loom over Jarrod. "Seems Daddy dearest is regretting his decision now, isn't he? Tell me, littlest one, wherever did you lose him? Has he met the Harvester personally now, or did he just realize he'd work better without a mewling child clinging to his sleeve?"

Jarrod shook with rage and fear, but he didn't dare speak. No one did.

When Nalem smiled, my face felt ready to split in two. "It will be such a pleasure working with you all. Now, if you excuse me, you may have a moment to dwell on your own little miseries. I've got enough of that with Retz here." He turned on his heels and shut the door behind him with a click.

"That was uncalled for," I told him as we walked down the hall.

"You brought it up, so you only have yourself to blame." He reached up behind his head, as if to adjust something in his hair before remembering it was my body, which seemed to have shorter hair than he was used to. He grumbled.

"All right, so now that you've scared the people we're supposed to capture—which, by the way, I'm really not wanting to do now—and insulted my brother repeatedly, what now?" I imagined myself clawing into a solid surface, like he did when he scraped the inside of my skull. *"Going to blame me for my own death, since that was a thing? Start your next plan for world domination and kissing up to capitalist snakes?"*

Nalem shook his head and whistled as he strode out the hotel door. *"I do believe the next course of action is pancakes."*

Jarrod found me an hour later, and I gave him the rest of my breakfast.

He'd waited until I told him I was me again before sliding into the booth with me. I had half a pile of pancakes drenched in syrup, since Nalem had decided that all the talking had made him hungry. My mental roommate had eaten, texted the lamia what he'd learned of our driving plans so far, and then retreated into my skull for further plotting.

I just poked at the contents of the plate before passing them to my brother. "I'm surprised you're here."

"Had to come pick you up. You're driving, after all." Jarrod took my fork and tried to scrape some of the syrup off. He had fresh bandages on his hands.

"Do you guys still want me along, considering what just happened?"

Jarrod didn't answer for a moment, taking a bite of pancake to buy himself some time. He grimaced; I hoped it was just from how sugary-sweet Nalem had made the pancakes. "If it was just you, sure. Nalem...as I explained to the others, he can be a force to be reckoned with, but he's never out for long. It boils down to being patient and not reacting."

I didn't buy it. Neither did Nalem, who smirked as he listened in. I said, "It doesn't excuse anything he does."

"That's true. I'm just saying, I expected an outburst sooner rather than later." He bit his lip before speaking again. "Are you all right?"

"In case you forgot, I'm the one who insulted you, not the other way around."

"No, I meant the dying thing." Jarrod looked up at me, eyes a murky gray behind his glasses. "I suppose it came as a shock."

I shrugged. It had, but the last place I wanted to have an existential crisis in was a small-town diner. There'd be plenty of time to freak out over knowing that I literally couldn't live without the monster in my head. "If anything, it explains a lot. Like why Dad was so intent on fixing me. He wanted to erase how badly he fucked up." I wanted to think Dad had meant well, but trying to justify the good intentions made me feel sick. Would he have done it, if he'd known what Nalem was?

"He still plans to fix everything. This only complicates things a little." Jarrod sighed through another bite of pancake. "That's the other reason I'm bringing you along. Alexander wants to see you."

Nalem raised an eyebrow, and I did the same. "Me? You mean me, not Nalem? Why isn't he here now, then?"

"Alexander is…preoccupied elsewhere. Part of why we lost contact." Jarrod eyed my water, so I passed it to him. He drank deep before sliding it back. "I don't have details yet, but I think he's got a new plan."

I'd love to see him try.

I ignored Nalem. "So you're just dealing with me because Dad said so."

"No. I'm dealing with you because you're my brother. Alexander's why you're coming along right now, despite how much you scared the others." Jarrod managed a smile, the wryest one I'd ever seen. "We spent most of the last hour convincing the furaribi that you wouldn't kill them. The other half was Farris apologizing for making everyone talk."

"Yeah, is he an amnesiac or something? Just wondering." He was odd either way; Dad was the only other human I'd ever met who saw the supernatural and remembered it afterward, and he wasn't enough of a daredevil to hack at a unicorn with a sword.

Jarrod nodded. "I can explain later, but yes. All we've got on him are vague hints, nothing conclusive." A long string of syrup dripped from a forkful of pancake. He sighed and set it down. "Let's not get off track. I've got the others on board. After we get the furaribi to safety, I need to bring you to Alexander."

"And you'll come home after that, right? To see Mom?"

This, more than anything I said earlier, took Jarrod aback. Something in his face fell. The tightness in his body slackened as he said, "I don't think she'd want to see me."

"Of course she would. She misses you guys." I reached over and brushed some of his hair out of his face. "She'd agree with me that you could use a trim, though. And some conditioner...you have heard of conditioner before, right?" I brushed against his skull when I moved his hair, and I used that for a quick glimpse of his skeleton. Again, the bones of his limbs and neck all felt off, as if they weren't made of the right materials. It was like perfecting a vanilla milkshake and then realizing someone's poured mayonnaise in your drink. His bones hadn't been that way ten years ago.

He pulled my arm away by the sleeve before I had a chance to ask why. "A lot has changed."

"That's how the world works, by changing." I tapped his hand with mine, just for a closer look. Even the joints in his fingers were knotted and rough as bark.

Jarrod pulled his hand away again, teeth gritted.

"Okay, sorry. Look, I'll see Dad, whatever, just come home and see Mom afterward. I'll even keep Nalem out of your hair as best as I can, just please, promise me that."

That was what made Jarrod back away, where Nalem had ultimately failed. "Retz, don't. You shouldn't make promises you can't keep."

"Do you really think I care right now?" I was having a hard time keeping my voice down. "I've kinda been through a lot in the past twenty-four hours. I just found out that you're still alive and that I apparently died once. I've fought and saved lives, two things I never do, and I've been forced by a psychopathic necromancer to insult my brother and buy pancakes. Oh, and if I ever get said necromancer out of my head, I'm dead again." I reached over and grabbed Jarrod's shoulder, hard enough that he winced. I forced myself to loosen my grip so I didn't hurt him already after so long apart. "Mom misses you. I do too. If you want me to come along and see Dad, then dammit, you're returning the favor and coming home to see Mom. Deal?"

Jarrod started to smack my hand away but stopped himself at the last minute. He looked distressed, body all tense as if ready to flip at any moment, but then he let go with another sigh.

"Fine. It's a deal." He stood. "Now that that's settled, we should get moving. The lamia may already be on our trail."

I followed him. Right. The lamia. Really, that's why I had to delay my freakout and keep my wits about me. I was already quaking inside at the thought of what the others would do once they realized I was working with the lamia—and what Nalem would do if I didn't.

8 - JARROD

I didn't consider that Retz driving his own vehicle might be a bad idea until I sat down in the back seat. The car sputtered to life, gears and pistons grinding together as Retz and Farris took the front seats. I found myself wishing to sit anywhere else. It wasn't that I didn't trust Retz's ability to drive; I doubted his reflexes in case his car decided to crash and break into a million rusted pieces, which sounded more plausible with each passing second.

"I've traveled this road more than anyone else in this car," I argued, "and that includes in the dark."

"Yeah, but you're also drunk," Retz retorted from the seat I should've been in. "I'd rather not get pulled over and let Nalem deal with the highway patrol." A smile fled over his lips, a ghost of Nalem's likely gleeful memory of such an incident.

"I'm not that drunk. I always have a beer in the morning, and any ill effects on my motor skills have passed. Trust me." I admit I'd drunk more than usual that morning, but only to numb the sting of my burns. I might've needed a bit more to hold a steering wheel for seven hours, but thanks to my huldra-inherited endurance, I tended to hold my alcohol pretty well. "Okay, then why don't I get shotgun?"

"Because the only way he could fit three people in the back is to fit a short stack in the middle," Farris teased from the passenger's seat.

Sadly, he had a point, since I was the shortest one in the car. While Retz's build was a near-skeletal take on Alexander's, I'd inherited our mother's shape; sturdy but short, a badger compared to the ferret that is my brother.

Farris winked at my brother and said, "Don't worry, he's always like this. He even asked to take over for a bus driver once."

"That was once," I grumbled, arms crossed, "and it was clear that the driver had never dealt with mountains before."

Aimi patted my shoulder as she slid in. "Don't let 'em get you down. I'm glad you're in the back, okay?" She and Isamu were wary of us—mostly Nalem—but as we'd already helped them, they seemed to recognize that we were their best bet to reach San Francisco and safety.

She had a point. There was a second reason to keep someone in the back, and that was to keep an eye out for anyone possibly chasing us. Retz or I were the best bets, since we could fight at range—unlike Farris and his apparent phobia of firearms—and could do so without setting the whole car on fire, which the furaribi would risk. Seeing as Retz didn't trust anyone else to drive his scrap heap, there I was in the back.

Isamu was the last to enter the car, and while his appearance and demeanor had improved after the unicorn horn, he was still feverish. It wasn't as bad as wearing the leather duster and scarf in a desert, but another reason to pine for one of the front seats. I ignored it by focusing on the rearview mirrors instead. They were smudged and adjusted to Retz's height. The Buick growled its way onto the highway, a corpse given life to complete one more unholy mission.

We had decided on San Francisco for our destination, and it was eight hours away, if traffic and the car's vitality approved. The first hour went smooth enough, if warm. The sky settled into night. My brother, Farris, and Aimi bonded over their love of ear-rending pop music. Isamu tried to sleep through it, gave up, and critiqued the ridiculousness of the lyrics in order to handle the noise. I'd shifted to face the back window, trusting the others to warn me if any cops were close enough to see. They were in the middle of some Lady Gaga song when I saw a white blur cross the road behind us.

"Unicorns again," I muttered, already reaching for my pistols.

"No, hon," Farris chirped from the front, "Highway Unicorn's a good song, but Retz already said the skip button's broken—"

"No, literally, there's a unicorn behind us."

Retz's eyes went wide as he glanced in his rearview mirror. Then the Buick swerved as another blur passed in front. We rammed right into the head of another unicorn; Aimi found a horn inches from her nose. I reached over and snapped the horn off, causing the unicorn to fall away from the car and collapse in a heap on the side of Highway 99.

Retz slammed down the gas pedal; the unicorn in the rearview mirror kept up for half a minute before lowering its head and charging. Three others followed behind it.

"I thought unicorns were rare! There's a whole herd here!"

Aimi turned around to watch. "Yeah, I sensed them earlier! The one you killed must've been their scout or something!"

They chased us in an elongated V formation, with an empty spot on the left side.

"They're chasing us because we killed their companion." I sympathized with them; if anyone killed Farris, I'd gun them down too. But my job was to get Aimi and Isamu to safety, meaning the unicorns had to go.

"Think we can outdrive them?" Retz asked.

"Maybe, but we'll run out of gas at some point, and they won't. And I doubt they'll be kind enough to wait for us at a gas station." Farris reached for his sword stashed under his seat. "Ready, babe?"

"If you must play action hero, wait until the car slows." I might've been able to stand it, but Farris was only human. I leaned over Isamu, half in his lap and apologizing under my breath, as I tried to open the window. It wouldn't, so I elbowed it full force to shatter it. "I'll buy you a new window later if the car lasts, 'kay, Retz?"

"What do you think you're doing?"

"Evening a few odds." Having removed enough glass to avoid cutting myself, I climbed into the open window, with one hand on the frame and Isamu holding my legs to keep me steady. One pistol in hand, I aimed for the unicorn in front. I wanted to shoot out the kneecaps and disable it, but the legs were moving too fast in order to keep up with us. I aimed between the eyes instead.

The bullet hit its mark, but the unicorn wasn't deterred. Even as blood and bits of brain splattered the road behind it, it kept running. I'd figured some brain damage would at least slow it . Wrong. I might as well have been fighting zombies. I fired off another shot at the horn, but didn't get to see where it landed before the Buick spun out, sparks flying across the road. Two other unicorns rammed into the front of the car, crunching the engine and hood. Retz and Aimi both screamed, Farris was raring to jump out of the car, and Isamu turned into fire again.

I pulled my legs from the furaribi and held on to the window frame for dear life. The unicorns were aimed right for me, and I dived and hit the ground with a roll. I got to my feet as one unicorn broke from the path to strike. I wasn't fast enough to get out of the way. I turned so it stabbed through my arm instead of my chest, the horn tearing through muscle and scraping the bone. It also scraped against the curse tied into my skin, awakening the vines. They lashed out and wrapped around the unicorn's horn. The unicorn snarled as it tried to pull away, shaking its white head and bloody mane. I reached up, grabbed the horn, and snapped. The unicorn froze, then crumpled to the ground.

It was muggy on Highway 99, with no wind to alleviate the heat. The road was empty; even trucks avoided this back road. We'd passed through a couple towns, but only fields and trees surrounded us now. Farris fought off two unicorns with a sword and surprising dexterity, while Aimi and Isamu, both on fire, had another unicorn each. I wasn't sure where the last unicorn was until I heard another crash. Retz was standing on the roof of the Buick, his equine adversary stomping over the broken engine, hooves breaking through the front window.

The corpse next to me twitched. The skin split as the spine tore out of it. Sharp vertebrae flew to Retz's hand, a possessed whip floating in his grasp. He struck, flogging its shoulders as he tried to aim for its face. I wasn't sure whether my brother or Nalem was in control, and for the moment, it didn't matter.

I ran to help Farris, who parried the unicorn horns with his sword. The arm the unicorn stabbed was useless for this fight, so I grabbed my pistol with my other hand, unable to unstrap the shotgun with only one hand. I shot the kneecaps of the unicorn closest to me, managing to disable the front two legs. With it out of the way for a moment, I joined Farris as he slid his blade into ribs.

"Nice of you to join me, hon." He pulled the sword back out, slick with bubbling blood. The unicorn's breath heaved, I assume from a punctured lung, but it reared up and tried to stomp us. Farris and I darted in opposite directions. I tried to shoot the horn, but got an eye instead. It screeched and tried to stab toward the source of the pain. I dodged easily enough.

"They tried to pick you off first. Bad move," I said.

"Wasn't it, though? So rude." Farris pierced the unicorn's neck to keep it still. I holstered my pistol and ripped off its horn. It fell into a heap. "You all right?"

My answer was interrupted by another screech behind us. We turned to find the crippled unicorn trying to charge us despite its pain, but held back by a spine-whip around its neck. Behind it, one unicorn lay across the front of the ruined Buick, its spine torn out and under

Retz's command, while the last two unicorns burned under the furaribi's touch. The golden glow lit the night.

"Good job, Retz." I pulled off my fourth horn of the night, glanced around the battlefield, and none of the fiends moved. The Buick wouldn't anytime soon, either. I pocketed the horn and waved the others over. Retz jumped off the roof, nearly falling as soon as he hit the road. The furaribi returned to their human forms, though the smell of burned flesh and hide clung to them.

"How is everyone?"

"This one's ready to pass out, but I'm fine!" Aimi wrapped an arm around her brother to keep him steady. "I didn't realize they were so rude."

"I'm surprised they managed to follow us." Farris wiped the blade of his sword on the corpse closest to him. "I mean, how obvious was it we killed their friend?"

"I'm not sure that's it," Retz muttered. The spine-whip fell to the ground and shattered. "One of them tried to run me down earlier, on my way to town. I think they would've chased us even if we hadn't killed one. They...don't seem fond of me."

Another weird coincidence. The unicorns appeared to Retz before Aimi located them and called us. But why? Did they have an idea we were coming—or did they sense Retz and Nalem within him? I wasn't sure what to think.

"I just hope that's the last of them," Isamu murmured, leaning against his sister. His hair and eyes still had flecks of orange in them. He narrowed his eyes when they met mine. "Hey. You're bleeding."

"It's not too bad," I protested, though my arm refused to budge without a shock of pain. "We should leave soon, though. Hitchhiking will be a bitch with five of us, so we need another plan. Anyone opposed to catching a bus?"

Isamu grimaced. "We'd get found, chased, and other humans would get involved." He tried to step forward but stumbled, Aimi barely catching him. "Shit, thanks. That's why we didn't take a plane. People might get hurt—or the Harvester might be looking our way if anyone got hurt and axe us too."

He had a point. I tried to think of another idea, but pain raced through my arm. Retz held it, bandaging it with a first-aid kit he'd pulled from the wreckage of his car. The speed with which he worked surprised me. He was biting his lip hard enough that the skin turned white. He tugged at my sleeve, and I realized he wanted it off to bandage it better.

"I've got an idea," Farris said. He helped remove my duster and then put a hand on my shoulder—it served as a nice distraction as Retz patched me up. "I can find a car for us. Something sturdier, an SUV or something. If we're quick enough, and maybe switch the license plates, it'd take a while for us to be caught. We'd definitely have a few hours, and that's long enough for us to get to Cali, ditch the car, and go from there."

"I'm guessing this isn't the first car you've…borrowed." Aimi giggled, though the worry rang in her voice too. Her eyes flickered to my bare arms, and the cursed vines sewn into them. The vines had settled down once the fight finished, so they resembled interlaced tattoos. She was wise enough not to ask what they were. "Stealing a car doesn't sound bad to me. I mean, we've already burned bridges and blocked up a highway with dead unicorns. How much more illegal can we be?".

Retz finished bandaging me and helped me put my duster back on. "There. Should hold us over for now." He turned to the others and said, "Can't we rent a U-Haul and drive in that?"

"We don't have time," Farris insisted. I figured he really wanted to steal a car—it was something he mused on more often than I thought healthy. I would've discouraged it if it didn't come in use on occasion. "It won't take long. Let's just find the nearest town. You guys get cleaned up, and I'll find us a sweet ride. What d'you say?"

"I say go for it." Aimi walked down the side of the road, pulling her brother along. "And if we get caught, I'm claiming you guys kidnapped me so I don't get in trouble. Fair's fair, right?"

Isamu chided her, and Farris followed behind them.

I looked at Retz, who was rooting through his broken car. "You ready?"

"Yeah, just making sure I got everything. Need a hand?"

"I got an arm stabbed, not a leg." I kept to the back of the group, keeping rear guard. Retz wandered by my side, a bag slung over his shoulder. I told him, "You handled yourself fairly well in that fight. That common now?"

"Not until yesterday. But it's actually kind of fun, weirdly enough. Say, what if instead of a spine-whip, I included the head and made it a flail? That would be"—Retz must've caught a glimpse of the disgust that passed over my face—"a horrible idea that I would never consider, of course."

"You made a sand castle out of fish bones and shark teeth when you were six. I'm almost glad to see that your twisted artistic sensibilities haven't changed."

"Hey." He mock-punched me in my good shoulder. "It's better than doing nothing at home. And it's nice hanging out with you again, even if it means saving your ass."

"You too." I took a deep breath of the air and wished it was colder. "Ten years is a long time."

There was shouting up ahead. I reached for my pistols, only to realize it was just the others telling us to hurry up.

"We should catch up." I shoved the hand of my injured arm into my pocket. "Think I'm injured enough for this to be a fair race, or are you that out of practice?"

This time when he smiled, it was all Retz. "Guess we'll have to find out."

We walked around four miles along the highway and another mile after that to reach a town even smaller than Cottage Grove. This one was little more than a main street and a handful of fast-food restaurants and gas stations. Farris wandered off to find a car, so the rest of us found an off-brand Mexican restaurant to wait in. Retz ducked into the bathroom; seeing as huldra bodies essentially burned through anything inside them and thus eliminated the creation of waste, I assumed he went in to be alone and out of sight. Likely dealing with Nalem, or allowing himself a chance to finally register all that he'd dealt with in the past day. It was just the furaribi, myself, and a plate of nachos that were closer to salt-laced shards of plastic.

Aimi watched Retz as he wandered away from us and then turned to me. "Hope you don't mind, but your brother's pretty cute."

"I can't tell since he's my brother, but I'll take your word for it." I tested the cheese to see if it could redeem the nachos. Now the plastic was slimy too.

Isamu did not agree with his sister's attraction. "Not my type, that's for sure. He looks like death warmed over. Plus, if you made out with him, he'd poke your eyes out with his nose. Ah, no offense or anything," he added, glancing at me. I shrugged; Farris had voiced similar concerns about my nose, which Retz and I both inherited from Alexander.

Seeing that he didn't have to eat his words, Isamu waved his nacho, deciding against eating that too. "Then I'd have to deal with a blind sister and, if I don't find some glasses soon, a half-blind me." He poked Aimi's cheek with the tip of a chip. "Vetoed. Disapproved. Do not pass go."

Aimi chuckled and pushed her brother's hand away. "But he's so nice, even if he isn't entirely...you know. Himself. I mean, I wouldn't ask him out and risk accidentally smooching Nalem instead, but it's a real shame that they're a package deal." She sighed and said, in a more somber tone, "I can't imagine what it'd be like, living with a nightmare like that all the time. At least Lady Delight left us alone sometimes."

"Which reminds me," I interrupted, remembering the arguments in the hotel. "You'd heard of Nalem before. Can I ask how? I was raised human, so I'm a bit out of the loop of common supernatural knowledge."

Aimi blew on a cheese-dipped nacho, causing it to bubble and I assume warm up. "Nalem's left his mark all over the world. A few creatures are even said to be his work. Japan alone's got the...gashadaka?"

"Gashadokuro," Isamu corrected, finally eating his nacho before making a face at its taste. "Giant, cannibalistic skeletons. Or there's the bakekujira, which is a skeletal whale…" Yes, those were the kind of fucked-up shit Nalem would spite others with. Isamu added after a moment, "Nalem's connected to the Harvester too. More often than not, where Nalem goes, the Harvester follows. Except, even when all other supernaturals bite the bullet, Nalem's still standing."

I nodded. "There's a relationship there. The Harvester brought Nalem into our lives, after all."

"I've heard that it looks after him, though no one's ever figured out why." Isamu shrugged before telling his sister, "And if you think that's cute, I'm sorry, but you have a few problems even I can't fix. I have no idea where I went wrong raising you."

"Jerk." Aimi giggled as she made small braids in her brother's hair, with no resistance on his part. When she finished, he even mimicked a judge at an award show as he gestured at his tiny braids. I managed not to laugh at them, but I might've cracked a smile. It reminded me of when Retz used to braid my hair, back when we were kids and my hair had been long enough for him to play with for hours while I kept my nose in a book. Though he'd had Nalem then, I hadn't been scared of him warping my bones while he'd played, because Nalem had laid low those early years, and Retz had been too innocent to consider using his powers on me.

Now…well, he was still my brother. I still trusted him. I just didn't trust that Nalem hadn't grown stronger in my absence.

Aimi's voice broke through my thoughts again. "Hey, think you guys will keep in touch with us after this is all over?"

I raised an eyebrow, finally returning to the nachos. The taste was shit but better than nothing. And better than syrup-drenched pancakes; the only thing more dangerous than Nalem's morals was his sweet tooth.

"Only to get our pay or if you have another job for us later. Why?"

"Oh." Aimi swung her legs again in her seat. "I just thought it'd be nice. We no longer have friends who understand what we've been through, and those we did have probably think we're dead. Plus, you guys are pretty neat."

"You mean, you think my brother's cute and want his number or something." I didn't understand how one could expect to formulate a meaningful relationship built on phone messages, but perhaps I'm old-fashioned in some ways. "You'll have to ask him, not me. I tend not to befriend my clients."

"And friends tend to tie you to one place," Isamu grumbled, even as he kept still for Aimi to play with his hair. "Remember how this started in the first place?"

"I do," Aimi said, and then she didn't say any more.

The conversation drifted off, so I munched on the nachos as civilians filed in and out for their late-night meals. Aimi tried to convince her grumbling brother to return the favor and help fix her hair; he eventually relented with slow, fumbling attempts at braids.

Once Retz finally wandered back out of the bathroom, he paused in apparent confusion at the sight of the furaribis' attempts at hairstyling. He shook it off and tapped me on the shoulder. "Hey. Can we talk a moment? Outside?"

"Don't see why not." I got to my feet. "Aimi, you and your brother behave."

"Because we're planning so much trouble right now." She winked at us, more at Retz than me. "No need to worry. We'll grab you if your knight shows up on his shining steed."

I snorted; if anything, I was Farris's knight, not the other way around. I followed Retz outside and to a patch of trees and bushes; out of earshot from others but keeping the restaurant in sight. The clouds were clearing, leaving patches of stars overhead.

"I've got a confession to make, Jarrod." Retz leaned against a tree, digging his heels into the parched grass. "I think Nalem's plotting something."

"Trying to cross us, you mean?" I wasn't surprised by that, but impressed that Retz was actually risking telling me. "Any idea how?"

"No, not exactly." Retz rubbed the back of his neck, brushing the water drops away. "But he's up to something. Might have something to do with that Harvester." He glanced at me. Since it was summer, his eyes were actually greener than the dried-up plants around us. "I've got a question too. Of course you and Nalem don't get along. At all. But say he actually had a plan that might be good. Would you consider going along with it?"

My first instinct was no, and it left a bad taste in my mouth to hear him ask. He knew more than he was letting on, but if I called him out on it, he'd stop.

Whatever plan was hiding under his cryptic questions, I had to wheedle it out. "Depends on the plan, the goal, and the means."

Retz sighed. "I'm still figuring that out myself, but remember how I mentioned that he got a call from an old acquaintance of his? It's not someone he's fond of, and he wants to use them or thwart them. Not sure which. Maybe both."

"And you're debating whether you should help him, considering his track record. Right?"

Retz nodded.

"How much of the plan has he shared?"

"I'm getting snatches here and there. He's mostly telling me things I need to do. Not much else, except it might get violent."

I mulled the information over, though it wasn't much to go on. Nalem was by all definitions a sociopath. Yet even the most foul-hearted person could have a good cause, couldn't they?

"If I were you, I'd get more of the plan before committing to anything. But if he's honestly trying to do something good, well..." I shrugged; my injured shoulder was already healing. "Hell, I'd almost go along with you just to make sure you two didn't get too out of hand."

"You mean it?" Retz practically frolicked out from the shade of the tree. "Thanks. You still give good advice after all these years, I guess."

"I wouldn't call it good, but I assume I'm better than talking to a wall." A dark green Pathfinder, an older model, sped into the parking lot and lurched to a stop. "Five bucks says that's the cavalry showing up."

"I'm not gonna doubt you on that one. Should I be scared of letting him drive?"

"Mortified. I'm a better driver drunk than he is sober." We started back to the parking lot. "And Retz? If you think that Nalem's preparing to put something in action, you tell me, okay? I don't want him jeopardizing this job."

"Already on it, trust me." He kept a few steps behind me, even though his legs were far longer than mine. "And I'm sorry for what he did earlier."

"Earlier when?"

"All of it."

I appreciated the words. Really, I did. But there's a difference between hearing the apology and seeing the proof that makes up for it all. I could try to trust my brother, but even if Nalem handed me my dreams on a silver platter, I'd be searching for the knife he'd plunge into my back.

Some people call me paranoid. I prefer the term prepared.

There once was a man and a boy. They worked together on everything, because all they had were their guns and each other. They worked to save others. They worked out of fear. Justice and mercy was the thin line they trod, unaware of the gravity of their two-person war.

But one day, the two were lost. They had just fought a battle, and the man left a trail of blood wherever he went. Instead of the nearest town, they found themselves in a land of roses, where the sun never shone and the stars were ruby droplets in the sky. The thorns grew longer and sharper the farther the two walked.

Finally, the man had to rest. He closed his eyes, and the thorns ate him alive. They climbed into the wound in his side and pulled him apart. His limbs snapped and reconnected. Vines broke through his skin. White roses burst from his eyes. The boy could only watch as his world fell apart. The clovers at his feet were stained red.

The man got back up. He was no longer a man, but a dual creation of life and death, flora and fauna, magic and madness. He discovered that he was stuck in his world of roses, so in a fit of devastation, he ordered the boy to fight, to right every mythic wrong asked of him.

His words grew roots in the boy's body, even in the bones. The boy tried to refuse, but when he did, the roses tried to claim him too.

When the man saw what he had done, he was filled with shame. He tore his own throat until he could speak no more. He tried to tear the words out of his son too, but to no avail. He was trapped in the roses that made him. The boy had to leave with the weight of his father's mistake on his shoulders. He became the only soldier in their war, and if he ever tried to leave, the thorns would claim him too.

The boy learned not to ask too many questions. Keep his head down and work, because fighting orders wasn't an option anymore. He couldn't tell anyone the full story, because they would use their words to order him around too. His lover wasn't even told all the details, and the boy trusted him more than anyone now.

Whoever said that only sticks and stones hurt needed their tongue ripped out, and no one could convince him otherwise.

9 - RETZ

I wasn't sure what scared me more: Farris's driving skills or the ticking time bomb in my hands. As another sharp turn crashed me against the door, I gripped my phone tighter and tried to keep it out of sight. When I ducked into the bathroom earlier, Nalem had texted Lady Delight our plans and coordinates. I'd get a text when they were in position.

Another turn pressed me against Aimi, who sat in the middle seat.

She giggled and said, "I'm usually not a fan of puns, but I've got to say, I don't think we've been this close before."

Next to her, Isamu groaned at the joke. I just nodded, scared of my voice giving me away.

We were almost to the Oregon-California border. The path we ended up on led us through a winding mountain path with a steep incline. Trucks crept up the road or pulled over to the gravel-covered side, unable to go on.

Farris must've thought he was in a NASCAR race by how he drove, switching lanes and swerving along corners fast enough to break necks without crashing.

Jarrod didn't seem disturbed, though he did quip, "Have you ever noticed that other pedal at your feet, the brakes? It's not a figment of your imagination. It exists. Pretty damn useful too."

"Yeah, I've used them once or twice. Don't you worry. I've yet to meet a better driver than me!"

"And how many other people have you met?"

Farris tapped his fingers on the windshield as he counted. "Depends. Do clients count?"

Jarrod shook his head.

"All right then, I know you. But I get us to our destinations in a decent amount of time. Therefore, I'm the best."

Jarrod shook his head and, instead of arguing with his boyfriend, fiddled with the radio again. A bit of country music and apparently a sex interview tried to break through the static, but what won out was a song of pounding drums and electric guitars. It was riddled with static as the car climbed four-thousand feet over sea level, but Jarrod refused to budge from the station, preferring "shit-quality metal over shit-quality shit."

My phone, set to vibrate, buzzed in my grasp. I had to elbow Aimi off of me during the next curve so she didn't see the screen.

The number was unlisted. The message: *Ready. Keep on highway. We wait at the checkpoint.*

I chose not to reply.

The checkpoint had to be the one just past the border, where the bored clerks made sure those coming to California weren't bringing plants from out of state—Dad had mentioned it once. Meaning, it was too late to warn them and take a different exit. I told myself I'd make up for what I was preparing to do by stopping Lady Delight afterward. A plan was coming together, and it might even work. Especially if I convinced Jarrod to go along with me, assuming his earlier words weren't just talk. I was sure that if I explained things, if Nalem would let me try, he'd understand. He wasn't Dad, and he could see the greater good, right?

Nalem purred, *'There's a principle you need to start operating on, and it's that everyone's as much of a selfish, lying sack of shit as you are."*

"Does that include you?"

"So I've told you. Your ears aren't just decorations, are they? Don't trust in people, but in their weaknesses. It's the only way to be sure you can manipulate someone to do what you want."

Question was, what did I want? I didn't usually do things for me, just what Nalem made me do. Was Nalem really giving me advice, or was this his roundabout way of pointing out how much power he had over me? I shoved my phone into my pocket and tried not to think.

When we reached the lamia, all I had to do was watch and wait and then explain things to Jarrod and Farris. Keep focused on the goal ahead, that's what I told myself.

The headlights illuminated the Welcome to California sign; Farris and Aimi cheered, Farris punching the ceiling of the car.

Jarrod checked the Pathfinder's clock and said, "We're making good time. We should be in the Bay Area before dawn, if traffic's not too bad."

"Of course it won't be! You're driving with me, after all." We hit the downward slope of the mountain, where a couple of vehicles with faulty brakes rested on the side of the road. I halfheartedly prayed for an avalanche to take us out before Nalem's plan did.

"It's been a while since we lived in California," Aimi mused. She rested her head against my arm with a small yawn. "I've missed it. You ever been, Retz?"

I shook my head. "Nope. Stayed up north my whole life."

"Staying in one place sounds so weird. How do you not get bored?"

"Sometimes things staying the same is comforting." I closed my eyes and failed to block everything out. The road speeding past us, the static-filled radio and conversations around me, Aimi's touch warm against my arm, all of it.

"I can't do this."

"If you don't, I'm taking over. You hear me?"

I reached my senses across the mostly empty road. Just a few miles ahead were a cluster of lamia, some in half-human forms and others in full snake-form with multiple heads. A few humans were curled up in fear, but none of them were dead. That was the checkpoint, and every car bad to stop there before passing on to the rest of the state.

"Fuck," I muttered under my breath.

Aimi sat up, but I interrupted her before she had a chance to ask what was wrong.

"Guys, ambush a—"

That's all I got before everything started going numb. Nalem's threat was legitimate, and he took over with frightening speed. I watched my body as Nalem shoved his heel into Aimi's foot and froze her skeleton to keep her from fleeing, leaving her glued to her seat, while he reached one arm onto Farris's shoulder and took control of his legs. A scowl stretched over my face, and that was the last thing I felt before I went numb. It wasn't my body, but Nalem's, and I was sitting far away and watching it all in a theater. It had been a long time since he'd taken that much of me over.

"Keep. Driving." It was obvious how taxing controlling two and a half bodies at once was by the growl my voice took on when Nalem spoke. "You'll thank me for this later."

"Jarrod? I kinda can't stop the car." Farris tried to pull away from Nalem's hand but nearly swerved off the road and sped up. Farris stopped fighting it once he realized it was the only way to keep Nalem from forcing us to crash.

Jarrod unbuckled his seat belt with a deep breath. "Isamu, pull your sister away and get out of the car. Fly before you hit the road or anything." He reached and grabbed me by the collar, pulling us face-to-face. "Let go, Nalem."

"Let go? Sure thing." Isamu was opening the door while pulling Aimi away, so Nalem controlled her bones to make her practically leap out of the car, taking her brother with her. They didn't have time to take their fire-form and fly off; I heard them scream and hit the road, but didn't see anything. I tried to wrest control back but was shut out with a mental snarl.

"I expected that you'd spring a trap on us, but not this soon. My mistake."

I expected Jarrod to try to choke me or something, which would've given Nalem enough contact to control his bones and maim him. But as he let go of my shirt, his scarf unfurled from around his neck, completely of its own will. It seemed to turn itself inside out—too fast for my eyes to quite catch what happened—but instead of wool, the scarf was now made of leaves and vines. One end wrapped around my neck, and the other around my arms to bind them together. Jarrod's neck, now bare, was covered in strange green runes with small leaves and thorns poking out from the skin. They were the same as the marks on his arms.

Nalem tried to breathe, but the scarf-leaf around his neck tightened. "Well, that happened. You're more Fae-tainted than I thought." He smirked. "Too late, though. Look where we are."

The road ahead merged into one lane, forcing us toward the checkpoint. We had to go through, and the lamia were waiting. At the checkpoint window, I recognized Zalin, my attacker and guide when I'd first arrived at Lady Delight's castle, in half-human form and hiding her tail.

"Fuckin' ratfinks." Farris tried to speed past, but then a snake-form lamia with three heads, large enough to eat the Pathfinder if it tried hard enough, curled up in our path. We came to a halt.

Zalin slithered over to Farris's window, tapping on the glass. When he refused to open it, she allowed another snake-form lamia to wrench the door apart with its teeth. She peered in, sneering when her eyes caught mine. "What do we have here? I thought you were bringing our prizes, boneboy."

"They fell out not even a mile away. If you hurry, you can get them before they become roadkill." Nalem tried to pull away from the scarf-leaves, but they only tightened farther. "I did what your lady asked. I just have these two complications. Would you mind?"

"Not at all." Zalin nodded, and the lamia that ripped the door off returned. It looked ready to bite Farris, but Zalin barked, "No! This one's human. We're not botching this mission with a Harvester sighting."

The lamia instead wrapped its tail against Farris, pulling him away even as he reached for his sword and tried to stab through its scales.

Once he was removed, kicking and screaming, Zalin turned back to my brother and me. "So, we've got you and a Fae-marked freak. Don't see many of those."

"I'm sure he'd fetch a pretty penny," Nalem said.

Jarrod reached for one of his pistols but had no time to draw it. Zalin tackled him, pinning him to the passenger-side door. The vines, still wrapped around my body, crashed Nalem into the back of the passenger seat.

"Damn leaves. Hey, careful here. This one's half human too."

"Figured as much. Don't worry; our Lady wants him alive." Zalin licked her lips and opened her mouth to bite. Jarrod kicked her in the stomach and, while she was winded, pulled his uninjured arm away and retrieved his pistol. Zalin stared at it for a moment, sneered, then backed away to make room for her ally. The door-crunching lamia bolted in, having passed Farris along to some other snake, only to be shot at point-blank range. Blood, guts, and shards of bone dressed the dashboard. Jarrod's face twisted in disgust, but he let me go.

Nalem rubbed his wrists, which I assume were sore from being manhandled—er, scarfhandled, I guess. "I'm surprised you didn't snap her neck. You must be strong enough for it."

"I hate killing others as it is. I don't need to be an animal about it too." He glanced out the window, where the lamia hissed and screeched over the death of their comrade, and Farris screamed too because he was being held upside down twenty feet over the road. "I don't suppose there's an easy way out of this."

"Nope. You're fucked." Nalem opened the door closest to him and stepped out. "Sorry, everyone, my pet had an accident. I'll make sure to give Lady Delight my apologies when next I see her. Speaking of which, since you've broken the ride I obtained, mind if I ride back with one of you?"

Nalem had smiled when he spoke, but it faded and I didn't understand why. Then I noticed the world going black, meaning he was passing out too. Nothing attacked us, but I got a murmured thought from Nalem before we lost consciousness completely.

"Tranquilizer darts."

I woke up, arms and legs tied together, the floor underneath me cold and slick. Metal. It bumped; I was in the back of a truck of some sort. It was too dark to see, so I closed my eyes again and whimpered.

Nalem stirred awake at the noise. *"Shh, little one, shh. Don't shut down."*

I nodded, bit my lip, and focused on not hyperventilating. *"Your stupid plan got us captured."*

"They probably didn't want to take any risks with us," Nalem told me. He was trying to sound reassuring, but an unfamiliar note of worry hung in his voice. *"One of their own was just killed, after all. Most are not as familiar with death as we are. It's just a precautionary measure, little one."*

As much as I hated it, his words did calm me. Nalem gave me grief, but he had also comforted me more times than I cared to admit. He heard all my thoughts, after all. A small shred of him seemed concerned for me or at least keeping me calm enough to stay useful.

"Retz? Is that you?"

I opened my eyes again when I heard Jarrod speak, but the darkness hadn't gone away. "Yeah, it's me. Are you okay?"

"Oh, he's fine, just peachy keen. And injured. And nearly fuckin' choked to death by your scaly friends back there." Farris wasn't even trying to mask his anger, and I couldn't blame him.

"Farris, that's not going to help us now. Calm down." Shuffling came from somewhere ahead of me. "Retz. Or Nalem, if you're there. Explain."

I sighed. Nalem noted my reluctance, and I felt a pressure in my jaw. I got the hint and nodded, letting him take over my voice to explain. "The old ally I was visiting was Lady Delight. She asked me to find the furaribi in time for her exposition, and I agreed, with the intent to double-cross her." I tried to sit up as he spoke, but moving was slow. "Do believe me, I approve of the menagerie no more than you do. I had plans to stop things before Arcadia, but—"

"Arcadia?" Jarrod's voice cracked.

"The exposition is taking place in Arcadia. Your clients are meant to be two of the centerpieces. Or were." I reached out my senses. Jarrod and Farris were tied up the same way I was, though Jarrod had managed to sit up. We seemed to be on a forested road again, judging from the amount of wildlife and lack of people; the static from what life was around gave me a headache. In what I assume was another truck just at the limits of my senses, I found the furaribi, curled up with hands and feet together, bound like the rest of us. Aimi seemed to be talking, and Isamu didn't move beyond the occasional twitch. "They are still alive. Probably with a nice road rash, though."

"You... I can't even think of an insult that matches how gross you are," Farris growled. If we weren't tied up, I'd bet money that Farris would try to choke me. "Is playing with people's lives just a game to you?"

"What better game is there?"

Before another fight broke out, I took back control of my voice from Nalem. He was tired from the whole past day, so he relented. I said, "Sorry. But that's what happened. I had no idea you'd be there, and I never meant to hurt you."

No response.

"Please believe me."

"Arcadia," Jarrod repeated, low enough that I think I was supposed to miss it. "He knew somehow. He knew."

"Who did? Who knew?"

I didn't think I'd get an answer. I sensed Farris nudge Jarrod, heard the quiet whisper of "tell him, he's your brother" that not even the growl of the engine could block out. Nalem stirred in my head, curious.

"Alexander." Jarrod sat up straight, back pressed against the wall. His voice shook when he spoke. "Alexander died too. But he didn't stay dead. We ended up in a place in Arcadia, and...he changed into something."

There was an unsaid last word, something *inhuman*. I imagined him saying it as if he was still in mourning over what happened.

"I met with him a few nights ago. He wanted to see you again, said he'd find us in Arcadia. Hours later, Aimi called me. Coincidence?"

"Fate," Farris muttered. "Everything ties together."

"Indeed it does." Nalem took my voice again, catching me off guard. "That is who gifted you your curse, is it not? Your own father couldn't handle not being there to control you, so he planted a curse to keep you leashed to his orders. Is that right?" Silence and gritted teeth, the sensation buzzing in my bones. "That's what I thought. Your father bit the dust but managed to avoid the Harvester by becoming a Faerie instead. Which would leave him with..." Visions from Nalem flashed through my head, blurring greens and reds. "How interesting. And ironic. My favorite combination."

Jarrod seemed to try to keep the hope out of his voice. "You have an idea what he is? A...Faerie?"

Farris piped up, "What, you mean some sorta' Tinkerbell?"

"Oh no. The Fae are something far worse." More images flashed through my head, slower this time, of beings that I doubted were ever human. A sentient tree-man looming over a forest, hundreds of fused carnivorous faces, a living statue of stained glass. "Those who die in Arcadia fuse with the land itself, wielding immense power but unable to leave their world for long. They have a tendency to go...mad, let's say." A masked figure with limbs of cello strings and piano-key teeth. An antlered woman in a dress of blood. "You just have poor luck. Fae who can curse are a rare and annoying breed."

The vehicle we were in bounced. My body ached in protest as my teeth slammed together.

"We're almost there," Nalem mused, slinking back into my head. I told the others, but was sure they'd already

guessed. *"Ask for the particulars of your brother's curse before we depart. It may be useful."* I sighed and did so.

"If a supernatural task is asked of me..." He paused. I'm sure he was questioning if he should trust me.

Farris nudged him again. I checked their bones closer; a few of Farris's ribs were fractured, one actually broken. I'd fix it, if he let me get close enough. I doubted he would. Jarrod's bones were stronger, but still felt worn.

"If a task is asked of me and it's in my power to complete it, I must do so. So if you're still planning on double-crossing the lamia, I'm with you. I need to get those furaribi to safety."

"And if you don't?"

The noise he made startled me. It was a strangled, defeated laugh. Next to him, Farris cringed. The truck under us slowed to a stop; we'd arrived at the castle.

"I'll turn into a rosebush. Can you believe that?" The back door of our container opened, flooding it with light. The first thing I saw was Jarrod's face, and he looked so tired, at first I swore I saw Dad instead. "He didn't bother to curse me with something useful. Just a fucking rosebush."

The lamia slithered in past me and dragged Jarrod and Farris out. Farris looked ready to bite, but Jarrod shushed him. Other lamia tried to figure out how to handle me.

"Hey, be careful," I called out to Jarrod, as if that'd fix anything. "I'll get you out. I—"

"Don't make promises, Retz," Jarrod called back, before he was dragged out of sight. "What do you think got me into this mess?"

And then he was gone, and the lamia were untying my feet and telling me to walk. They had guns and sleeping tranqs aimed at me, and at the front of the group was Zalin, her makeup smeared and mouth curled into a snarl. I started walking.

Nalem sighed, stretching as if he'd been the one tied up instead of me. *The plot thickens, and you remain as pathetic an imbecile as you've always been. Why am I not surprised?*

"Not right now, Nalem. Please." I looked at the other truck.Both resembled blank white U-Hauls. The lamia were carrying out the furaribi, keeping fire extinguishers pointed at them. Aimi was pulled out first, and as soon as she saw me, she glared but stayed quiet. Two lamia went to get Isamu but didn't come out until a third entered with a tranquilizer. He was still writhing when they pulled him out, even as his movements slowed and his eyes shut.

"Regret? Guilt? What a sappy human you are, little one."

I found myself back in Lady Delight's dining hall. My captors placed me in the same seat I had sat in less than two days earlier but did not untie me. I didn't get a chance to see where the others were taken.

At the head of the table rested Lady Delight. This time, she wore a black dress with violet trim. The table was clean and empty, but the smell of blood intermingled with her lavender perfume. She rested her chin on her interlaced fingers and didn't invade my personal space, though she licked her lips when she smiled at me.

"You finished earlier than I anticipated," she said to me, her voice a low purr. "I am so thankful, my dear Nalem and vessel."

"You sure have a funny way of showing it," I responded. I tried to ease my hands out of the rope but only succeeded in chafing my wrists.

"Do forgive me for the rude way you were brought here. I had to take precautions that you wouldn't hurt my dear staff—though I was unable to anticipate your brother. Poor Zalin told me how traumatizing it was." She sighed through her teeth. "But that is not why we're here. Now you have succeeded, we have a small problem. I owe you a favor, and—" She slithered over to me, not actually touching but leaning in close enough that I smelled the rot in her breath. "—I do hate being in debt."

Nalem took over my body again, edging away from her as he contorted my face into a grimace. "So I become your tied-up hostage. Going to make me work for you instead, with no hope of repayment?"

"You see, I considered that." She raised one finger and scratched the nail down my lips. "I almost accepted the exchange you wanted. Deal with the hassle of taking you to Arcadia and you being my responsibility—you would be my guest, after all." Two claws ran down my neck. "Or I can make you work for me. Your powers are invaluable for both battle and tracking. And there is the matter of the Harvester to consider...but you and he are double-edged swords." She leaned in and whispered, "Like father, like son, hmm?"

I tried to pull away from her and almost knocked my chair over with me in it. I planted my feet on the floor to stay steady while Nalem said, "I would behave myself at the expo. Acting out in Arcadia is more difficult than I care to admit." His face—and thus, mine—contorted into a snarl. "Are you so foolish to assume I'd ever stoop low enough to work for you?"

"Not *for* me. With me." Lady Delight placed the tips of her nails under my chin. "I do believe your dream is foolish, but I could assist you. Give you the resources you need. Even an army, if you asked. You would just need to help me in kind."

"I thought you said you didn't want anything to do with my plans."

"Business equals compromise. So does love."

Nalem groaned, leaning back in our seat to pull away from the claws. "If I ever really and truly loved you, I would never have let you even consider opening this menagerie. And, need I remind you, I only married you to get you out of the brothels, and you are technically a widow now. Let me tell you, dying's a lot easier than divorce paperwork."

"Whether or not I count as a widow when my husband regenerates is another matter entirely." Lady Delight pursed her lips together, crossing her arms and curling her tail around herself. "You speak as if you saved me from my old life for no reason."

"I did it because you were a pathetic child."

"You are quite skilled at lying to yourself. You did it because you loved me. You just love your obsessions more."

I considered speaking up, point out that I'd lived with Nalem all my life and never felt a shred of affection for anything from him. If he ever acted nice to anyone, he planned to use them later. This included me, my family, and definitely Lady Delight if he'd rescued and married her. But I said nothing, because even if Nalem didn't care, Lady Delight still seemed to hold a torch for the bastard—and I'm sure she'd painfully silence me if I pointed out how foolish that was.

Lady Delight's tail lashed out at the legs of the chair, sending Nalem and me crashing to the floor. She loomed over us. "But that can all be fixed. I have yet to tell you my new plan, after all."

"Does it involve kicking me while I'm down?"

"I am pleased that your sense of humor remains intact." Lady Delight clapped for one of her servants, who handed her a plate. She picked something up from it and leaned over, dangling it delicately over my face. "I will explain, but you really should eat first. You're skin and bones, after all."

It was the raw rabbit I'd refused the other day—had it really only been two days?—and by the looks of things, it hadn't been refrigerated or anything. Just smelling it, combined with the blood and lavender perfume of Lady Delight, made me want to hurl.

"You eat it," I told Nalem. *"Your wife prepared it just for you, after all."*

"Little one, I am revoking your sassing privileges, starting now."

10 - JARROD

"**H**ulderkind. Twenty-four years of age. Female."

"Born that way, not staying that way," I protested. "I mean, I've taken testosterone for years now. Do you have any idea how long it took to grow this beard?"

Seeing as I was both injured and a new acquisition, I was dragged into the infirmary and strapped to a table. The room did not have the freakish white veneer of the mortal hospitals I abhorred, but was a light yellow and perfumed with pine layered over sanitizers and blood. I supposed the room was supposed to look golden, sunny. It just made me think of bile and piss.

The lamia in the white lab coat in the back ignored my commentary. He lectured to the other lamia, who jotted down his every word. None of the lamia worked on me. They had a handful of humans doing so. Those humans worked in a daze; I'm sure their minds were broken due to constant supernatural exposure they were unequipped to handle.

"As we already saw," the lamia intoned. "This specimen is stronger and more durable compared to the average human but weaker than the average huldra. She also has a tail—yes, the bovine variety, that is correct—but does not possess a hole in her back. We can thus assume that she has all of her internal organs. No, we cannot dissect her to check, the Lady would be displeased with us."

"I'd also prefer not being cut up," I grumbled, keeping the leaves of my scarf tightly crossed over my bare chest. They had tried to remove the scarf but realized it was fused to me, even though they couldn't see that it was actually made of leaves. I wasn't meant to be tied up, but I had punched out the doctor who tried to remove my boxers. Said doctor was now in surgery in another room. How many other rooms were there, and were Farris, Retz, or the furaribi in any of them?

"Can anyone tell what kind of markings those are?" A lamia raised her hand, answering in a voice too low for me to hear. "Yes, Fae-marks, correct! As we can tell from the patterns, these indicate a binding curse, with a transformative element..." My scarf tightened around my chest, and I wished it covered all of me. All these traits I tried to hide were being turned into an educational lecture. They just looked and my identity was laid as bare as my body. Made me want to retreat into my head and go numb for a bit, as Retz had once described doing when Nalem was in control.

I pulled at my restraints, which were metal to hold my strength. My injured arm still ached. The bandage had been removed, revealing reddened skin and tissues trying to knit the hole from the unicorn horn shut.

"If there's a test on this, I hope you all fail."

The head lamia—was he a doctor, or just a cruel professor?—turned to me at my comment. The sick hospital lights made his green scales look the color of vomit. "Excuse me. These hatchlings must learn all they can about other beings, so they have the knowledge of how to engage or care for them, whichever their future career requires." He waved the other lamia closer, until I was surrounded. "For example, huldra have an advanced healing factor. But as we can see, hulderkind do not have all the physical traits of their nonhuman parent. Question is, how fast does this one heal?"

The lamia whispered amongst themselves, as the human doctors continued to prod me and take measurements. I glared at the lamia around me, their details blurry due to my lack of glasses. A few recoiled and backed away. One, however, picked up something presumably sharp and slunk over.

"There's a shoulder wound here," the student intoned, "but we have no idea when the injury first occurred. Even if she told us, she might be lying."

"Tuesday evening," I answered, just in case I'd been out longer than I thought and it was no longer Wednesday. "And I do have a healing factor. There's a freebie on your exam. And extra credit, I'm not a woman, stop calling me one. See the beard and all that?"

The student stared at me, then raised a scalpel. The teacher rushed forward, protesting. I had a moment of hope.

"You cannot do that. Half humans may still summon the Harvester. While it usually arrives only when a human perishes, it may arrive unbidden if Nalem or one of his allies are injured. Here, let one of the humans here do it, that's less likely to draw unwanted attention."

In human hands, the scalpel glided across the skin of my stomach. Blood bubbled up to the chorus of pencils scratching on paper, with crescendos of oohs and aahs as the wound knit itself shut in under a minute. Even I got a sick fascination out of watching sometimes. Reminded me of Wolverine from the X-Men. Not that I enjoyed being cut up for the amusement of a class, of course.

"Do it again," someone whispered.

When the scalpel next came down, one scarf-leaf unfurled from around my chest and wrapped around the doctor's arm. He hissed as I twisted the limb, pointing it toward the lamia.

I said, "This is a class, right? So inform me. How fast do you guys heal?"

The students backed away, their teacher reminding them that I was tied down though he slithered away himself. The human doctors swarmed, holding my scarf still and reclaiming the weapon. I tugged against the restraints and felt them loosen. Just a bit more—

Pain shot up through my foot. I bit my lip to keep from shouting, but the pain wouldn't stop. The part of the scarf around my chest constricted, even as the doctors tried to pry it away. Another doctor at the foot of the table lifted up something red and dripping.

"Yes, that's why we usually take a toe from our specimens. They have nearly every ingredient we need for tracking purposes, but do not detract much from the overall appearance." There was pride in the teacher's voice. "In fact, the furaribi were reclaimed by someone who tracked them by their bones, if you can believe it. We may even get to look at him..."

"Don't touch him," I snarled, which got the lamia to jump. "Don't you touch him or anyone else. You think this is fun? Do you think—"

Too late, someone applied the anesthetic. A strong one, too. My tongue went numb midsentence, and the rest of the world went soon after. The blurriness gave way to darkness. I wondered how long it'd be before I got used to blacking out.

At first glance, I thought I'd fallen into another vision of Alexander's. The grass was soft and green, and the sky overhead was dark. But I saw stars, not the glowing red roses that obscured the skies in his realm. And when did I get my glasses back to see them with, anyway? My tail twitched. Even the ground felt wrong.

"Mornin', hon." Farris plopped down next to me. He was dressed in a white suit, which only confused me further. "How're you feeling?"

Good question. The anesthetic left my body tingling and sluggish. My skin felt too thick. Feeling my feet wasn't an option. I glanced down to find a pair of white socks cleaner than any pair I owned, and my little toe was missing from my left foot. I was dressed in white too—a T-shirt and pants, not a dress, thank the stars.

"I feel like a marshmallow," I finally responded, words more slurred than I cared to admit. "Where are we?"

"I've heard everything from a temporary holding area to a personalized habitat. I'm starting to think the lamia crossed "cage" out of their dictionaries." Farris leaned over and smoothed hair out of my face. "If you look behind you, you'll see the glass. The furaribi are across from us."

I considered looking, but moving didn't seem feasible. I focused on Farris as I collected my senses. "At least they're close by. Seen Retz?"

Farris shook his head. "Heard some mutterings from the guards, and I think he's being moved into the menagerie with us, but ain't going on the expo." He took a deep breath, reluctant to continue. "We are. You've got a price tag on your tail."

"For the love of..." It took my confused body a few tries, but I managed to grab hold of my tail and check the golden tag on it. Different angles showed prices in different measurements and languages. In dollars, I was worth just under twenty thousand. "Judging by this menagerie's standards, I should probably feel insulted. How much are you?"

Farris lifted his wrist. A tag dangled from it, but it had no numbers. It instead read "Special Auction."

"But you're just a human."

"Human royalty, turns out. You think I'd remember that. They keep calling me the White Prince, but I'm not sure if that joke's because of my skin or these duds." He gestured to his outfit and gave me a sheepish smile. "Of course, I haven't asked. They assume I'm not an idiot who forgot who the hell he is. Soon as they noticed me, they pulled me out of the doctor's office and stuck me with the tag and this monkey suit."

A prince? I tried to imagine it. If nothing else, it explained my boyfriend's complete disregard for authority; who'd dare boss around a prince? "It's a start, at least. I'm sure someone will explain." I decided that sitting up would be a good plan, though my body was less than cooperative. Considering it took copious amounts of alcohol to achieve this effect, and how fast I passed out, the anesthetic had probably been meant for a far larger creature. A rhino, perhaps. "So how'd you get me here?"

"I said you were my consort, and that if I wasn't given you and your stuff, I would do a few choice, horrible things." Farris placed a hand on my back to help me up. "I never got around to what horrible things I'd do, but hey, results are results."

Once I was sitting without fear of falling back over, Farris retrieved my stuff. There was my duster, binder, all guns—though emptied—and a few other supplies. The unicorn horns, of course, were not among them. Farris covered for me while I got redressed.

I said, "So, all you learned is that you're royalty. No idea where from, or what family, or anything else."

"Don't have the foggiest, nope. But don't worry, I'll ask." Once I had my coat on, he put a hand on my uninjured shoulder. "More importantly, you okay?"

"The numbness will pass and the pain after that. I guess we'll find out if I can regrow body parts."

Farris didn't say anything. The concern didn't leave his face.

I groaned. "This mission's got me worried. I have no idea how we're going to rescue anyone else, much less ourselves, and..."

Farris put an arm around me, again avoiding my injured shoulder. "Don't worry. We'll get out of this. And if we can't come up with a bombastic escape plan first,

I'm sure I can pull out the consort excuse to get us sold as a package deal."

Escape. I looked at the cage around us; it was large, and fairly secure. If other creatures couldn't claw their way out, I doubted I could. There had to be some weaknesses. It was just a puzzle to solve, same as any other case. But my mind was still sluggish, so I leaned against Farris and closed my eyes.

"Am I really your consort?"

"You can be. If you really want to be, I guess."

I wasn't sure. I loved Farris, but there was still so much of him that remained a mystery. His past. What he was meant to be the White Prince of. The spiraling tattoo on his left shoulder, his myriad of strange habits and skills he didn't even realize he had. His insistent belief in Fate. Why he forgot it all. At least he had an excuse for not telling me these things. How much of myself did I really share with him?

I said, "Let's focus on getting out of here first. After that, we can talk."

It was always night in our cage. It was designed to resemble a forest clearing with white castle ruins, and a full moon overhead. I tried to learn more from a staff member; she said it wasn't built for us, but the only fitting "habitat" for a human prince and a hulderkind on such short notice. When we pressed for details about Farris's royalty or where Retz ended up, she slithered away without a word. The guards in front of our cage were even more reticent.

As Farris said, the furaribi were across from us, too far to hear but close enough to communicate with through the bastard child of sign language and charades. They remained in fire-form at all times; I don't think they were allowed to change in case guests came through. There was a strange sheen to the glass of their cage, which I assumed meant it was fireproof. It was decorated in reds and violets with hanging fabrics and wisps of smoke that reminded me of an opium den. Aimi was more communicative, signalling that she and her brother were not harmed. Isamu barely spoke but sulked around the cage in search of a new exit.

Farris and I checked our cage but also had no luck. The grass was fake with hard stone underneath, so digging wasn't an option. The structure was sound, and as expected, the glass was too strong for me to punch through. I tried once I shook off the anesthetic, even though my shoulder and foot still ached.

I was unsure how much time passed, but the lights of the menagerie slowly dimmed, until only soft orange glows lit the walkway for the lamia on patrol. The chattering of creatures in the menagerie lulled. Isamu stopped his skulking and curled up next to Aimi, the two of them drifting to sleep. Farris yawned and suggested we do the same. I tried, though my rest was uneasy, and

I'd gone long enough without a drink that I felt the phantom sensation of bugs crawling all over my skin.

I did not remember my dreams. I recall waking up, Farris's arms still around me. There was tapping at the glass.

I pulled away and slipped on my glasses before approaching. The tapping continued. It wasn't the guards, whose heads hung as if they were asleep. It came from a staff member, not a lamia but human in appearance. He was in janitorial grays, leaning on a mop, his hat unable to contain a mess of black curls. His skin was dark, and his eyes bright yet silver.

No, wait. One was green. It was the one in his neck.

"Not you."

"Yes, us. My my, how you've grown." The figure's grin was uneven, teeth filed to resemble a shark's. "Come closer, would you?"

I shook my head. The Harvester. Usually when I saw him, he was a monochrome blur, a blink of a thousand eyes gone just as quickly. But he looked the same as I'd first seen him, almost human. I slunk away from his soft voice.

"Don't be that way." He was no longer behind the glass but right in front of me. I hadn't even seen him move. Neither did the guards—out of the corner of my vision, I noticed one's neck was slit, blood slowly trailing down her chest. My visitor said, "We are not here for you. We just figured, while we were here, we would speak with you. Make a request, you might call it." The eye in his neck blinked.

"A...request?" My scarf tightened around my neck. "Last time you did that, Nalem ended up in my brother's head."

"A fair exchange for saving a life. Mostly." The Harvester sighed, rocking on his heels as I had seen Nalem—and Retz by proxy—do many times. "We can guarantee this request requires no possession."

Just being near him made my skin crawl, but with my curse intact, I didn't have much of a choice. I glanced over my shoulder at Farris; he was still asleep, oblivious. Across from us, the furaribi continued to slumber. The Harvester looked around the cage, but the eye in his neck stared right at me.

"What's the job?"

The Harvester reached into nothing, pulling out two pairs of eyes. He juggled them. "We can both assume Nalem will end up in Arcadia in the near future. As you must be aware, he can regenerate. Arcadia is the exception to this rule, and there are those who wish to exploit that."

"You want me to make sure he doesn't die there."

"Correct." He caught the four eyes; they sunk into his palms, then blinked, part of the skin. "It is most unfortunate this is the life you have grown into. You would have pleased us greatly as a scholar."

"And it seems you're vying for the circus."

The Harvester smiled again. "Oh, we wish, but we're just so busy. Otherwise, we would look after Nalem ourselves, as we used to."

I mulled over earlier discussions and memories of the Harvester and Nalem. "I'll have you understand, Nalem and I don't see eye to eye often. Why me, and why him?"

"One. You are the one closest to, and most equipped to protect, his vessel." Of the remaining eyes, he tossed one and caught it in his mouth. His next words were muffled. "Two. Nalem is our responsibility, but so are the mortal inhabitants of this world. We lost our ability to watch our son well before the population hit seven billion." Down went the second eye.

"Your—" As much as that explained, it only raised more questions. I did not have time to ask. My scarf was on the verge of constricting me in its impatience for my agreement. "I will do my best."

Squish. The Harvester chewed the eyes as he reached into nothing again. He pulled a pair of gloves covered in shimmering blue scales out of thin air and swallowed as he put them on.

"You didn't even ask what you would get in return. Foolish or selfless, we cannot decide." He offered a hand to me. The scales of the gloves bore many scrapes, and the leather was rough from years of use. "Still, we shall not cheat you. We offer one save in return. One revival, a death completely ignored, no questions asked."

I could say no. Decide that my own life was less important than curtailing Nalem's influence. I knew Alexander had a plan to save Retz, and if he was in Arcadia, that might involve killing Nalem too. Two birds, one stone. I would protect Nalem by proxy of protecting Retz, but if there was a way to separate the two, I would be the first in line to wipe Nalem off the face of the Earth. However...

"The free revival. Can I use it on someone else?"

The night I met the Harvester was one of many firsts. It was also the night I met Nalem. The night Retz died. The night I learned how far my parents would go for my brother and me.

But before all that, it was the night I first killed something.

They were called revenants. Ghosts who had become strong enough to possess a body, living or dead, to continue their mission. Usually, ghosts could only visit places important to them when they were alive; possessing a body bypassed that limitation. And while Alexander claimed he'd retired from paranormal investigations in order to be a husband and father, he still took the occasional case. Exorcisms were common. This one hadn't gone quite right.

I'd been five, still thought I was a girl, and my first kill had been a teenage boy. I never found out if he was already a revenant or not, but when I tackled him in self-preservation and slammed his head against the floor, he still bled. Alexander had said not to harm others, but he and Erika had both said that it was okay in self-defense. The boy had a knife. I didn't need one.

I cracked his skull open on the floor. I didn't understand death, not until that night, but there was blood and bits of brain and bone all over my hands, my pajamas, the floor. I threw up. Part of me knew I'd gone too far. Tears washing away the filth on my face, I went to find my parents. I found Erika tearing one revenant off from biting her shoulder while she punched another into a wall. Alexander shot the dead ones in the head, and performed quick exorcisms on the living ones. I watched the fight, quiet.

When it was done, Erika noticed me first. Scooped me up and cleaned the blood off my face. Alexander checked over the bodies, asked me if I was hurt. I said no, but a bad man tried to hurt me, and I made him stop. I remember disgust and grief contorting my father's face.

Then we heard the crying. In the heat of battle, we'd forgotten my baby brother.

My parents ran, Erika still carrying me. We almost ran into Alexander when he stopped in the doorway. All the color drained from his face, then Erika's, and there was an emotion on their faces that I'd never seen before. Horror. I was confused until I looked into the room, at what was standing over Retz's crib.

This revenant's body was dead. The skin of his fingers had rotted and given way to bone. His fingers were poking through my baby brother's mouth, through where he'd broken through the skull. Huldra can take a lot of pain, but the energy that fuels them is concentrated in their heads; they're as weak to decapitation or blows to the head as any mortal. There was no blood; even before Nalem, Retz never grew organs or veins.

I later learned that Alexander had faced the revenant in life, was the reason for its death years ago. In that moment, all I knew was the creature was going to taunt us, and then Alexander shot it in the head. And the body. And arm. He wouldn't stop shooting, and the noise echoed in place of my brother's crying. I clapped my hands over my ears until he stopped. And when he did, he just stood there, staring at Retz's tiny corpse. The body was ripped apart. Mom held me tight, too shocked to even cry.

Then there was a gloved hand on his shoulder, someone who hadn't been there before. "Poor little one. Never even got his milk teeth in, did he?"

Alexander pulled away and aimed his gun at the stranger. The figure was shorter than him but taller than Erika. He resembled the grim reaper from pictures I'd seen, but instead of a skull was a human face with skin like worn leather. His hood was covered in scales. He leaned on a scythe of gray lightning, its blade inset with eyes. It stared at me and blinked.

"The Harvester," Erika breathed. She stepped back and held me tighter to her chest. "Please spare us. They were possessed. The little one, she did not know."

"Oh, don't you plead. The fault was not yours, but our own." The Harvester's smile was serene as he reached into the air and pulled out a teacup. He drank from it; the cup was also adorned with an eyeball. "As an apology, we are willing to make an offer with you. May we offer either of you a cup of tea while you listen?"

"You shouldn't exist," Alexander muttered. "They said you were a boogeyman. A fairy tale."

"Now, those are two completely different things, and we are neither. Not to be rude, of course." The Harvester's grin didn't quite reach any of his eyes. Not until he looked at Retz; for some reason, the sight of that empty, motionless body gave him his most human emotion.

I wanted to hide my face in my mother's bloodied pajamas, but couldn't bring myself to look away.

"Our offer is this. We can fix your son's body, keep the soul intact. But the spark of it has been snuffed. The life of another will need to join his, in order for the body and soul to function."

Erika shook her head. She muttered no, we shouldn't listen, the Harvester only destroyed. But Alexander stared at Retz's corpse, one of his still hands clenched into a tiny fist.

"I'll forfeit myself," he finally said, "if it will save him."

"Our apologies for not being clear. We already have an individual in mind." The Harvester took a last sip from the teacup before tossing it into the air, where it blinked and vanished. "You just need to say yes. And if you change your mind—well, it's as easy as killing him again."

"Alexander, don't, please." Erika's face was wet with tears. I didn't understand why, not back then. "Nothing good comes of the Harvester. We can have another child, just say no..."

The Harvester's smile drifted away. Patches of his skin seemed to fade, revealing the swirling gray underneath. "We are only trying to save...one dear to you, another dear to us. That's all we ever wanted. But the stories evolve and neglect that, now don't they?"

Alexander said nothing. Just offered his hand. The Harvester shook it, still smiling, then took off his gloves. He opened his mouth. The skin around his jaw went gray, distending as he reached in. Rows of filed teeth filled the gaping maw, his fingers scraping against them. He pulled out two eyes, slick with spit and bile, flashing between colors so quickly it was mesmeric.

The Harvester tapped them with his fingers, said, "Be good this time," and placed them in the back of my brother's head. The body knitted itself back together. The tiny fingers flexed.

The eyes opened, splashed with color like an oil stain. What I later learned was Nalem grinned, his malice already contorting my brother's face. But then the eyes faded to green again. Retz gurgled a not-quite word, watching the three of us as he sucked on his fist.

The Harvester slipped his gloves back on and patted my brother's head. "There we go, little one." He said what I thought was a blessing in a tongue I didn't understand, and then he was gone. Same as the teacup, no trace.

My stomach churned. Vomit and bile rose in the back of my throat, but I was scared eyes would roll off my tongue if I dared open my mouth.

I clung to Erika tighter, and she held me back. We were both crying, though I had yet to comprehend all that had happened. Retz's babbling was muffled by the fist he slobbered on. Alexander didn't move, as if he really had given his life and turned into a statue.

At the lack of attention, Retz cried. With mechanical motions, Alexander stepped forward. Smoothed the wisps of black hair. Checked to see if the skull really was fixed. The baby continued to cry, so Alexander picked him up.

"Shh. It's all right. You're alive again."

And with the voice of a child who hadn't even said his first word, Nalem responded, "Bastard knew I hated babies."

11 - RETZ

lmost every step back to the menagerie, I had to stop to hurl. Cold, raw rabbit tastes even worst the second time around as warm chunks. My guards jabbed me in the back with small clubs to push me forward; they didn't want to risk physical contact with me. I was handcuffed, and while I was allowed to walk this time, I had just lost my toe to the infirmary. I should've been upset, but all I could focus on was how ironic it'd be, if someone tracked me down the way I'd tracked down the furaribi. Besides, I could always replace my missing toe with other bones. Not like I took my socks off much. But more than anything, I wanted to at least wipe the blood and vomit drying on my face.

"At least your face is finally starting to look as disgusting as you are on the inside."

All I managed was a groan. A guard shoved me, causing me to lose my footing and crash into the plush red-and-blue carpet. Soft but not comfortable to crash into headfirst. I hoped that if I didn't move, they'd leave me for dead, but they kept prodding me until I got back to my feet.

By the time I'd expelled all the dead rabbit from my system, I would've rather fallen unconscious again. But then we passed through the menagerie doors. I felt multiple beings tense at my presence, some even freezing to watch. I didn't meet anyone's gaze.

"Nalem? Why'd she bring us back here?"

"She said she had a new plan for us. So I assume she will propose it in front of either the furaribi's or your brother's cage, so she can use them as a threat against you." Nalem was pacing in my head, steps slow from tiredness. His footsteps clacked against the base of my skull, the pressure simultaneously irritating and grounding.

Lady Delight, who had gone ahead of us due to impatience with my puke breaks, was almost where Nalem expected. We passed the furaribi, and Jarrod and Farris across from them. Aimi and Jarrod pressed against the glass to watch me, a mix of worry and resentment in their eyes. Isamu tensed, the flames across his body flaring up, as if my very presence caused him to flare up. Farris examined a corner of his cage, ignoring my presence.

But we didn't stop at their cages. No, the one we stopped at was a temple of bone, though even the briefest check with my powers confirmed they were fake. The temple was on a small cliff, with water lapping at the base and steps to a small beach. It was dusk inside, tiny pinpricks in the violet sky indicating stars.

"What do you think?" Lady Delight asked when we approached. "There's a throne in there and everything. And if memory serves me correctly, you once said you grew up by the ocean. Pacific, I believe. You can even see the sea serpent's tank from here."

Nalem stopped pacing in my head. He didn't snark, didn't even move, just stared through my eyes. "You're caging me."

"For your own good, of course. You may have many enemies, but they cannot reach you here." Lady Delight raised a finger to her lips. "It may also bring my menagerie some renown, having the legendary Nalem captured within its halls where he cannot inflict his wrath, or that of the Harvester's, on anyone else. But that is just an added bonus."

My chest felt like it was caving in with emotions that weren't mine. Rage kindled in there, of course Nalem was angry, but more than that, there was a murky sadness that muddied it all up. Nostalgia for what should've been, but all the details were wrong. It....hurt, and that, more than the prospect of being caged forever, scared me.

I spoke up for him, "But if the Harvester looks out for Nalem, won't he break us out?"

"Nalem only provokes the Harvester when in danger. And none shall confront him here." Lady Delight slithered around the cage, running a claw along the glass. "Our dear friend has the same problem every time, you see. He relies on others until he gains power. Then he tosses those alliances aside if they refuse to comply with his schemes." Her words were bitter, even in her honey-coated tone.

"So you think caging me is going to change my mind?" Nalem took my voice back with a shout. Others turned to watch. "You have some nerve! If it weren't for me, you would still be squandering for fucks in the gutter. This is how you repay me?"

Lady Delight bared her fangs with a hiss. "This is how I save you. You took me from that gutter and showed me what the world held."

The guards pressed their clubs against me, preparing to open the cage and shove me in.

"Now, allow me to—"

"Cut the crap." While my hands were bound, my feet were not. At Nalem's request, I kicked backward into one of the guards, using the contact to access his skeleton and snap his neck. The other guard prepared to swing, only to find her buddy's ribs breaking out of his body to pierce her, through the lungs, through the heart. With those out of the way, I backed up and put the corpses between me and Lady Delight.

And then I ran.

With every new misfortune another kick in the head, I wanted nothing more than to curl up somewhere, cry in pain—the lamia hadn't been kind enough to give me any anaesthetic—and then pass out. But I got everyone into this mess, and if Nalem's plan backfired us into a cage, then I had to stay strong and get us all out. Hopefully, the threat of summoning the Harvester would keep the lamia from targeting me during my escape, and then I could figure out a different way to rescue the others. Maybe see if Mom or any of her contacts might help. Maybe figure out what happened to Dad, since I'm sure he'd want to keep Jarrod safe if nothing else. So I bolted, the two lamia corpses trailing behind me.

When I passed the others, I heard Aimi shout, words muffled by the glass, "Behind you!"

I turned, too late, and a tranquilizer dart pinned me in the chest.

"Stay awake, little one. We have to get out of here. Stay awake—"

The carpet wasn't any softer the second time I hit it.

At first, I thought I was dreaming.

I ran up a hill, and someone held my hand, but I somehow wasn't able to look back to see who it was. I didn't stop until I reached the top, which is when I heaved for breath and caught a glow out of the corner of my eye. There was a city, and a fire spreading fast. People scurried around the streets, and they were so small.

The thought that passed was, *"Not ants, though. They aren't so organized. More like fleas. Clusters of lecherous fleas."*

"The Monsieur always said he wanted to see it in lights," said a familiar voice, though with more of an accent than I remembered. I faced Lady Delight, the younger one I'd seen from earlier flashes of Nalem's memories. Her dress was gaudy and torn, and her makeup was smeared. Her smile was fragile; I got caught on how red her lips were. "I don't think this is what he meant, though."

"He asked, and so he received. Now he knows his intent means nothing." That was my mouth moving, but not my voice. It was Nalem's, stronger and not as ethereal as when he spoke in my head. He reached out with a skeletal hand and touched Lady Delight's cheek; I got a brief glimpse of her young but already-battered bones. "How do you fare?"

I think she answered, but I lost focus as her features shifted. For a split second, I saw a different woman in her place, one with dark skin and a darker mane of hair. Her eyes were gray, blank until she smiled. Her sadistic grin looked the way Nalem's felt.

"You just remind me of someone," Nalem responded to a question I didn't hear. He swept an arm along the countryside on the other end of the hill. "We'll cross these until we're in Spain, and that is where we'll part. I need to secure a ship."

"A ship?" The young Lady Delight purred, even as her face betrayed her nervousness. "I was born at sea, not far from here. And where would you go, my bold sailor?"

He started to answer but caught himself. There was another flash of that woman, and Nalem's fists clenched. "I believe it's called the Americas around these parts. I have business there."

"Then take me with you. Please." She ran her fingers, not yet decaled or trimmed into sharp points, through her hair. "I could be a valuable asset in so-called business."

"Not the kind of asset I need," Nalem answered.

Lady Delight frowned, seconds away from sobbing.

"Hold your tears. Just because you aren't, doesn't mean you won't be."

Lady Delight nodded, dabbing at the corner of her eyes so as not to further disturb her makeup. "I see. Thank you. May I ask what business you have in the Americas?"

The smile felt too wide on my face. "To put it simply, I'm going to fix the world."

"You get out of there, little one."

I felt myself being pulled backward, and then I opened eyes I didn't realize were closed. I looked up at a dusky sky, waves lapping somewhere under me, and sighed. I had ended up in the cage after all.

"I must really be slipping with my defenses," Nalem muttered, pacing again in my skull.

"Memories? I thought they were dreams. Sorry." I sat up, though my limbs didn't really want to cooperate. I found I was dressed in white, which only further accentuated how pale I was. I didn't have shoes, and there was a slit in the back of my shirt. I reached to feel it and found the ribbons that kept my back closed were missing, though the corset piercings themselves were still intact. Anyone looking inside my body would see bones floating in a void, defying all biological sensibilities. *"But while we're on the subject. You did save Lady Delight?"*

"Ages ago. She was a pathetic hatchling, I helped her out. Married her to get her on board the ship with me. Helped set her up, assuming she would be of use to me, but she only focused on her own gain, so I left." He spun on his heels, pausing to look at the sky over us. *"And here we are. It does resemble what I told her I wanted, at least in part. Yet it isn't right at all."*

I stretched my arms and cracked my knuckles. *"Who was that lady, the curly-haired one?"*

Nalem didn't answer. He rarely did when his past came up. The most I'd gotten out of him over the years was that I was not his first vessel, he'd always had his powers, and he claimed to be young when Mesopotamia was in its prime. I did the math once and realized that meant he was a few thousand years old, and when I later told him he should act his age, he just laughed at me.

Seeing as I wasn't going to get an answer, I decided to do some exploring. The bone temple was small, just enough to hold a throne and a room barely big enough for a bed. If I walked down to the beach, the water was warm as if heated by a day's worth of sun, and I was able to touch the glass. The other three walls were painted over, so I could only look out of the front one, and even then, I had to press my face against the glass to look down the aisle at other cages.

When I say there were guards everywhere, I mean *everywhere.* Each cage had at least three, armed with clubs and stun guns as they led creatures out of their cages and down the halls. Lady Delight herself was at the cage Farris and Jarrod were in, and seemed to be talking to them, though they were too far away for me to hear anything. Jarrod looked worried as he pleaded something, while Farris had a hand on my brother's shoulders. Lady Delight focused on Farris more, but when I reached out with my powers to check on them, all three felt tense. And Jarrod was missing one of his little toes, same as me.

Nalem pointed out, *"But Farris is not. Because he is human, I assume. But there has to be something more, for Lady Delight to keep him. I wonder why..."*

Before I could remind him that I had no idea, the three turned around. I couldn't see what they were looking at because it was on the same side of the aisle as me, and the glass was too thick for me to hear, but I was able to reach out with my powers. I was hit with a flash of heat and movement; Isamu was trying to take out the guards. None of them were around Aimi, just him. A few guards felt poised to fire tranqs at him, but then Lady Delight slithered forward and spoke. She pointed at Aimi, bared her fangs. Isamu went slack and cold, and the guards could finally grab him. Aimi ran forward, but a third guard stepped in and kept her back. She shook where she stood.

"They're being separated?"

Nalem stirred in my head, and I felt a wave of unease. *"It appears so. I do so hate unwanted complications."*

I was still pressed against the glass, so I was able to see Jarrod staring at me. I waved; he gave a small wave back and mouthed something. I guessed that he was asking if I was okay. I nodded and flashed him a thumbs-up. But then Lady Delight moved to leave, and two of her guards opened the cage. Farris grabbed Jarrod's arm and pulled him along. My brother mouthed a few more words before they left the cage and followed Lady Delight. Farris held his head high, projecting confidence and poise that didn't match the jokester of the past few days. It was enough to keep the chains and tranquilizers at bay.

Soon, the guards were gone, save for the amount usually on patrol. Most of the creatures went too, most of them in chains or forced into smaller wheeled cages for transport. Even the unicorn from earlier stomped and tried to pull away from the chains pulling it along, out of the menagerie to gods-knew-where. Aimi and I were amongst the few creatures remaining.

"Now what?"

Nalem hummed as he thought. I kept feeling flashes of unease, maybe even something close to fear. He had an idea, but it was one he didn't want to use. I walked along the beach as he thought, and I realized I'd never been to a real beach. I dug my toes into the sand and wondered if I ever would.

"Oh, you will. Stop being so melodramatic." Nalem glanced around through my eyes and yawned. *"I'd prefer having more energy for this, but it will have to do. We'll have to work fast once we begin."*

"What're we doing?"

"I will explain, but first, a question. Would you rather I warp the bones of your face or your ribs?"

I had to wait until night, after the creatures for the expo were removed and those remaining were calm and asleep. Even the guards seemed lulled, and the ones in front of my cage kept themselves awake by talking amongst themselves. Wondering what they'd done to deserve guarding Nalem, I bet.

"Are you sure I can't take my shirt off first?" I asked Nalem as I paced around the cage. I wandered around the cliff

outside the temple, staying close to the part of it touching the glass walls.

"I already told you; if you take any such precautions, the guards will realize this is planned." Nalem stretched his limbs in preparation for his escape plan. *"Remember: pretend you aren't cooperating. Maybe even attempt to fight back. Not that it will work, but they'll be none the wiser."*

I ran a hand through my disheveled hair. *"I can do that. I might even win. What if I—"*

"No, you can't. Besides, that'd ruin the plan. And we can't have that, now can we?" With no warning, Nalem started his scheme—by throwing the brunt of his powers against my knees. I crashed into the glass on my way down. In case that wasn't enough to grab the guard's attention, I scraped a hand down the glass, finger bones jutting out of the skin, sharp enough to produce the proper nails-on-chalkboard sound. The guards jolted to attention and turned to face me.

"Help!" I shouted as loud as possible to be heard through the glass. "Nalem, he's trying to—" I interrupted myself with a scream as Nalem made my ribs pierce through my chest, tearing through both the skin and shirt. I continued scraping against the glass. *"You don't have to make it hurt this bad!"*

"What, and take on the pain myself? I have to be lucid for this plan to work. You should just be happy your lack of organs is such a boon in this case."

I groaned and pulled myself up to my knees, making sure to show off my warped skeleton to the guards. I didn't have internal organs to pierce or blood dripping from severed veins, something I'd inherited from Mom, but, unlike other huldras, I did have my bones. I started to stand, but Nalem took a whack at my spine, sending me toppling almost off the cliff. I had to bite back a smirk of success as I saw one of the guards whip out a key and charge into the exhibit, the other two trying to warn her before following anyway.

The first guard didn't take long to reach me, tranquilizer gun trained on me. "What's going on here?"

"Nalem! He's trying...trying to kill me! So he can escape!" I winced as Nalem kicked the base of my skull. *"You're having way too much fun with this."*

"Oh, I'm sure I'll regret it in the morning." To help the charade, he took over my head for a moment—I mentally laughed as he felt the pain he'd just inflicted on my head. "You can't keep me in here! I will not allow it!"

The remaining guards caught up, and all three aimed their tranquilizers at me. Nalem gave me control of my head so he could take one last bash at my spine. It was strong enough that I flung myself off the cliff—and out of the way of the tranqs. And while I busied myself with the landing, Nalem took a knife of bone—made from a few metatarsals and such no longer needed thanks to the removal of my toe—that we'd hidden atop the temple, and used his powers to fling it at the guards. The knife buried itself in the back of one guard's skull, and he slumped over once the knife reached his brain. I hit the water as the knife flew through the air and buried into its second target, piercing into her stomach and up to her heart. The blade finished by coming out through her mouth.

The water was shallow, but I still flailed before my head got above water. I wasn't a great swimmer, even when not in pain from my bones getting the marrow kicked out of them. The bone knife floated in front of the final guard's face, fresh with the blood from her comrades.

I shouted, "Right, that was fun! Now, you're going to do what I say, or the same happens to you and all your friends. I'm not getting caught off guard again."

The guard aimed her gun, hands shaking. I sighed as the bone-knife sliced into her neck, just deep enough to bleed. "Don't think I won't. I'd love to set up your bones as pins, and your head as a bowling ball. Keep myself from getting bored." The guard got the hint and lowered her weapon.

"Glad that bluff worked. I hate bowling." Nalem urged me to my feet and waved the guard to join us with my exposed ribs. The guard winced as she slithered down to join me.

We met on the beach, and Nalem ordered, "Here's what we'll do. I need a mirror, and you are going to march me to a room where we can find one. I will pretend to be handcuffed, and if anyone asks, you will claim you are taking me to the medical ward. Say that Retz is injured and I am refusing to let him fix his own bones."

The guard said, "They won't believe me if I'm alone." Her face was hidden by a helmet that matched her security uniform, but was already crying.

Nalem answered in a faux-sweet tone, "Oh, you're never alone. See?" The murdered guards stood up under Nalem's command, their red uniforms obscuring the blood of their wounds. If they stayed behind us and out of the way, the shadows would cover up the rest. "Your friends are still with you. And they'll be the first to fight back, should you disobey. Clear?"

The guard nodded, too scared to speak. I strode up to her and put my hands behind my back, as if they were tied together. She put her tranquilizer against the base of my neck, and out the door we went.

"Wait, Nalem, how're we going to get Aimi?"

"A good question. Here's the answer." He waited until we passed Aimi's cage, then muttered instructions to our guard. She and the entourage of corpses behind her came to a halt. The guards in front of Aimi's cage tensed while she watched us from the glass in fire-form.

Our guard told the others, "I'm taking Nalem and his vessel to the medical bay. They fought, and Nalem is refusing to heal his own injuries." She gulped and added, "But he requested...company. Of the feminine variety."

Aimi's guards glanced between her, our guard, and me. One asked, "Why doesn't he pick, ah, you?"

I piped up, "Nalem has a thing for legs. Nice, long legs. With, ah, powerful thighs." Nalem had never actually been attracted to anything as far as I'd noticed, but the excuse seemed to convince the guards. They muttered amongst themselves, but with Lady Delight and most of her higher-ups either heading to the expo or gone to sleep for the night, the guards didn't seem to have anyone to ask. Aimi's three guards retreated into her cage, coming out with her moments later. Unlike me, she was actually handcuffed, though still on fire. They shoved her into the arms of one of the dead guards, which we controlled just in time to catch her.

"At least someone'll finally get the goods from her," one of the guards said, and his companions laughed. I felt sick, and we left the cage as soon as possible.

It wasn't until we were out of the menagerie and into a side hallway that Aimi spoke up. "Okay, what the hell are you doing?" She sounded both angry and scared, which only made sense

"Well, first off, we're not going to the med-bay and Nalem doesn't actually have a thing for your legs. I mean, you've got nice talons and all in your true form, but that was just an excuse."

Aimi raised an eyebrow, and my skin felt warm. Well, she was on fire, so of course it would.

I focused on fixing my bones, including getting my ribs back into my chest. "We're breaking out of here, so we can rescue our brothers."

Aimi dug her talons into the floor. "Why the hell should I trust you? You already double-crossed us once. Maybe you'll get to the expo and trade me for your brother."

I shook my head. "Yeah, we double-crossed you, but that was meant to be temporary to get Lady Delight's trust. We were always going to break you back out. Promise."

Aimi stopped walking, digging her talons into the floor and glaring at me. Flames lapped from her eyes.

So I told her, "Look, saving you and your brother will keep mine alive too. Otherwise, we're all lost. Even if you don't trust me...trust in me saving him."

Her eyes flared, but she started walking. "Fine. I'll follow you, for now. But if you're lying again..." She snapped her fingers, and a ball of flame ignited into existence in her hand. "Then I'll burn you and Nalem both out of existence. Don't think I won't." Only after her threat did she notice that the guards behind her didn't even flinch. "Uhmm...are these guys okay?"

"Nope. They're dead. Don't worry; Nalem made it quick, for once." Nalem told me new instructions, and I told the living guard, "Nalem says the room with the mirror should have a light switch or be really dark. A bathroom would do the trick; is there one around here?"

The guard nodded, too scared to speak.

Aimi muttered, "Okay...why do we need a dark room and a mirror?"

"Dunno. Nalem said it's a surprise." I glanced back at her; she didn't look hurt, so I asked, "You okay? You and your bro kinda took a nasty fall if I remember right."

"Just got a road rash. You can only really see it in human form." With a more bitter tone, she added, "And otherwise, more than a little pissed I ever called your family for help. Now everything we've done, it's been for nothing. Any idea how that feels?"

"All too well," Nalem and I both muttered. I did a double-take when his words matched mine; he just taunted *Your own thoughts echo mine now, you jinx,* and bade us to keep walking.

One of the guards reached for a walkie-talkie while watching; we hurried along

Our hostage did in fact lead us to a bathroom, a small and private one with a lock. She stood next to the open door and prepared to stand guard; I grabbed her wrist and dragged her inside with us, leaving the dead guards to keep watch. I undid Aimi's handcuffs and had her turn the lights off so the room was only lit by her glow. Following Nalem's orders, I told her to step back and pushed the guard in front of us, knife hovering above her chest.

"There. This should be the right setting for her." Nalem took control of my mouth and the bone knife. "None of you interrupt, unless you want your arms wrenched from their sockets."

"Her? Nalem, what are we doing?"

"You'll see." He cleared his throat before calling two words. "Bloody Mary."

The knife pierced the lamia's chest, sliding down.

"Bloody Mary—"

Blood bubbled out of the new wound. Aimi had her hands over her mouth, and in the mirror's reflection, I saw the guard's heart. She screamed, but no one answered. Her tranquilizer gun fell from her grip and clattered against the tile floor.

"Bloody...Vairi, I'm calling and sick of your game. Get out here. I've got a present for you."

The mirror rippled. A hand reached out, skin mottled like blood splattered across sand. The heart floated into its grasp, and the guard fell to the floor, clutching her chest. The hand was followed by a red sleeve, another hand, two mottled legs covered by a red dress sliding onto the countertop between the sinks. In a matter of seconds, there sat a woman with eyes and hair as red as her dress, pointed ears, and antlers poking out of her head. With this and the way her skin was patterned, she resembled a fawn.

"I do love presents. Is it my birthday?" She tilted her head and cradled the still-beating heart in her delicate hands.

I almost sensed her bones, but Nalem persuaded me not to unless I wanted the strongest migraine of my life.

"It must not be. You would not call for something you deem so unimportant. So why does my brother call me when he prefers to forget?"

My skin felt cold and too tight around my bones. *"You have a sister?"*

"Two, if you must acknowledge this one. I prefer not to." Taking more control of my body, Nalem prodded the guard with his foot, starting to remove the bones. "I have business in Arcadia. There is an exposition happening somewhere, a market of sorts. Don't suppose you've heard of it."

"Such is not of my interest, but yes, I am aware of it." Vairi shrugged and took a tiny nibble of the heart. The blood clung to her lips, staining them bright red. "Do you require a ride?"

"Yes, and my companion here as well. I've paid your toll already, so no horsing around." Nalem passed control of the bones to me; I let them float aimlessly at my side, keeping them away from Aimi. The fires of her eyes flared as she watched, hands still clasped over her mouth.

"I am reminded how rude desperation makes you." Vairi took another bite of the heart as if it were a peach. Her mouth seemed to be filled with rows of pearl needles instead of teeth. "I will, of course, require equal payment for a return trip, if you choose to take it."

"As I'm well aware. Look, can we go already? The guards have seen us and may be here any moment now."

Vairi hummed as if considering the weather. "But wouldn't that be fun? We can fight them and then have a competition of who can make the best creation from the corpses."

My attention was hung up on the heart she was eating; it reminded me of the raw rabbit and I wanted to hurl again. But Aimi was not so disturbed.

She stepped forward and said, "Excuse me, miss, not to be rude, but a bunch of people have been captured and forced into this expo, including my brother. We need to save them before they get sold off. So if you don't mind..."

Vairi's expression turned puzzled as she slid off the counter. The heart floated up over her shoulder, encased in a globe of blood. The blood from her hands, but not her lips, joined it.

She was taller than Aimi, so she had to lean over to look her in the eyes. "Such boldness. Hello, beautiful stranger. What name have you been given?"

"Aimi Kurusaki. And it's thanks to your brother that mine is in this mess." Aimi took to the air until she hovered an inch or two over the tips of Vairi's antlers. "I understand if you're reluctant to help out this double-crossing bastard, but we really need this."

Vairi's eyes went wide. The heart floating over her shoulder wavered, threatened to fall. She composed herself right afterward, but Aimi unsettled her. Nalem racked his brain trying to figure out why.

She finally said, "I approve of this one. Feisty." She nodded at Nalem and me. "And I am intrigued by your young vessel, brother. With such entertaining companions, who am I to say no?"

It was at this point that fists and clubs slammed against the door. We'd been found.

Vairi smiled with her teeth and waved us to the mirror. "I permit you to travel with me. Quickly now, we must depart."

Nalem had me run for it, with Aimi hot on our heels, pulling the dead lamia bones behind us to use in case we needed protection. I asked Nalem if we'd be safe wherever we were going.

"Why do you think I was reluctant? It's the most dangerous place I could go."

12 - JARROD

Our fellow captives were led out of the menagerie. The transport cages were lined with thorns along golden frames, with a space at the top for air that was too small to escape through. Many creatures walked into these with heads bowed and tails between their legs. Some fought to escape; Isamu took out two guards with his flames before threats on his sister calmed him. Others fought to stay in their enclosures.

"Not that I can blame them," Lady Delight admitted to Farris and me as we followed her down the hallways. Farris somehow held enough sway to avoid traveling in a cage. I, as his supposed consort, had to stay with him. Thus we followed the queen of the menagerie as she explained her false paradise. "I try to make my habitats as ideal to each creature as possible. They are all custom-made with each being's needs in mind, after many extensive studies."

I nodded, absent and discontent because her words had an ounce of truth. Many of the creatures we'd passed by seemed content. No screaming or sobbing until they had to be moved. When the guards entered for food or sanitary purposes, they weren't bothered, and some were even greeted with enthusiasm.

The furaribi were an exception. "But it is mostly the boy's influence, which is why I have to sell him off. He is such a hassle, and I can't have that, now can I?" Lady Delight winked at us and added, "The girl should calm down without him. I expect that she can become a prize jewel in my collection. Did you hear she's the only one of her kind that's ever been found outside of Japan? She's truly an exotic specimen…"

Farris smiled and muttered something in agreement, but he held my hand tight enough that my fingers were constricted. I squeezed back.

He asked Lady Delight, "So, my consort and I are being sold together, right? Or, well, auctioned?"

"Of course not. I am allowing you the gift of each other's company for now. Once we reach the exposition, all bets are off." She hissed a laugh. "Though if you are bought by an ally instead of your enemies, perhaps you will be pitied as the prodigal son you are." She put a delicate, clawed finger to her lips. "Which reminds me, you are quite a ways from home. What business did the White Prince have here, I wonder?"

Expression never wavering, Farris answered, "That's classified, m'lady. Couldn't tell you even if I wanted to." I had to admit, Farris had the most convincing poker face I knew. Even worked during actual poker. "It was going pretty well, though. Too bad I have to set it aside for now. Unless there's some way I can convince your majesty to change her mind?"

Lady Delight made a gesture of being flattered, even as she shook her head. Either she'd called Farris's bluff on how little he knew or the lure of his price was too great for even an apparent prince to overcome.

We strode down the bright and boiling hallways to the front of the castle. On the other side of the moat were transport vehicles, trucks with treads better suited for tanks. The cages were being loaded by legions of lamia and a few humans. I caught a glimpse of a unicorn in one, a fellow huldra in another. I found Isamu slumped in the bottom of his, too tired to keep up his fire-form. I tried to remember which truck it was, but they all looked the same, without even license plates to differentiate them.

Each truck had four seats up front. Farris and I joined Lady Delight and the driver, a violet-haired lamia I recognized from the attack at the border. I was told her name was Zalin. She licked her teeth when she saw me, as if trying to figure out where to bite me first.

Lady Delight explained as we took off that Arcadia was only accessible in certain in-between spaces. Crossroads and natural borders such as rivers were common, particularly at dusk or dawn. I wasn't sure how long we'd been at the menagerie, but the sun was setting as the trucks eased down the mountain. But instead of going to the main road, they rumbled through a different path cleared through the woods. Branches and too-slow animals crunched under the treads. After a few minutes, we came upon a small lake with a silver-leafed tree growing out of the middle.

Our driver grinned. "Roll up your windows, bitches. And, uhmm, my Lady. We're going in."

Reminiscent of some of my boyfriend's "finer" driving moments, Zalin slammed on the gas, and we gunned forward. I clung to the seat as we drove right into the lake, submerging as we approached the tree...

Only to come up on the other side of the tree in a golden lake surrounded by liquid trees resembling spilled oil. They glistened in the light, droplets falling from drenched leaves. Animal parts were embedded in some of the trees. Oil oozed over the corpses, until even the bones might be mistaken for strange branches.

"Another reason dear Nalem is not coming on this trip." Lady Delight turned to us, gesturing to the world outside. "Welcome to Arcadia."

The Arcadia I knew was a twisted forest of thorns, where roses glowed and vines came alive. After the oil-coated land, we drove through a field of graves, where the ground was shattered tar and concrete and half-buried cars were marked with plastic tombstones. As Lady Delight explained, these realms and more were all part of Arcadia, strange caricatures of the world grown rampant.

But I didn't want to listen to Lady Delight, whether or not she was being informative. Her voice was velvet when she described the value of others as if people were pretty baubles to collect. Every time she spoke, her words crept under my skin and into my fingertips. I had an urge to choke her until her face was as purple as her corset. But that was an urge to shove deep, deep into the dusty corners of my mind with all the other ignored instincts.

I did have inhuman instincts. Huldras, so long as they deemed someone as evil, had no qualms against murder. It was as simple as dragging the offender out to the woods and giving them a farewell fuck before those offenders were crushed, throttled, or even old-fashioned beatings until they croaked. I had heard plenty of stories from Erika. On rare occasions, I even considered emulating them—especially on someone such as Lady Delight, who bartered with lives as if they were nothing more than coins.

But it wasn't right to judge a life and decide whether it deserved death or not, same as how it wasn't right to declare a life's worth like a commodity. Alexander had taught that lesson from day one. I was not a monster, and my body was not a weapon. Especially not when my hands were shaking from both ire and sobriety.

Farris rested his head on top of mine. "Are we there yet?"

"Didn't I make you swear to never say that?"

"Not that I remember. So, are we there yet?"

I looked to the window. We had passed the fringes of the automotive graveyard. The new area we entered had no discernible features. It was the strangest thing, looking at the ground but unable to register what was there. There were things in the distance; crystal spires rose out of the ground to touch lightning bolts while in another direction loomed a blinking face carved out of a mountain. But here, there was nothing. It made both my eyes and brain sting.

"This is one of the Liminal Lanes," Lady Delight explained. She examined her nails instead of looking through the glass. "Unformed spaces in Arcadia. They may be...unsettling, but they remain unclaimed by Fae, so we utilize them as much as possible." She ran her nails along the dashboard. "Fighting a Faerie, after all, would disrupt both our schedule and our cargo. And possibly our lives."

"Sorry, ma'am," our driver muttered as she rubbed her eyes, "But I'm starting to prefer a fight to this place. Gives me the creeps."

I had to agree. To distract ourselves, I let Farris examine the contents of my coat pockets, none of them useful for fighting or escaping our present situation. I absently explained what the various artifacts and herbs were for, but my mind was elsewhere. In desperation, I tried to contact Alexander.

"Sir, it's Jarrod. I have been captured and am to be sold in Arcadia. I found Retz, but he has been locked away in a lamia's castle." I had never managed to summon Alexander; it was always him summoning me. To be honest, my attempt consisted of thinking as loudly as possible and focusing on memories of my father and his realm as they appeared in visions. *"We seem to be in an empty area of Arcadia. I am unsure of how to escape."*

The world faded into a flash of sensations. Running against wind. A false sensation of writhing snakes under the skin. The low chittering of a thousand voices at once. The world was a blur of green. I needed no words to describe this; Alexander had heard me and was on his way. I felt a moment of relief.

Then I woke up to reality and found myself slammed against the truck door, pinned moments later by Farris crashing into me.

"The fuck?!" I assessed the situation as I shoved away from the door. The truck was now sideways. Our driver was bleeding from the head, and Lady Delight had wrenched her door open and shifted to full snake form as she left the truck, hissing and screeching. Something roared overhead in the empty space.

"You sure picked the wrong time to pass out." Farris rolled off me, bracing himself against the backs of the seats. "From what I heard the snakes screaming, we ended up too close to a Fae's stomping grounds and now we're being stomped."

"Understood." With Farris off me, I climbed up to the window to witness the fight. Lady Delight and other lamia, all in snake-form with a multitude of heads, surrounded a crystalline Fae that resembled an arachnid, about as large as Lady Delight was. Electricity coursed from its head down its legs, which tapered into sharp diamond tips. Instead of eyes, it had eight mouths of gnashing teeth. The contents of at least one truck had already decorated those maws with metal and blood. The other trucks sped away as fast as possible.

"We're not fighting that thing, right?" Farris wore a nervous smile the way a hyena laughs out of fear.

"Only if we have to." I climbed into the front and checked the driver's pulse. Her skin was cold, and the heartbeat was weak.

"Babe, she was a captor. Don't bother with her." Farris tugged me away from the driver with a sigh. "So we're running, hoping nothing else decides to eat us?"

"Not yet." I climbed through the open door and offered a hand to help Farris through. "We have to check for other survivors."

Farris grabbed my hand, its tremors calming with the rush of adrenaline. "Sometimes, I wonder why you have to be such a hero."

He knew full well why; the only alternate to heroism was villainy, and I couldn't be like Nalem and Lady Delight. I pulled Farris up with me, and we crawled along the car's wreckage to check the cages in the back. There was a gaping hole in the side of the trailer; the crystal Fae made a similar hole through the body of an attacking lamia. The lamia might have had superior numbers, but fangs, poisons, and constriction had no effect on that beast.

I climbed into the back of the truck to find broken cages with equally broken bodies inside. I ran to the few still living and tried to help them to their feet. A foo dog with an injured paw snarled as I approached until it realized I meant no harm, after which it let me pull the shards of glass and metal out of its paw. It licked me in thanks as I led it to the exit.

Farris was at the hole punched through the side, helping others up and off of the truck. His eyes narrowed at the foo dog. "Amazing as I am, I can't lift Fido down there, hon."

"Allow me." Someone strode to the other side of the canine; in tandem, we helped it scramble out of the ruins. I looked over to find my helper was another huldra, tail bent at an unnatural angle. "Many thanks, forest-brother."

"To you as well." How long had she been trapped in that menagerie, away from the woods of her home? How long for all of these creatures? The thought made me sick, even as we climbed out and I figured out what my new plan of action. The creatures we saved ran in every direction, too frightened to trust each other in this void. The huldra followed after a loose cluster of other creatures, and I wondered whether she meant to help them or was just searching for someone.

The foo dog, unable to hide its bulky orange form, became a target for the Fae. It tossed lamia aside to chase the poor escapee, charging far faster than a creature its size should've been able to move. It was about to bite when Lady Delight, with her golden scales and five heads, tackled the Fae. Both crashed against the void, oddly soundless. The foo dog ran toward the distant mountains past the edge of the void and didn't look back.

My conscience nagged at me. Even if it was an enemy, there was still one person to save. I told Farris to keep out of sight as I crawled back to the front of the truck. The driver was resting in a pool of her own blood, clinging to life. There wasn't much I could do, but I searched through my duster, finding a bandage and a bit of yarrow to staunch the bleeding. I rolled her over to find the wound and patched it up with what little I had.

I hadn't realized the crystal Faerie had noticed me until I heard Farris shouting to run and saw the diamond-tipped limb crashing down. I grabbed the bleeding lamia around the chest and escaped into the back seat. The crunching of the engine wracked my ears as we barely avoided the same fate. I tried to get the back door open, but it wouldn't budge. The Fae watched me from the front. It made a strange series of humming noises with its many mouths.

Was it trying to talk to me?

I didn't have a chance to figure out why before the Fae's tone switched to high-pitched static. Vines shot out of the ground and wrapped around the crystal limbs. The beast was immobile, and its electricity couldn't shake the vines away. A familiar figure perched atop it and reached a flora-coated claw into one mouth, grabbing the jaw and wrenching it apart with a series of grinding pops.

All other fears temporarily forgotten, I clambered out of the truck. Lady Delight had left the fight and was scrambling to regain as much of her runaway "cargo" as possible. The crystal Fae was tied to the ground by Alexander's vines, two of its eight mouths broken. Alexander looked ready to wrench open a few more as his cataract eyes settled on me.

And then vines broke out of the earth and through the crunched-up truck, wrapping around my legs. Alexander leapt off the Fae and ran, and the vines carried me after him. Farris screamed again, and I realized too late that the vines hadn't grabbed him too.

"Sir! We forgot Farris! We have to go back!" But he didn't listen to my pleas. The plants constricted me the more I struggled, so I soon stopped. Perhaps Alexander hadn't heard me. Or we had more immediate matters to attend to and would save Farris and the furaribi later. I couldn't think of any other reason to leave Farris behind.

As we sped through other realms of Arcadia, too quickly to gather any details, Alexander signed to me. Retz had made it to Arcadia. We were going to pick him up—the term he used was "rescue from danger," though what danger, he did not say—and would then return to Alexander's territory. We would talk more there.

"And then we'll get Farris back, right?" I asked. "And the furaribi I have to save. The curse will activate if I don't."

I didn't receive an answer. Since when had my father been able to move so fast? We zipped past entire realms in Arcadia—the mountains the escapees had fled toward, a lake of porcelain with shores of sunlight, into a forest of white trees with stained-glass leaves...

There was something silver in the distance, skittering along thick webs the size of train tracks. It was long and had insect legs, like a centipede, but made of metal. There were strange markings on the side, but again, the speed at which we moved made details difficult to see.

Alexander made two signs; brace yourself, and train. Yes, the locomotive variety.

I had to wonder, in what world was that thing a train?

Once, Alexander almost shot Retz. On purpose. If he'd been enough of a monster to pull the trigger, it would've been the second murder of the night.

I'd been fourteen at the time and Retz ten. Before the incident, we were both restless despite it being a school night. I'd been going by Jarrod for the past few months at home, and I was awake with anxieties over going to school, being teased, and having to respond to a girl's name. It was a daily existential crisis of mine. Retz was simply not tired. So, as he often did when he was awake but our parents were not, he slunk out of his room, down through the house, and out to the backyard.

I remember it being a clear night, with a full moon. It was mid-October and brisk after dark. As usual, Retz sat on the swing set our parents had built us, watching the stars and the slow decay of the trees. Sometimes he'd actually swing and jump off at the highest point, trying to land on both feet. I was sick of wallowing in bed but too tired to leave my room, so I watched him from the window.

That night, a man showed up at our house. He was one of the school janitors, and he'd had to clean up after some of Nalem's outbursts. Activities such as weakening a football jock's bones before a game so they'd all snap or making the dissected frogs dance through the science lab and terrify the students were amongst Nalem's favorites. And while most humans forgot supernatural incidents as soon as they left the source, there were exceptions.

The janitor entered the backyard with a pistol and a cross made from a hammer and shovel tied together with rope. I was too far away to hear him, but I saw the janitor make threats, point his gun, wave his cross. I hadn't learned how to fight yet, so I ran to get our parents. Erika was strong, and Alexander slept with a gun on the nightstand. We ran downstairs ready for a fight with a madman.

The janitor was already dead.

His chest was pierced by sharpened bones, ones we later identified as from our neighbor's buried dog. Blood dribbled from the wounds and from his mouth. His limbs were completely curled, all the bones in them broken.

"He tried to kill me," Retz explained, still sitting on the swing. "So I got him first. And Nalem sometimes says he'll turn people into pretzels, so I tried that, but I don't think I got it right. I don't eat a lot of pretzels."

Erika, who thought this was an acceptable way of dealing with intruders, rushed to hug her son. I wanted to follow, but the display made me sick, and Alexander wasn't moving.

"You did this," he said. His hands shook. "Not Nalem, but you, Retz, did this."

"Here. Start packing. I'll explain to your mother before we go."

I ran back to my room, heart racing

13 - RETZ

"Are you enjoying my most humble abode?" Vairi asked, her voice and face as earnest as a kid's. "I built it myself, in case you were curious."

The notion made me even sicker. We were in a train, and everything was stylized to match. Well, it was if you ignored the stitched mishmash of carpeting that covered everything. And the bloodstains which came from the blood vessels running alongside vines and strings on the ceiling. Or the pulse of muscles and organs underneath the thing veneer of fabric on the furniture. The mirrors, cracked and stained, that covered the walls and made it hard to tell where the actual windows began. The metal insect legs clacking us along a track instead of wheels. Otherwise the same as any other train, yeah.

"You built this." Aimi hugged herself as she looked around, refusing to land and touch the floor. "I can't imagine how."

"With a combination of magic and technology, there is nothing that can't be accomplished." Vairi spun around, her dress twirling around her. "All the blood and muscle helps me control it. Though I admit, I had some help from my siblings. Long ago, Nalem even helped me with schematics for the train—though there are no actual bones anymore. Safety precautions. But isn't it so pretty now?"

"Charming. I feel so honored." Nalem's voice dripped with sarcasm. When he spoke, my features in the mirrors shifted, as if it was trying to photoshop my reflection to resemble someone else. I caught a glimpse of a dark, empty, and cold face before it snapped back to my own. My white clothes were stained with dirt and lamia blood, and the bones of the guards hovered close behind me.

Vairi watched from one of the window seats. She shook her head at the display before motioning for us to join her. I sat opposite her, regretting it as soon as I felt how warm the seat was. It moved as if it was breathing, and smelled of dust and open wounds. Vairi watched Aimi until she sighed and joined us, fire-eyes dimmed to showcase her reluctance.

"It is good to see you again, brother." Vairi ran delicate fingers along her antlers. "Even if you do not agree with the sentiment. And the exposition you speak of is close, but not so close as to cut our visit short. But how are you? How does your plan fare?"

"Plan's going well. You will hear nothing of it."

"But your goal remains the same."

"And it will remain so until my task is completed." Nalem crossed his legs and steepled his fingers. "That is one of few things we have in common, you and I: persistence."

Vairi pulled her hand away, and with it came the red from her hair. It coalesced into globules of blood floating above her hand, leaving her coiled hair stark white. "We share more than you would care to admit. But let us not argue this night. It is rare that we have such a peaceful meeting. Which reminds me..." The blood globs morphed until they resembled a sphere, near perfect except for a series of craters: a literal blood moon. "Samhain is drawing ever closer."

"You once said that every moment is always drawing closer. Some of your time-is-a-construct bullshit." Nalem pressed his fingers together until the joints popped. I emulated the action.

"Yes, but it has been so long since you have appeared. The others have missed you. They always do." The blood moon stretched out to resemble a face with a frizzy mane of hair. "Were you informed that she is visiting this year? Won't she be so disappointed if her dearest brother does not arrive?"

"It isn't always my choice." Nalem snarled and pushed his fingers hard enough that they bent at unnatural angles. My own started to hurt until Aimi pulled one of my hands away with hers, which were warm but currently not on fire. "I will, however, do my best to attend. Just understand if I happen to end up...preoccupied, considering current events."

"I am not the one you will apologize to."

Nalem did not seem to have a response to that. And Aimi and I, we weren't sure what to say that wouldn't accidentally offend our creepy savior. The room already smelled of charred flesh and cloth, since most of Aimi was still burning. Oh, and that cloying stench of blood, couldn't forget that.

Then Vairi laughed. It wasn't even that at first, just a snicker, but it grew louder. Not because of Vairi, but the train. The train itself creaked and rumbled, the muscles inside quivering. An artery overhead burst, falling to the ground before Vairi caught it and sent the blood back up. The laughter didn't stop until I was scared her train would quake itself to pieces. When I hazarded a look out the window, we were climbing a web quite far over the ground and definitely swaying.

"What," Nalem snapped as he dug his fingers into my skull for support, "do you think is so funny?"

"What isn't funny?" Vairi smoothed the cushions of her seat as if petting a beloved pet. This eased the quaking of the train, but we still rocked as it rumbled. "That is your problem, brother dear. You are so wrapped up in your obsessions, you are unable to see the humor and wonder in life. You chase a goal you've convinced yourself will make things better. But why not see what you are trying to improve on first?"

"Can we start by improving the shocks on this thing?" Aimi asked. The train responded with a sudden swing to the left, which would've caused me to fall and crash against the other wall if Aimi wasn't holding my hand. Even Vairi braced herself as her eyes widened in surprise. "You can't even predict your train? Is it alive somehow?"

"It has the bodily functions to be so, but no brain. Make of that what you will." Vairi got to her feet, rocking the train to balance. Her eyes went glassy, which combined with her posture, reminded me of a ceramic doll. "I do believe there is an intruder on my train. Oh, and someone familiar at that. I peeked into his realm, so now he returns the favor, is that it?" Those red lips of hers curled into an expression I'd felt on my own face, and that's when it really hit me that she and Nalem were related. "Brother, we can have that corpse competition now, if you wish."

"I'd rather not." Nalem pulled the bones of the lamia, which we had grabbed before entering the train, around us like a protective cloak. "You recall how well I deal with this realm and its inhabitants."

"Only too well." Vairi twirled away from us and made for the door. "Beautiful stranger, do look out for my brother and his vessel. And remember, stay in this room. You will find the rest of my train is not as kindly as me."

She left us with flounce and flourish, the door clicking shut behind her. The train stabilized, but swayed and dangled over the Arcadian ground. The broken artery in the ceiling dripped again, fresh blood reeking and splattering a paisley piece of carpeting.

Aimi took a deep breath and let go of my hand, allowing hers to smolder once more. She burned my palm by accident in her haste, but I said nothing.

"If, for whatever reason, you and Nalem ever invite me to a family reunion, remind me to say no."

"Sure thing. I'd ask the same of you, but..." Where Nalem went, I'd be there too. Not wanting to spend another minute on a seat that I swore was breathing, I stood up, Nalem keeping the lamia bones around us. "At least she's giving us a ride. Once we hit our stop, we can save our brothers—Farris too, I guess—and hightail it back to San Francisco or something."

Aimi raised an eyebrow as she floated in the center of the room. "Sure she's not lying? And even if we make it to this expo, how'll we get back to the real world?"

"Vairi is incapable of lying," Nalem told me, though not why when I pressed him. *"We paid the toll; thus, getting us to our destination, in this case the expo where the others are to be sold, is her sworn task. As for how we'll make it back...I'm sure we can find another heart. Or steal a lamia's truck."*

I repeated this to Aimi, whose flames flared and fists curled. "You make it sound so easy! Are you saying you can just kill someone to use them as a train ticket and not feel anything?"

I shrugged. "I guess so, yeah. Everything that lives has to die at some point. It's what keeps us all connected, right?"

Aimi flapped her wings and floated up to the ceiling, putting a burning finger to the leaking artery. Cauterizing it, I guess. "Keep thinking like that, and there'll be no one left to be connected to. Besides, if you don't regret murder, what do you feel for those left behind?"

I couldn't answer her. It wasn't the first time I'd been asked that question, and when I was honest, I was called a psychopath at best.

"I almost wish I was you," Aimi continued. "I want Lady Delight out of the picture more than anything. But when I imagine killing her, even her...I dunno, makes me feel kinda sick. I mean, who am I to say someone shouldn't live?"

"And who are we to say that someone should?" Nalem said. Images of the young Lady Delight flashed through my head again, watching as sparks met with stars in innocent eyes. *"I chose to save her when she would've died with her face in the gutter. Look how she's repaid us."*

I mused on this before remembering Aimi was lucky enough not to hear the voice in my head. "Nalem said, it's a choice to let someone live too, and that's not always a great option either. Look at me; I should've stayed dead, but I was given life again. And, well...this life isn't like the board game, that's for sure."

The look Aimi gave me was pensive and sad; I didn't understand why, so I ignored it.

"There's that, I guess. Two sides to everything, huh?" She floated down, wavering a few inches over the floor to look at me eye-to-eye. When I tried to look away to avoid both staring and melting my eyeballs, she drifted back into view. "Personal question. If it was your choice, and you knew who Nalem was...would you still choose him over dying?"

I was going to lie when tapping came at one of the windows. The others heard it too. We all turned toward the noise; a certain someone was clinging to the side of the train, tapping with one burned hand and one leaf that resembled a bright scarf.

"Jarrod!" I stumbled to the window and tried to open it. It was locked, but Nalem manipulated a few lamia bones to act as a key and pick the lock. I was hit by a blast of sweet, cloying air as it swung open and Jarrod slipped inside. "What're you doing here? I thought you were being dragged to the expo."

"I was. Alexander didn't approve of that plan." Jarrod shook his head and tried to get his windswept hair out of his face. The train rocked as if struck; I almost lost my footing, though of course Jarrod was unfazed. "Enough talk. We need to get you out of here for the meeting. Then we can save the others."

Nalem's reaction to this plan was to mock it with tart phrases such as *"Daddy's little bootlicker, aren't you?"*, which I refused to voice.

I asked instead, "He didn't even grab Farris? Thought you two were inseparable."

Jarrod's body tensed, but he only allowed himself the curtest shake of his head. "We had more pressing matters to attend to. He understands that I'll come back for him." He stepped out of the way of another broken vein's leak, wincing as the blood splashed his bare, bandaged foot. "Look, we have to leave, and we have to do it now. There are enough footholds on the side of the train that we can climb out."

I went to the window and looked down. There were vines and thick multicolored strings twisted into weird patterns, like a tangled embroidery project. They clung tightly to the train. "All right, Spider-Man, sure we can't just walk through the train like normal people?"

"The other rooms, at least the ones I passed, are filled with other creatures. I suspect that many of them are Fae." Jarrod grabbed the windowsill and slipped over, gripping the tenuous strings with ease. "Just pretend we're kids climbing trees again."

"Trees usually don't move while you're climbing them." Plus, he seemed to have forgotten the fact that I was always the one who fell out of the trees, sometimes hard enough that Nalem had a few bones to patch up afterward. I asked Aimi, "Do you want to go ahead, and I'll, ah, guard the rear?"

"Did you forget I can fly?" Aimi strode past me and jumped out the window, wings catching her so she hovered a few yards away from the train. "If any rear needs guarding, it's yours. if you don't mind a few burns, I'll catch you if you fall."

Nalem took the first steps, grabbing hold of my body and swinging it over the edge of the window. He then left me dangling there, though he took the pain from the burn on my hand, leaving it in my control but numb.

"You're welcome. Get moving."

"Why can't you?" I asked, even as I took the tiniest baby steps across the strings. Seeing me move, Jarrod took that as a cue to climb ahead with a speed and ease I'd never be able to emulate. Show-off.

"Arcadia...disorients me. I do not belong here, thus my senses are shot when I am in this realm." He sighed and twitched his hand as if he could shake out the pain of the burn. *"And no, I am not explaining particulars right now. Walk."*

"You never explain anything." I inched my way along the strings, holding the threads so tight that they bit into my skin. They felt warm to the touch, humming with energy. *"You're as bad as Jarrod, you know that? You only talk when it's convenient and expect me to jump when you say so."*

There wasn't an immediate reaction, but a pause to think. I wondered if I'd somehow escaped Nalem's wrath, but then he took control of my foot and misstepped, leaving me clinging to the threads and on the verge of falling. The train was at least fifty feet off the ground, gliding across a giant web as if it was just a spider.

"I can end you at any moment. Without me, your pathetic existence is nothing. You obey because you must."

I hazarded a look down. Seeing me dangling precariously, Aimi flew under me, hovering in wait for my inevitable fall. And up ahead, Jarrod paused his climb to watch me, braced to scurry over and save my sorry ass.

I wrenched control of my foot back, and while it took a few tries, I stepped onto the strings. The others relaxed in relief. *"At least I have friends. What do you have?"*

"The power to snap the bones of your little friends and send you both plummeting." Nalem reached up, then pierced his skeletal fingers into that point of my skull and ripped down. The new migraine caused me to waver again. *"Don't let allies give you false confidence. And don't badger me into speaking. You cannot comprehend the gravity of my cause."*

"Probably 'cause it's something stupid and petty." I knew pushing him was stupid. I knew I should back down. But damn it, after all I'd been through in the past few days, I didn't need Nalem's drama on top of it. *"You want revenge on someone who insulted you and left before you had a chance to maim them? Someone turn you down once? Did you—"*

I expected him to make me release the strings, to let me fall and then follow up on his promise to break anyone who caught me. Nope. Instead, he pressed my hands against the side of the train and burst the bones of my wrists through my skin, warping them into spikes. He oh-so-kindly gave me feeling back in my hands, so I felt the sting of my skin tearing to make way for sharp bone, and the sudden disconnect between my fingers and the rest of me. The spikes curved inward, making it near impossible to pull them out of the hole they'd pierced.

"You feel so empowered because you have friends who can rescue you? You think that makes you better than me?" Instead of attacking my head from the inside, he took control and slammed it against the wall. I heard noises from inside, the pulsing of the train and the movements of people. *"Then continue to be a burden they must save. Having others willing to rescue you is not a power you can retain for long."*

He tried not to yawn, but I knew how tired he was. He gave back control of my body, but he countered my attempts to fix my hands. Wouldn't even let me touch my fingers. So I was stuck, palms and wrists ripped, fingers dangling and connected only by skin, bones hooked into a living train that still hadn't reached the ground.

At least I wasn't going to fall. Silver linings and all that.

The others were at my side in seconds. Aimi hovered close by but not close enough to touch. Jarrod climbed over and reached with a scarf-leaf, using that to examine my hands. I tried and failed to bite back a cry when he nudged my useless fingers.

"What did you do this time?" Jarrod asked, trying to rescue my hand.

"I got a little fed up with him; we argued; he won by turning my wrists into hooks." I shrugged and tried to sound lighthearted. "Better than lying that I fell down the stairs or something, right?"

"We don't have time for this." Jarrod's knuckles were white against the vibrant strings as the train rocked again. "Retz, you can fix your bones, even if some are...temporarily removed from you. Right?"

I nodded quickly.

"Aimi, get behind him. He's probably going to fall."

"I am? How am I—"

"Sorry." He lashed at where my bones met the metal, striking as hard as possible. If someone like Aimi or a normal human had tried, this wouldn't have done anything. But Jarrod had the huldra strength of Mom and her family. Horseshoes were bendy straws in their hands; breaking bones were no problem. The bone spike shattered, freeing my hand but also blinding me with pain. I even felt Nalem hold back a shout.

I didn't have time to dwell on this pain, though, because Jarrod freed the other hand, and I fell backward. I spun through the air as I plummeted, heat radiating near me as Aimi swooped in to catch me. I reached for her even though my hands were busted beyond all use.

Something else caught me. Bark bit into my skin; had I crashed into a tree?

No, trees didn't curl their branches around things. I looked up into a pair of milky white eyes in a familiar face, one I hadn't seen in years. Said face was also covered in blood and thorns. Nalem swore something in my head.

"Hey, Dad," I muttered as the rest of my body shut down from pain. "What big claws you have."

The better to tear me apart with, I bet.

I don't remember much of the trip to Dad's realm. I was too busy trying to fix my bones without passing out. Dad carried me the whole way like I was a kid, and like back then, he seemed taller than I remembered. He smelled of roses, crushed grass, and blood.

"Sadly, my distraction did not work as well as I wished." Nalem muttered this, curling up in the base of my skull as if he were a worn-out cat. He answered without me asking, *"I felt him and Vairi fighting. I hoped if I kept you long enough from reaching him, she'd defeat him and I wouldn't have to deal with his schemes, but alas."*

I stared at my palms, watching the skin grow back. Between this and the earlier escape from the menagerie, I was ecstatic to have that speedy huldra healing factor. The lack of organs to heal helped too.

"So you weren't really angry?"

"I shall explain my plans soon enough; there's no reason for me to throw a fit over that. But it is fun to watch you squirm."

Was he telling the truth, or just trying to brush off his outburst? Neither answer made my hands hurt any less. I decided to leave it alone and let Nalem sleep, except Nalem stayed awake, watching.

When I asked why, he said, *"You think your father won't try something? I thought I taught you better, little one."*

In Dad's realm, trees made entirely of thorns with glowing white roses reached up and obscured the sky, and I almost mistook the roses for stars. The thorns were thick and clustered into walls with clearings and pathways within. Figures scurried in the shadows, but none close enough to tell if they were human or something else. My head still ached, though it was mild compared to my burned and torn hands or my fingers readjusting to being connected to my wrists again. I didn't need surgery to reconnect lobbed-off parts thanks to my powers and bizarre anatomy, but like other hollow huldras, the energy that kept me alive needed time to flow through my fingers again.

Dad set me down and held out a hand to me before running off; I assume that meant to wait, because he didn't seem the sort for high fives. A cluster of vines set Jarrod down nearby, and Aimi...wait, where was Aimi?

"He forgot to grab her," Jarrod answered before I even asked. "He only had eyes for saving you and me. I think I saw her fly back to the train, but I'm not sure." He sighed, pinching the bridge of his nose. "You all right? Nalem seemed to be…acting out."

"I've been through worse. Just argued with him and pushed the wrong buttons. But I'm all right." My hands stung enough that shoving them into a beehive would've been less painful, but I wouldn't give Nalem the satisfaction of whining.

Jarrod nodded absently, but kept staring out into the distance.

"Something up?"

'I don't remember there being other people here." Jarrod didn't sit down, but watched with his hands in his pockets. "There weren't when Alexander and I came here. I've never seen them in visions when we've met. So why? And who are they?"

"We are his followers." said a stout young blonde who wandered over from the thorns. She had a belt full of bottled salves, most of which were noxious shades of green. She looked human, except for the pointed ears and the green rune tattoos covering her arms and chest. "He rescued us all from horrible situations, in exchange for our assistance. All of us are happy to help after all he has done for us." She bowed before kneeling next to me and examining my hands.

Jarrod's eyes narrowed. "Alexander wouldn't do that. He never demanded payment of any sorts for his work. The money wasn't what mattered. Saving people was."

"As I said, we don't mind." She looked up at Jarrod while rubbing strange green liquid over my broken skin. "Master was the one to save us; repaying him with a bit of work is the least we could do."

"*Master, huh?*" I briefly checked the blonde's bones; human but fuzzy around her arms and chest, same as Jarrod's limbs and neck. Dad had cursed them both, then. "*He's starting to sound like you.*"

"*I don't do curses. Or force you to call me Master—not that I would mind if you did. Master Nalem has a nice ring to it.*"

The girl wrapped bandages around my hands, though she must've noticed that I didn't bleed, but I didn't catch her name before she left.

I flexed my fingers, which felt stiff, but my hands did feel a bit better. "Well. Never figured Dad would hire a secretary."

"It still doesn't make sense." Jarrod knelt opposite me, pulling his glasses off to clean them. "We've had offers of help before, but Alexander always denied them. It was just us. So what's so important that he recruits clients into servitude?"

"People don't always change for the better," I told him. I was the perfect example, but I didn't think Jarrod would appreciate me saying so. It'd just remind him even more how he and Dad had failed to save me.

It wasn't long after that when Dad returned. My mental haze passing, I noticed how much becoming a Faerie had changed him. He still looked mostly human in his face, though the white eyes and the vine hair were both new. But the rest of his body was a sick fusion of flesh and plant matter. He didn't have hands, but twisted roots the consistency of bone combined to vaguely resemble fingers. A few glowing roses decorated his joints and right over where his heart should've been. He was splattered in blood.

I said, "Between how much I've been torn up today and how creepy Bloody Mary turned out to be, this whole day's made me glad I'm unable to bleed." I caught his gaze and tapped the side of my cheek. "You missed a spot. Right here."

Dad moved as if he chuckled, but it was expressionless and soundless. He pointed at me, tapped his face and then his head. Jarrod translated, "He's asking how you are. And Nalem."

"Right now? Not a happy camper. It's been a rough few days." I sat back up, wrapping my arms around my knees. "Overall? Fine, I guess. Trying to lay low and keep Nalem out of trouble—it's his schemes that got us into this mess. And before you ask, Mom's good. She misses you."

Dad made an X shape over his heart and then mimed a tear; I wasn't sure if that meant he was heartbroken, or that he thought Mom was being overdramatic.

Before Jarrod could translate, I asked, "So you're mute now?"

"If he speaks, his words tend to...stick in unexpected ways." Jarrod waved one of his scarf-leaves as an example. "So he stopped, last I heard. Though, sir, forgive me for asking, but I saw someone else here with a similar curse. Was that..."

Dad put a claw to his lips, signaling Jarrod to shut up. He then slunk over and examined me, looming as he looked me over. Tapped my chest a few times, I don't know why, not like I'd grown a heart in the past ten years.

"This isn't exactly the reunion I expected," I said as I tried to brush his claw away. "I mean, you've never been the hugging type, but at least some indication that you're happy I'm alive, apologizing for dropping off the face of the Earth..."

Jarrod winced as I spoke, but Dad wasn't affected by my words.

"Maybe just a lunch date? Or, well, I'm sure you don't go to restaurants a lot now that you're made of plants, but maybe we can find a coffee shop that doesn't mind if you blend in with the shrubbery."

Exasperated, Dad shook his head. He made a few more signs, which Jarrod translated, "He says maybe later, after he's...fixed you. He can't explain that plan, but he does have something that will help for now." A long pause. "He wants to talk to Nalem."

Tell him I'm not here right now. "Nalem curled up tighter and buried his face in his arms. *Call back later or leave a message at the tone. Beep.*

Pulling Nalem out wasn't something I did often—I preferred to be in control of my own body more often than not. But Nalem was worn out, having taken over too much without rest in the past few days. Hooking me into the train had drained what little energy he did have. So getting Nalem to take control was as easy as losing focus on my body, letting it go numb and essentially stepping out of it.

Nalem blinked a few times before scowling. "Insolent vessel. Fine. What do you want with me? Want to tell me your plans so I can tell you how foolish each one is? Desperate enough to attempt an exorcism? What fix will you attempt this time, Alexander?"

Dad crouched in front of us. And to my surprise—and Jarrod's, judging by the way his eyes went wide—he spoke. "I have an order for you, Nalem."

"For me? You think you can order me around?" Nalem chuckled, digging his fingers into the earth and tearing the clovers. "What, going to curse me the way you did your little mistake over there?"

"Yes." Dad noticed Jarrod steeling himself to speak up again. "Silence until I am finished. Only I can speak."

The whole area listened, all sound fading out. No wind, no rustling leaves in the thorns, nothing. Jarrod tried to talk, but his lips moved with no words to back them up. And what was stranger, I didn't hear Nalem in my head either. All I heard was the phantom ringing that comes with silence.

"Nalem. You are the son of the Harvester. Death. Some say you should inherit that role—I argue the opposite." The roses covering Dad glowed brighter, and Nalem scrambled to his feet to run. "No. Do not move until I am finished. Only I can move."

The world came to a total halt. Even the leaves stopped midmotion. A wave of fear rolled through me. Dad pierced his claws through my skin and I couldn't move, couldn't do anything to stop him.

"Nalem. You will kill no longer." As Dad spoke, white roses used their thorns and roots to crawl down his arms. It almost looked cute, at least until they burrowed into my skin through the holes created by my father. "You may use your powers on the already dead. You may even hurt others, in self-defense. But death is no longer yours to deliver."

The wave of fear was replaced by one of indignation. Even if our body didn't budge I felt as Nalem ravaged through my skull, not even leaving impressions of what his body might be like, thrashing out with jabs of pain and pressure. He screamed but no sound came out, which only made him try harder.

"If you do kill, these thorns shall hold you fast. Your body will be consumed and immobile until I can find and capture you. By then, my plan should be ready."

Dad pulled his claws away. He kept a blank face, as if there was nothing wrong with what he'd just done. "The curse is placed. I release you from your confines."

Sound and motion struck back in a cacophony, starting with Nalem shouting. It was a primal sound that scraped my throat, a noise I'd never heard from him before. And Jarrod, he covered his mouth with his scarf and didn't speak, just stared at me with wide eyes.

Nalem fled back into the depths of my mind. Feeling returned to my face first, then my chest with new holes in the flesh trying to knit themselves shut. But there was something deeper, clinging to my ribs and winding around my spine. Part of it even reached into my skull, curled up at the base the way Nalem sometimes would. There was a pattern to the way they hung from my bones. Numbness fled my fingers as I realized they were pricking themselves on the new thorns, trying in vain to tear the vines out.

"Stop. That only makes it hurt worse." Jarrod grabbed my hands and pulled them away, almost holding tight enough to fracture. "Believe me, I tried once. Before. You'll...you'll get used to it eventually."

I think he was trying to remind himself more than convince me.

14 - JARROD

I wanted to leave for the expo immediately, but, as Alexander pointed out, Retz needed to rest. He'd be useless otherwise, and we would need his help. After all, there'd be more monsters than the lamia at the expo.

"This was your plan all along, wasn't it?" I asked as I followed Alexander around his realm. None of his followers were in sight, but I caught rustles and the reflections of eyes from within the thorn walls. "Cursing Nalem to hamper his abilities, I mean. Is that the only reason you wanted me to bring Retz to you?"

Alexander nodded and signed, "Do you disapprove?"

"I...not necessarily." I wasn't fond of my curse, but Nalem's was for a good cause. We'd lived under the shadow of his threats for so long, I'd always wondered when—not if—he would snap, and which member of our family would be the first to die on the altar of his own self-importance. I should've been relieved. But other worries, subtle ones clinging under my skin and hiding in the spaces between my guts, were growing in this rose-lit land.

"Then there is no problem," Alexander signed. He'd explained he was getting better with his binding words, but still preferred to sign his conversations so as not to risk anything. Yet I understood him better in Arcadia, as if he were talking aloud when he signed at me. Did Arcadia strengthen some part of the bond that facilitated my visions, or were we getting better at understanding each other? . "It is only a temporary curse, regardless. Until the plan can be enacted."

"What is the plan?" I asked.

Alexander did not answer. That meant it was not important for me to know, or he didn't trust my ability to keep it secret.

"Understood. Do you think Nalem will find a loophole?"

"I would not doubt it. But it is better than no protective measures at all."

He did not sign more on the matter. I kept walking with him, almost jogging to keep up with his long strides. I had more questions but wasn't sure how to ask. Or if I should. I was glad to see him again in person, that my family was slowly coming together again. But with these new followers lurking around, and how he'd left Farris and all the other runaway menagerie creatures behind...had the roles been reversed, Alexander would've chided me for my selfishness. And I didn't know how he'd react if I accused him of the same thing.

"You seem troubled. Speak."

"Sorry, sir. Two questions. You said that you were better with your, ah, words. Have you figured out how to alter or remove them yet?"

He glanced at my scarf, which unfurled to reveal the marks underneath. He put a claw to them, then shook his head. "I have not learned. My words burrow too deep." He paused, flexing his claws as if trying to remember how they'd worked as fingers. "Removing them now would only cripple you, at best." This was followed by pointing to my limbs and neck, and a motion of them popping off.

So much for that thought—I needed my limbs to continue my work. And having a neck to breathe with was a little important as well. My scarf wrapped back around its usual perch. "All right then. Question two: The Harvester made me an offer, and his payment is a free revival. I wanted to use it on you."

"Your question is one of permission." Alexander tilted his head, eyebrows raising in interest. "What must you do in exchange?"

"Keep Nalem from dying in Arcadia. I figured I'd be protecting Retz anyway, so it's a given."

"And if my plan involved the death of Nalem, to keep the world safe from his influence? Would you stand against me?"

"As long as Retz was okay, then no, I wouldn't. Even if my curse remained and I turned into a rosebush, I'd make that sacrifice."

Alexander stopped and stared at my face. I wasn't sure what he was searching for, so I stared back.

He flicked me in the forehead with his claws, which felt like being struck with a metal pole. "Don't be a martyr. I have yet to determine if I can stop Nalem without killing him or myself in the process, but with that deal made, it is far more likely that your curse will activate. You should not have made the offer."

"I didn't have a choice in the matter." I jabbed the scarf. "Can't say no to missions. Besides, you didn't refuse the Harvester either."

Alexander responded by placing one hand just under my jaw. If he so much as twitched, the claws could easily pierce through my skull. My breath caught. He wouldn't, would he?

"My apologies, sir. I misspoke."

The claws slid off my face, the tips grazing my chin. "Better. I understand the difficulties of the refusal." He signaled for us to resume our walk as he continued signing. "As for the revival, I will not accept it. It is vital I remain as a Fae in order for my plan to come to fruition."

"Understood." We had circled the main clearing of the territory. The barracks, as Alexander called them, were in sight. Retz was sleeping in that fort of brambles; I hoped this break would be enough for him to recover and be ready for the expo.

Distracted by my own thoughts, I missed what Alexander signed next, save for the word "connected." I asked him what he meant. "Being a Fae. I have come to realize that this world, all worlds are just the motion of many lives moving as one. And now, I see the strings that keep them all moving."

"I'm afraid I don't follow, sir."

"Perhaps someday you will."

I didn't press him on the subject. The possible implications, ones I hoped he didn't intend, settled in my head. I focused instead on keeping pace. I wished Farris were around to make one of his stupid jokes, to distract me from those buzzing thoughts. But then I imagined him saying the wrong thing and Alexander silencing him. I imagined claws going through his jaw and out through his eyes.

I shouldn't have. Should never have imagined such violence from my father—he'd hurt plenty of other monsters, but he never hurt me on purpose. But the time in Arcadia was slowly changing him. There was a growing inhumanity in him, and even if it was just in the claws, I imagined the worst despite myself. Just in case.

"Are you unwell? You look ill."

"Just thirsty, sir. Don't suppose you have a drink around here?"

Once we were ready, Alexander did not come with us. He told us that he had research to do, order to maintain in his territory, but he might catch up later. I think the real reason was that he had to patch up after the fight with Nalem's sister; Alexander was still coated in blood when we left. I wondered if any of it was his, if he even bled anymore.

He did point us in the direction of the expo, so my brother and I started walking. The lack of familiar skies made telling time difficult, but I believe we traveled for at least a day, with a few hours of sleep each. It might have taken even longer with all the breaks we took. Retz wasn't one for prolonged physical activity.

"Isn't there a map of this place or something?" Retz asked during our last stop, where the land around us was a swamp with water like spilled oil and small flames floating just over the surface. "Maybe with an information kiosk and a helpful guide nearby?"

"Alexander once explained to me that Arcadia is always shifting. I think Lady Delight mentioned that too." I wasn't fond of being lost either, but my attention was elsewhere. I worried we were too late to save the others and wondered if they'd even made it to the expo. For all I knew, the three people we wanted to save were already dead. My job for the furaribi was just to get them to San Francisco; they never said it had to be alive.

"Hold up." Retz stopped in the middle of the swamp we were slogging through. He was soaked up to his calves, while the swamp reached just above my knees. He shut his eyes and stretched out his arms. The skin was healed, but the palms were still bandaged and moving looked painful. "I think I sense something."

"The others? Or another Fae?"

"It's...lamia. They're just on the edge of my sensing range." He took a step forward, a will-o'-the-wisp by his leg floating around for his attention. "There are other creatures. They're moving things. Wait...there's a hot skeleton. I mean, literally, warm. Judging by the build, pretty sure that's Isamu."

"Good. A lead." I put a hand on Retz's lower back to keep him steady, as he wavered where he stood. "Do you sense Farris? What direction are they in?"

"Working on it. And..." Retz pointed northeast first. Then he paused, and his finger slowly drifted up. There in the sky, far past where the swamp faded into a cluster of trees and ruins, was a billowing smoke cloud that seemed haloed in light. Was it from a fire or a factory? Hard to tell from so far away.

"Bingo. Farris. He's with Lady Delight. She seems to be...not limping, doesn't have legs after all, but she's not moving quite right. He seems fine." Retz opened his eyes with a loud exhale. "Okay, dizzy. 'Scuse me. Need to puke."

I turned around to give him some privacy while he dry-heaved. I was glad to have a destination, but Lady Delight was still in the picture and lingering around Farris. That meant tight security, especially if he was the White Prince, whatever that was. I should've asked Alexander. Plus, the expo was apparently in the clouds, meaning we'd have to climb without being spotted, break into the expo, and somehow rescue some of the priciest pieces in Lady Delight's collection and climb back down without dying.

The things I do for love. And to keep from becoming a rosebush.

Retz returned with an announcement of, "The pissy necromancer stopped moping long enough to come up with a plan."

Nalem had been quiet for the past day or however long we'd been gone from Alexander's. That didn't quell any fears I had. "Does it involve any sudden betrayals? Murderous rampages? Zombie outbreaks?"

"He says no, no, and skeletons are stylistically cooler. Zombies look funny once they've rotted enough." Retz cocked his head as if hearing something far off. "Okay, so Nalem wanted to go to this expo to give a speech. That's what Lady Delight first agreed to. So Nalem and I get in and give that speech as a distraction."

"You can't guarantee that it'll get everyone's attention," I argued. The will-o'-the-wisp gave up on Retz and floated toward me. I swatted at it with my tail. "Nor does that give us an escape plan."

"Maybe we can hijack a lamia truck to escape. Or wait, wait..." Retz listened again. "Okay, Nalem is loath to do this, but he's willing to call on his sister again. He'll cause a fight with his speech, and we save the others in the chaos. Then, once the fight gets violent and people die, we can use someone's heart to summon Vairi and pay for our passage. She's got a thing for those."

I mulled over the plan. "There are too many variables. And how can we be sure that Nalem isn't setting up another trap—or that the mob, once violent, won't turn on us?"

Retz shook his head. "He's going into this as blind as we are. He just wants to give his damn speech and get out of here." Retz started walking again, toward the smoke in the distance. "Arcadia's not a fan of him, you see. Plays havoc with his senses, makes him sick. I'm getting bits of it here and there, and it's not pleasant."

"I see. Then until I come up with something better, I suppose that's the plan." I waded through the swamp to catch up with Retz and his stupid long legs. "And I will come up with something better."

"Nalem's laughing, but I don't doubt you." He glanced at me over his shoulder, brow creasing with concern. "You scared?"

I wondered why he'd asked, until I realized my hands were trembling. "No, just sober." I decided to fix that in case an ambush cropped up, and fished the one drink Alexander found amongst his followers out of my pockets. The lukewarm hard lemonade tasted as vile as I'd expected, but it would soon soothe the shakes from my limbs.

Retz raised an eyebrow. "Being an alcoholic's better than being scared?" I thought he was going to chide me for it, but he reached over and ruffled my hair instead. "Guess you're still following Dad's footsteps. That'll never change."

"Your habit of lording your height over me also hasn't gone anywhere," I grumbled as I pushed his hand off my head. "Hurry up; the others are waiting for us."

We resumed our trek through the swamp, wisps of fire continuously crossing our path to lead us astray. Retz complained about how the muck got between his toes. I asked if he'd rather go back to the menagerie, and though I regretted the comment as soon as I made it, the complaints stopped. The swamp eventually gave way to broken slabs of concrete poking up from piles of coal and ashes. A small river rolled through where a road should've been. The farther we went, the more concrete there was, with crumbling ruins of office buildings and houses. Holes were rent in corrugated metal roofs, as if giant claws had torn them apart.

The smoke I'd seen earlier came from a glistening factory tower, made out of obsidian instead of steel.

Pipes and chimneys spewed brimstone; I had to cover my mouth with my scarf to avoid breathing in the sulfuric smell.

"So, they're in that tower?" I asked Retz.

Retz tilted his head, his gaze drifting up from the tower. "No...they're in the smoke. There's a solid surface up there that they can walk around on, I guess." He pursed his lips together. "I'm not sure how we get up, though. Maybe there's an elevator."

"Keep wishing. It might work someday." Looking closer, I saw small forms—guards, I assumed—marching in and around the tower. The tower itself had plenty of pipes and footholds for climbing, but obsidian is smooth with little traction, and I had already seen how incompetent Retz was at climbing. Well, with Nalem interfering, at least. A rope would've been nice, but this area didn't even have plants anymore. It was all water, debris, and soot.

"I really should've kept those lamia bones," Retz muttered. "Left 'em in the train. If I had enough, then I..." He stopped again and I nearly walked into him. He really needed to give me a warning before doing that. "The train. It's here."

I didn't need to ask where, because Retz was already running toward it. Hiding in an alleyway between two rubble-strewn buildings, an impeccably clean train rested. A strange antlered woman sat on the nose of the train, watching Aimi pace. She was in human form again,

I wasn't going to question it. "He's not telling me much more about Atlantis and Lemuria. Just that they existed on Earth ages ago and now exist elsewhere."

Farris thought on this a moment, as if he was on the verge of remembering something, then shook his head. "Whatever. I'm going ahead to scope out a place to sit. Make sure we're not stuck in a caboose or anything." He planted a quick kiss on Jarrod's head before running off.

"He needs time to think, and sort out some of this mess without us," my brother explained. "I'm not surprised. After all that, I'd want to be alone too." Jarrod tugged at his scarf, loosening it enough for him to get more than gasps of air. "I always dreamed other worlds and stuff existed when I was a kid. If only the younger me knew what I was getting into."

"I remember. You wanted to escape into Middle Earth and be an elf or something. And we decided that Nalem was Gollum because it pissed him off so much." The very mention of it earned a string of protests from Nalem, which always lightened my mood. "Hey, maybe Farris is a nickname for Faramir or something."

Jarrod almost smiled. "Somehow, I doubt that. But I'm sure we'll find out soon enough." He stopped when we reached the doors of the train. I wondered why until his scarf wrapped around the lower half of his face; even after all the years of fighting, gore still overwhelmed him sometimes. He gritted his teeth while the innards of the train gurgled as it prepared to depart.

"Careful there, Jarrod. You'll wear those chompers down to nothing at this rate." I hopped up the steps to the train, waiting for him to follow. "Hey, I've been thinking. Since you're supposed to be watching me anyway—which you probably should've told me before I ran off—I'll watch your back too. If you're scared of Vairi, well, she can't do anything to me. I'll keep you safe. Okay?" It was the least I could offer after the trouble I'd caused.

Jarrod made an effort against grinding his teeth as he steeled himself enough to board the train. "I appreciate the offer, but I can look after myself."

"Nice tough-guy act. Real convincing."

"So long as I believe it, I'll act as long as I need to." As soon as his feet hit the floor, the glass shards from his earlier fights pushed out of his skin. His blood leaked into the carpet until his healing factor kicked in and knit the wounds closed. "Though I admit, this is...more than a bit disturbing."

"Sure is. C'mon then, Legolas, let's see if this creep keeps any Band-Aids onboard."

I found an odd amount of comfort when I sat in that bloody train a second time. When the scenery outside the window became a blur of color, I closed my eyes and felt the pulse of the train, beating in time to rhythm.

"It's mimicking a heart," Nalem told me. *"Feels so long since I had one of my own."*

"It's weirdly pleasant," I thought back. It wasn't as unsettling as the squirming vines inside me playing the part of fake organs, and the seat was so much warmer than my own skin. *"Distracting, but pleasant. Is this how most people feel, when they're alive with all their organs intact?"* Was this what I had missed this whole time?

"Kind of. But it's nice not having a heart. It is a big weakness, after all. One stab and it's over. Or one well-timed heart attack. Or just running into Vairi."

He had a point. I'd always thought organs were inconvenient because of their fragility, so I'd been happy not to have any. Still, there was something to be said for this fake heartbeat, something I almost envied.

I opened my eyes again to check on the others. Jarrod had fallen asleep, thanks to a cocktail of exhaustion and blood loss. Vairi had been kind enough to return long enough to clot his wounds so they'd heal faster, but I think she took an extra donation of the stuff, 'cause Jarrod had been pretty woozy afterward. Even Farris seemed impressed; he said my brother didn't sleep much.

Farris was still awake, staring at the polychromatic blur outside while stroking Jarrod's hair. He hummed off-key notes, which I think were meant to be an old Simon and Garfunkel tune, and refused to acknowledge my presence.

The train slowed. I hazarded a look outside, relieved to find that we weren't a billion feet in the air this time. It was dark out there, and tiny red rubies illuminated bare-branched trees. The tracks ran over a dirt road and through patches of mist clinging to the windows with trailing tendrils. The train scuttled to a halt in front of a bus stop made of old and splintering wood, covered in wind chimes and what I thought was a rusted sign. No, that was a mirror splattered with blood—must've been how Vairi had been summoned.

The furaribi stood in the bus stop but didn't sit down since they were in fire form. Between their flames and the light of the rubies, a third form was illuminated, slumped inside the lean-to; it shook, writhed against bonds I couldn't see.

Vairi stepped out and curtsied to the furaribi. Aimi lifted her hands with an offering, a heart. Vairi seemed to refuse it and laugh, and whatever she said shocked Aimi enough that she dropped the still-beating organ. It came to a stop just above the ground, then rose up to Vairi's lips. She took a bite. Aimi stumbled backward, and Isamu caught her. Pure light leaked from their eyes as Vairi spoke.

"They killed someone for that heart." Jarrod had woken up, and I hadn't realized until he stood next to me to watch. His arms were crossed and holding his coat together. "Bloody Mary must think it's funny, for some reason."

"It's because they didn't have to," Nalem explained, and I echoed his words for the others. *"Vairi never forces anyone to kill, just give her the body. Displaces the blame, or so she claims. She's laughing because they went through so much extra effort."*

"That's sick." Jarrod shook his head and backed away from the window. "Does she ever refuse an offered heart?"

"If she has a better use for the offering to stay alive, then yes. I've heard that she still rewards rides for the attempt." His sarcasm painted my own voice. *"She is, after all, oh so kind. In the same way that I am kind."*

A figure in the back of the lean-to with eyes glowing from multiple heads broke from its bonds and threw itself at the furaribi. They jumped out of the way, and Aimi kicked it in the face before allowing her brother to uppercut the puny Faerie. I guess it, too, was pissed at its murderers. The furaribi prepared to strike again, but Vairi raised a hand and spoke. The two of them stepped back as the Fae rushed forward again.

At that point, the windows clamped shut. While I imagined the shutters were metal on the outside, the inside was like the backs of my own eyelids, albeit with more veins.

Jarrod winced at the sight, then turned to me. "Are they safe?"

I reached out with my powers just enough to sense the furaribi, though the close proximity of Vairi and the Faerie threatened a migraine. "They're closer to the train now. I think they're going to enter, but whatever they're watching, it's got them distracted. Scared, too." I felt how tightly they held each other's hands, how they only lightly touched the earth so it'd be easier to flee. Vairi must've done something, because I heard a door slide open a few cars down and felt the furaribi run inside. I lost track of them after that because my brain snapped back with static.

"They're inside," I told the others. "So we've got that problem down."

"That's a relief. It seems Vairi has either taken a liking to the furaribi or to us." Jarrod tugged at his scarf in a vain attempt to loosen it further. "I'm not sure which is more worrying."

Farris crept over and tried to help Jarrod with his scarf. "Either way, she's got a weird way of showing it. Most people stick to the wine-and-dine approach, not the ride-and-die one."

Waiting for the train to start up or for news of the furaribi, we fidgeted and kept apart instead of wasting time with empty words. Farris and Jarrod stayed close to each other but didn't quite touch. Nalem curled up in my head, unable to hide his fatigue, but he kept one eye open instead of drifting off.

Vairi skipped in a few minutes later, the furaribi in tow. The two were in their human forms again, and Vairi had apparently found clothes for them—Aimi's red dress had been cleaned of blood, and a patched-together jacket and slacks had been found for Isamu. The siblings kept their heads down, but Aimi hazarded a quick glance at me. She'd been crying, but out of fear or coming down from that fight outside, I couldn't say.

"You are all so fortunate I gave young Miss Kurusaki a ride earlier," Vairi chirped. "I might have ignored her initial calls otherwise. But now, your merry band is reunited and paid for. So, where shall I take you?"

"Our first task is to reach San Francisco," Jarrod answered. He added to the furaribi, "After you two are safe, the rest of us will take on Lady Delight. We'll need time to prepare, though, and we'll be able to drive ourselves. I assume you and Nalem still remember the way, Retz?"

I nodded.

"Then there we go. We disembark in San Francisco."

"Such a short trip. And here I was hoping to spend more time with everyone. Other than a certain rude prince, you all entertain me so greatly." Vairi clicked her tongue before spinning to face me. "Now, if you'll excuse me, I have a train to conduct. It gets so fussy when I am not at the helm."

I wanted to stay with the others, make sure the furaribi were okay, but Nalem had other plans.

He tugged me to my feet and said, "Allow me to follow. We have matters to discuss."

"Do we now?" Vairi's face lit up as she grabbed me by the hand. "Then talk we shall! Just stay close, lest the other inhabitants make other plans for you." She pulled me along; assured I would follow, Nalem released his control on my body. Vairi called as she left, "The rest of you, we will arrive at our destination shortly. If you kill anyone in my absence, please take the corpse with you when you depart."

Aimi made a sound of protest and started to stand, but Isamu grabbed her arm and pulled her back down. He muttered something to her in Japanese; she sank onto the seat, only responding in broken phrases. Jarrod cast me a glance before reaching into the ruins of his coat. I had to leave before I could see what he was searching for.

As soon as we entered the other cars, I understood why Vairi wanted me to stick close. None of the creatures were human, though I had a sinking feeling that many had once been. In one room, a woman made of blades threw pieces of herself at a scaled beast, her audience shouting advice on where its weak spots might be. Another had a masked figure and a humanoid with arms of guitar strings and piano keys dueling with words, every insult resulting in bruises and cuts. In every room, all eyes flickered to me, some drawing out into stares.

"These all friends of yours or just other riders?" I asked, as we reached a crowd pinning a multilimbed insect down while an amalgamation of bone tore through the insect's guts for some unknown prize, the insect's cries rough as wind scraping a rusty corridor.

"Both, in a respect. By giving their all in my service, they have been rewarded with permanent positions in the train. And I care for them all so, so deeply." She waved to her minions as we stole into the front of the train.

Nearly all of the walls were replaced by windows showcasing the end of the ruby-lit forest. There was no furniture in the room, but in the center rested what I assumed was a map. There were two globes, one of which was cast in metal but showed a typical map of Earth, and the other was the largest ball of string I'd ever seen, unfamiliar continents rising out of the enigmatic tapestry. Between them rested the unholy hybrid of an Escher painting and a poorly designed travel map. It hurt my eyes just looking at it.

"This is the most complete map of the three realms," Vairi explained to me. "I made it myself. So far, it's been a five-thousand-year labor of love." She stroked the middle map, and it spun at her touch. "It even has most of the Arcadian gates. Speaking of which, it is most fortunate for you that San Francisco still has gates of its own."

"Indeed, how lucky we are." Nalem took control of my mouth again while I tried to find a comfortable place to stand. "But I am not here to discuss maps. I need you to tell me of our parents' plans."

"How typical. I am only your sister when desperation strikes." With her back to me, Vairi continued twisting the maps into strange configurations. "I am the child our parents trusts to not usurp them. Why should I betray them in your favor?"

"What's in it for you, you mean." Nalem pinched the bridge of his nose. "Well, I'm willing to make a deal, so what is your wish? A seasonal donation of hearts? More followers? A goddamn radio to make this abomination more tolerable?"

"May I have a promise that when instigating your plans, you will keep Arcadia safe? It has become more important than you realize, brother." She offered a wry, bloodstained smile. "I would ask for my own safety as well, but we're both aware how little you care for that."

Nalem swore a few times in my head before answering. "You know I can't guarantee anything. No matter how many calculations I make, how many theories I test, in the end...what we're attempting to do, it hasn't been done before. The closest incident was in reverse."

"But you can try your best, can't you?" She crossed the room and cupped my face. "Listen to me. The world you wish and work for, brother—it encompasses far more than you and her. There will be consequences you cannot account for."

"The same can be said of all actions. Case in point, our existence. Yours more so than mine."

"I told you to listen, and still you refuse. You never change." Her bloody fingers reached into my hair. In the back of my mind, Nalem flinched. "All I can say for now is that our parents are doing the same thing they've always done. They're protecting us."

"Protecting us from their own mistakes when we can fix them, you mean."

For the first time since I met her, sorrow and pity mixed in Vairi's bloodshot eyes. The same expression pulled at Nalem's face, though he urged me not to show it.

Vairi pulled her hands away as she asked, "Will you come to Samhain regardless? Please?"

The train shuddered as Nalem answered. Outside, the first morning rays reached San Francisco.

It shouldn't have surprised me that the gate into Arcadia was located in Golden Gate Park. The air was colder than I expected as I stepped off the train, thanks to the early hour and the nearby ocean. The grass crunched under my feet—this was California in a summer drought, after all. Vairi tossed a few clothes our way, claiming that otherwise, we'd be caught as vagrants and she'd have to come rescue us again. Nalem denied this the whole time I put my shoes on.

As soon as I stepped out of the train, I marveled at the sights. The city was already awake, cars slipping up and down the streets as sunlight glinted off the windows of the skyscrapers. I barely brushed the world with my senses and was hit by the static feedback of billions of bones.

"If you rubberneck any more, I'm pretty sure your spine's going to snap," Isamu quipped.

As I lowered my head so I wouldn't be mistaken for a tourist, I caught Aimi almost smile.

"Don't tell me this is your first big city?" Isamu asked.

I shook my head. "Visited Boise a few times and passed through Seattle, but nothing beyond that. I don't get out much." The thought of letting Nalem loose in a city, with so many people—and large cemeteries to accommodate them—was not one I wanted to dwell on.

Farris stepped off the train and collapsed as soon as he hit the California dirt. Jarrod raced to his side to help him back up. "Farris? Come on, Farris. We made it. You're safe."

"I'm all right. Just. Ow." Farris pushed himself onto his hands and knees. "Fuck. Y'think the dead wouldn't have nerves."

"True, but Faeries are far from truly dead." Vairi leaned against the doorway and watched, as if people writhing in pain outside her door was a common occurrence. Oh wait, it probably was. "Most are tied to Arcadia. A few hours outside and the pain of the living worlds are too much to bear. But thanks to your deal with Mother, such cannot stop you. How lucky you are!"

Farris made a noise indicating he was anything but.

"I shall be off, then. Places to go, summons to answer. Oh, how life goes on. But best of luck to you luckless lot. Especially you, brother dearest. Or should I say deadest?" Vairi curtsied as the door of her train slid shut. It hoisted itself onto its insect legs and skittered into the woods in a blink. I swore I saw Vairi wave out of one window as she departed.

Jarrod finally got his boyfriend up, one arm around his waist. "Grateful as I am for the ride, I'm relieved to see her go. But at least we have one mission down."

Isamu snorted as he watched the trees. "Remind me if we're ever invited to meet another of Nalem's relatives to say no and run in the other direction."

"I can remind you, but I have a feeling such advice won't do you any good." Jarrod glanced over his shoulder to make sure the train was gone before turning to the furaribi. "I'm sorry we took so long, but here we are. Unless you have any further requests, I believe this job is done."

Isamu nodded and reached into his pockets before remembering they were empty. "Yeah, it is. 'Cept you might have to wait on payment, all things considered. If you don't mind."

Those two discussed payment with Farris making unhelpful comments over their shoulders, but Aimi kept quiet.

I waved a hand in front of her face to make sure she hadn't zoned out. "Hey. You all right?"

"Sure. Fine." Her eyes dimmed from gold to a glassy black. "Ah, who am I kidding? I want to curl up in a hole and just lie there for a bit. I don't get how you do it."

"Do what, curl up?"

"Ha-ha, no. You told me that death and killing doesn't make you feel anything. I don't get how that's possible." She meandered away from the others, and I followed her toward the trees. She kicked at the ground as she walked, keeping her voice low as she spoke. "I refused to let Isamu be stuck in Arcadia forever or risk getting caught again. But I couldn't give my own heart for the train, and I wouldn't let him do it either. And no matter how much we walked, we always ended up at the same spot. That train stop."

"At least you didn't get attacked by a merry-go-round. I don't think I can ride one of those ever again."

"Those aren't alive. Well, probably. Arcadia doesn't seem to fit reality." Aimi reached the edge of the trees and her gaze followed them up to the pale morning sky; I almost thought she would take to fire form and fly away, disguise herself as a shooting star bright enough to be seen in the morning. "We found a lamia who was lost. I'm not sure if he was one of Delight's or not, but I didn't care. I figured, better him than us, right? So we pinned him down and burned him, and I thought he was dead when I went to get the heart, but then he started making noises, and..."

Aimi didn't cry, didn't tremble, and didn't break down. Just kept staring up at the tops of the trees. I wasn't sure what to do; comforting people was never my strong point. I wanted to reach out to her but stopped my hand just above her shoulder—it would be so easy for her to burn me, or worse, for Nalem to decide to add to her misery by ruining her bones.

I'd decided to go grab her brother when she asked me, "Did it ever get to you? Ever at all?"

My hand settled on her hair, smoothing it and sweeping the bangs out of her eyes. I settled into the conversational tone I used with clients at the salon. "The first time, yeah. And it's not as if I've killed many people myself. That's Nalem's job. But you get used to it." Even though being a hairstylist felt farther away than ever after the past few days, the chatty lies flowed with the role. "Not that you have to. Now that you're here—"

"Being here won't change anything." Aimi's fists clenched, and while she stayed in human form, I felt heat pool in her knuckles. "It might make us harder to find, but if we rely on that and get careless, what's stopping

Lady Delight from finding us again? Careful didn't stop her before."

"As it happens, she is going to be stopped. By me." When Aimi looked at me in surprise, I added, "Well, Jarrod will be there too. And Farris. And our dad, if he decides to actually be helpful this time."

"And you think you can really beat her?"

"We...don't exactly have a choice in the matter. We stop her, or we die trying." Well, more accurately, we'd turn into plant matter, but she didn't need those thorny little details. "So whatever happens, don't worry. We'll take care of it and make sure no one ends up in that gilded hellhole of hers again."

That golden glow sunk back into Aimi's sockets like the sun lighting up the sky. She pulled away from me and ran back to the others. "Sammy, we're not staying. They're going to fight Lady Delight, and we're going to help!"

"We are? But we just—" Isamu must've seen the look in his sister's eyes, because he stopped his protests. "Jarrod, would you mind...?"

"If you're sure, then we can use all the help we can get. But only if you're certain. I'll give you time to discuss." Jarrod strode away from them, Farris on his heels, over to me. "What did you do this time?"

"All I did was try to calm her down." I was honest, but something in Jarrod's stare said he didn't believe me. "Scout's honor. Cross my heart and all that."

"You were never a scout, and you don't have a heart." Jarrod bit his lip before asking Farris, "Think you can steal a bigger car?"

"Babe, I thought you'd never ask."

18 - JARROD

"Okay, so I thought the bullets would be a stretch considering where we are, but you managed. No surprise there. But seriously, how'd you find lamia antivenom so quickly? This city's huge, and that can't be common."

I couldn't help but feel a surge of pride at Farris's shock. I took a sip the beer I'd gotten as well, the first one I'd had in days, before sliding it back into one of my coat's many interior pockets. "It's a matter of having the right contacts. Plenty of supernaturals make their home here, so Alexander and I have been called here on numerous occasions."

"Hence your frequent flyer miles with the black market, so to speak." Farris ruffled my hair with his knuckles, not wanting to risk scratching my scalp. He was still getting used to his claws.

The two of us were alone as we broke through the crowds of San Francisco. We'd split from the others to get supplies and, on our end, to find transportation. I wasn't sure if the furaribi needed anything or went with Retz to make sure he and Nalem didn't cause a scene in their search for bones.

I still hadn't figured out how Retz convinced the furaribi to join us. When I asked, all he said was "Anyone'll jump at revenge if they think the odds are worth it. If they can mask it behind a noble cause, even better." I'd hoped those were Nalem's words, but the posture and expression weren't there, not even the purring, mocking tone. It was all Retz.

The words didn't sit well with me, and I'd asked the furaribi to reconsider and stay safe. But past all the fire, there was something dark in Aimi's eyes. She'd told me, "I got out of the menagerie, the market, and Arcadia at the cost of others. It's time I make it up to them. I'm not gonna rest until Lady Delight's out of the picture."

Isamu had nodded and said that where Aimi went, he followed.

"You. You're thinking too much. Stop it." Farris tried to elbow me the way he used to, but thanks to his Fae-induced growth spurt, his elbow reached my head instead of my sides. The cool smoke brushed against my cheek, though I had to focus to see it. The glamour that made my curse resemble tattoos and a scarf also hid Farris's shadows. To human eyes, they resembled long gloves and boots, with small bits of jewelry on his face and fingers. And, to my amusement, the metal-and-glass teeth manifested themselves as braces. It seemed I was the only one to see past the glamour to find the darkness underneath—one of the few benefits of bearing a Faerie curse.

I took another swig of beer. "That's what brains are for, Farris. Thinking. I apologize for getting so much more out of mine than you do yours."

"Ouch. If I still had a heart, you would've broken it."

Someone beside us stifled a laugh before being swallowed back into the sea of pedestrians. The summer sun glinted off the skyscraper windows and threatened to blind anyone who looked up. Cars wove through the maze of skyscrapers and one-way streets, occasionally interrupted by a bus or trolley. I'd told Farris both were off-limits for hijacking.

To console him, I offered him the last of my beer. He drank and grimaced, claiming he didn't taste anything, and tossed the bottle at a nearby trash can.

I pulled out my notepad—one of the few things the lamia left in my duster, which I hadn't let Vairi replace, though she had been kind enough to patch it up—and checked our peculiar shopping list. Antivenom, herbs for medicine and other concoctions, and ammunition— we'd found all our esoteric supplies, though I'd used up all my favors. Practical things like food, first-aid kits, and a car...we still had to work on those. The lamia left no money in my wallet, which left theft as our main option.

Farris and I had shoplifted small items on occasion, but enough to support a group? I wasn't looking forward to it.

Farris looked over my shoulder and said, "What if we hold up a corner store?"

"No matter where we go, there'll be too many people. We'd be caught."

"Yeah, but it'd take hours for the cops to get through traffic. I'm starting to think our best bet is stealing a helicopter."

"Even if you knew how to drive one, I wouldn't trust you to do it without crashing or setting us on fire."

"Babe, have a little faith. Besides, two of our five are dead-ish, two others have wings, and you...well. I'm sure one of us could save you from certain doom if I did crash. Which I wouldn't, 'cause I'm an awesome driver."

I reached up and put a finger to his lips. "We're not having this discussion, because we're not hijacking a helicopter. End of story."

Light footsteps fell into step alongside us. "Oh, and we were just thinking of how fun it would be if you two did. The rush of air, gears giving their last crank before the heat of combustion! More thrilling than a regular freefall, wouldn't you say?"

I jumped at the presence of our new companion, who was dressed in khaki shorts, sandals, and an obnoxious orange Hawaiian shirt with green decals. His curly black hair was pulled back into a ponytail, and for once, he only had two eyes visible.

"And who the fuck are you?" Farris asked as he flexed his new claws. "Didn't anyone ever tell you that snooping is rude?"

"Farris, can it. Greetings, Harvester. I didn't expect to see you here."

The Harvester smiled with his shark teeth—this time, I saw the similarity in that grin to those of his children. "We were in the area already and sensed a strange sort of death, so here we are." He walked backward, ignoring the people he bumped into, then reached out and prodded Farris's arm. "And how long have you been out of Arcadia, little one?"

"Hey, I ain't little. I'm taller than you, at least." Farris pulled his arm away. "And a few hours, I guess. Now wait, are you really the—"

"You should be dead by now. I mean truly dead, not this state of half-lives." The Harvester kept poking and prodding. "Fun fact: most Fae last an hour or two outside of Arcadia at most before suffering a unique and excruciating death! Most peculiar, isn't it?"

My heart came to a stop, as did the walk sign. "He's going to disappear?" Because I had brought Farris out of Arcadia, I was killing him? I darted my gaze to Farris, as if just mentioning his possible demise would make him disappear. He looked as shocked as I felt.

"Well, that's the thing. He should be dead, but he isn't. Let's see, we have a theory as to why…" Having avoided falling into traffic, the Harvester paced around me and to the other side of Farris. Farris bared his teeth and growled, but instead of being frightened, the Harvester just prodded the metal-and-glass fangs. "Most fascinating. How did you meet your end?"

"Your daughter kinda broke my heart. By eating it."

The Harvester shook his head. "Oh, Vairi dearest. Never was the best at manners, but we suppose that's our fault. Now, young Gallows, this is your wish? Let's see…" He prodded a few more times. When the light turned green, I had to pull them both along before angry pedestrians ran us over.

"Aha! We figured out the how, if not the why," the Harvester declared as we reached the other side. "He is currently under contract with the Weaver, even more than you are under contract with us." He prodded Farris's shoulder, right where his mysterious tattoo was. "There's a mark right here and everything. Keeps him moving until the task is completed, hence why he can survive outside of Arcadia without becoming a quivering corpse."

Farris's eyes narrowed. "The Weaver? Ain't that your wife stuck in Moonworld? Why the hell would I make a deal with her?"

A question I wondered as well—especially since that meant Farris had a stronger connection with Nalem's family than we thought, and we had no idea how or why.

The Harvester tilted his head. "How did you...ah yes, the children. They have such a tendency to blab. Well, we cannot tell you your own motivations. Just that this contract keeps you from death, but since you are under her sphere of influence and not our own, we cannot revive you. You were going to ask this of us, weren't you, little one?" He glanced at me, reading me all too well, and smiled with those pointed teeth again. "Ah, fear not. Once the quest is finished, we can assist. Or perhaps the Weaver will do so herself, as a reward to her hopefully faithful follower. As for now—oh, it seems we are needed down in the Tenderloin. We've always been fond of there."

"Wait just one second." Either not realizing full gravitas of who he was dealing with or just not caring, Farris grabbed the Harvester's sleeve and dug his claws in. "I lost my memory, and I have no idea what the hell I'm supposed to be doing for your wife. You seem to. So, answers, and answers now."

"What do you think we are, mind readers?" The Harvester was about to pry Farris's hand off but hesitated, instead pulling away and tearing his own shirt. "We sensed the mark on your shoulder, but it is little more than the seal of the contract, not the rules themselves. Those would be a secret kept by you and she alone, and if you cannot remember..." The Harvester slipped his scaly gloves on as he stood on tiptoe to look Farris in the eyes. A few pedestrians muttered curses as they had to walk around us.

Farris took a step back. "You may be a reaper, but you sure ain't grim at all."

"We also have skin and don't wear our cloak unless it's raining. Strange, how wrong such myths can be." The Harvester reached up, fingers hovering just over Farris's face. "No, not here. Too many people." He retracted his hand and said to me, "We may be able to help, but our time here is short, and there is work to do. We are certain that we will find you soon, though, yes?"

I answered, "We plan to be out of San Francisco by nightfall, and then we're off to Oregon to stop Lady Delight."

"Then, as mortals say nowadays, it is a date." His words barely left his lips when he turned around and escaped into the crowd. I caught a glimpse of black hair bobbing toward Tenderloin. That was all.

There wasn't a chance to absorb the encounter; the crowd refused to keep still long enough to let me think. The unease of the Harvester's presence, and the weight of his words, sunk in all at once. I found myself trembling and I kept close to Farris.

"Do you have any idea what just happened?" he asked me.

Dumbstruck, I shook my head in reply.

"Hey, you all right?"

I became all too aware of how cold Farris was. How...empty he was, without a heart beating in his chest. And the easy fix I thought I had? Why did I let myself bank on that? Idiot! This wasn't an injury that could be fixed with a bandage or a unicorn horn. He was dead. Still up and talking, but dead.

"Come on, let's get away from all these people for a sec."

Farris lead me through the streets, though finding an empty spot at this time of day was harder to find than anything else on my list. Farris settled for stealing an outdoor cafe table, leaving me only to grab a drink from inside. He also brought out some napkins and dabbed them against my face. I hadn't realized I'd been slowly crying as my last traces of calm wore out. The tea he pushed into my hands wasn't alcoholic, but it was warmer than him, and that helped ground me.

"I'm sorry," I said.

"Don't be." Farris tucked his sleeves over his shadowy arms, pulled his hair over the traces of brimstone along his ears. He put his hands in his lap, safely out of sight, and smiled without teeth. If I ignored the gray pallor already spreading across his freckled skin, I could pretend all was normal. "Babe, you've been running on empty since this whole thing started."

"And we still don't have time to rest," I countered. "We've still got to stop Lady Delight, and figure out what pact you made with the Weaver, and—"

"None of that's going to change if you take five minutes to breathe."

"It's another five minutes you're stuck like this. Seriously, why are we talking about me? Farris, you died. You're literally heartless. You can't keep smiling and tell me you're okay either."

His smile fell and his brow creased. "Guess you've got a point." He sighed, and looked ready to cry too, but didn't. Maybe he'd left his tears behind once he'd died. "Kept telling me how dangerous it all was, and now look. Some pair we are, huh?"

"Yeah." My hand was warmer from the tea and the summer sun. I reached across the table. Farris slowly raised a clawed hand and held back, claws resting against my knuckles. Still cold. But still there. That's what mattered. "We're going to get through this. That hasn't changed. No matter what Nalem or the Harvester or anyone else throws at us, you're coming back to life."

Farris mulled on that before asking quietly, "I know you don't do promises, but can you make one for me? Promise you won't get yourself fucked over, trying to save me? 'Cause if I get my life because you lost yours, then there ain't a point to coming back."

For once, I told the logical part of my brain, the part reminding me of everything that could go wrong, to go to hell.

"I can do that," I said. And then, as my promise, "I love you."

I expected him to startle at that. He squeezed my hand tighter instead. "I love you too. And as long as we can say that, nothing's going to stop us. Now, take your time with that tea. World's not going anywhere."

We met up back at Golden Gate Park, as planned. In addition to our previous acquisitions, Farris and I managed to smuggle out some bandages, a bottle of painkillers, two beers, and a few packs of beef jerky. Isamu had a bag full of combustible projectiles hidden under shoplifted meals, while Aimi had acquired a whole backpack of spare clothes, toiletries, and a few choice chemicals she claimed could be combined for flash bombs and knockout gas. Supposedly none of it was stolen, but "donated" the same way the supplies she'd gotten back in Cottage Grove had been. I didn't bother to question her further because we had a bigger problem on our hands.

Retz wasn't back yet.

"He said he was going to meet up with you guys, so I figured he'd sensed your bones and tracked you down," Aimi explained as we scoured the park, just in case he was waiting in a different location. The cloud cover had burned off, covering us in a blanket of heat. "You're sure you never ran into him?"

Farris answered, "Turns out, he's not the only deathly skinny white dude in the city. Who knew?"

The search continued in vain. The park itself was peaceful, with clusters of families and friends enjoying one of the city's rare patches of nature. We asked a few if they'd spotted my brother. They quickly answered that they hadn't, and went back to ignoring us and everyone else in the park. A man who was spray-painted silver and dressed as a pirate was the one person of use, claiming he'd seen someone who at least resembled Retz boarding a bus a few hours ago, but couldn't recall which bus it was.

"Even if I did, though, I wouldn't suggest looking for him there. No one pays attention to who goes where, and I swear, between the buses and taxis and the BART transit—well, turns these cities into even more of a maze." The pirate shifted pose, pointing a fake flintlock pistol at a group of girls who sniggered as they passed. "No better place to get lost than a crowd, I always say."

We thanked him, and in lieu of a monetary tip for his performance, I instead took a moment to correct his gun grip and stance. He gave me a strange look as we left.

It wasn't until we were out of earshot that Isamu said, "That's why I always clung to cities when I was younger. The anonymity of it all. Used to think it made us safe."

"Nowhere's safe from a dedicated hunter." I'd found myself on both sides of the chase before. "Even unpredictability can only get you so far."

"That's why we gotta stop Lady Delight," Aimi said. She was so wound up that she kept walking ahead of us by accident. When she stopped to wait, she bounced on the balls of her feet to keep moving. "Hey, Jarrod, will we actually be in the clear after that? Safe from other hunters and people like her?"

"Hard to say. I'm sure there are other hunters out there, but I don't know of any way they'd be aware of your kind. After all, Lady Delight was right about how rare you are. I guess as long as you keep on your toes and don't get too tied down anywhere, you should be ready for anything that might happen." I wished I had better advice for them, but after ten years of traveling and fighting, I couldn't remember how to survive being settled in one place. When I was younger, we'd had to move a few times to escape whatever chaos Nalem had caused.

"Paranoia's a hard habit to keep up," Farris added.

"I advised precaution," I argued, "not paranoia. Paranoia is thought-consuming and often unfounded. Jumping at shadows only leads to unexpected falls."

Aimi stopped to mull over this, gazing into the distance as we caught up. "Makes sense. But in your opinion, is it worth being paranoid over Nalem?"

"He may be the exception to the rule, yes."

"Then get ready to jump, 'cause here he comes."

We caught up to her at a street corner, where Retz had finally arrived. He'd somehow acquired a Dodge van, the sort usually reserved for soccer moms transporting leagues of children. It was silver with a stick-figure family plastered to one of the tinted windows, and a school award on the bumper. Retz pulled up to us on the street, ignoring the cars honking behind him.

"Okay, so I know the plan was to find a car after we found everything else, but I kinda needed the trunk space." His eyes were wide and his breath was quick as he flipped a switch to unlock the car. "Pile in. I'll explain later."

"I'd prefer an explanation now," I said as I went for the passenger seat. I realized why he needed the van as soon as I hopped in: the trunk and the third row of seats were piled with bones, obscured by the tinted windows of the van. "Please tell me you didn't ransack a graveyard."

"Not yet. Too conspicuous around here, and I wanted to make sure you guys could fit first. Well, at least you and the furaribi. I figured we'd strap Farris to the roof or something if worst came to worst." As soon as the doors slammed shut, the van rushed back into the traffic. The bones in the back clacked and jostled with each stop.

"I might just ride on the roof anyway," Farris muttered, edging toward the door and away from the bones. Some sort of animal skull fell onto his lap at the next stop. He slid it over to Aimi, who chucked it back into the pile with lightning speed; the force of the toss caused another group of bones to dislodge and slide into her brother's lap. Isamu covered his mouth as he brushed them off and tried not to hurl.

"Children, behave before I turn the car around," Retz ordered in a manic singsong tone fueled by adrenaline. "Okay, I didn't reach a graveyard, even though Nalem really wanted to, but we found this place in Berkeley that had a whole museum full of bones. Real ones at that, not casts like regular museums, all on display and sale! So I found a van to put them in, drove to the back, and Nalem paid for all the bones by not killing the staff members. I mean, he can't kill anyone now thanks to Dad, but I wasn't going to tell them that."

I wasn't sure if I should be disturbed as usual or proud of my brother's resourcefulness. I decided on a mix of both. "How'd you get the van?"

"Skeleton key." Retz waved his left hand; his ring finger and pinkie were completely deboned, the skin torn at the tip and flapping. "It's only temporary, don't worry. I've done this before. Now can anyone direct me to the highway? Nalem's directions seem to be a century out of date."

I searched through the glove compartment on the off chance that it had a map. "I've been here a few times, but my memory's a bit fuzzy on directions. If I remember correctly, our best bet would be to take this next left to reach the highway. Judging how frantic you are, would it be safe to assume we're being followed?"

"Not that I can tell. But hey, if you committed grand theft auto to transport a bunch of bones that you also just stole and then had to drive through an unfamiliar city with a bunch of people you'd screwed over, trust me, you'd be panicking too."

Farris piped up, "At least you aren't on fire, yeah? Everything's worse when you're on fire. Er, unless fire is your thing," he added as soon as he noticed the raised eyebrows and pointed glares of his seatmates.

I decided to speak up before the car descended into further chaos. "Peanut gallery in the back, shush for a minute. We're going to get out of this city and to our destination just fine. If you have the energy to talk and think, save it for planning our attack, not making smart comments." I added to Retz, "As soon as we're clear from cities, we're pulling over in a secluded area to hotwire the car. I'm sure driving without two fingers is painful for you, and it creeps me out. And before I forget—no, Farris, you can't teach Aimi how to hotwire. That's the last thing she needs to learn."

Isamu flashed us a look of gratitude in the mirror while Farris and Aimi silently lamented us ruining their fun. I did my best to keep Retz calm and on track as we navigated the California traffic. We turned on the radio once we hit the stop-and-go traffic.

"...three dead and at least seven others injured, including one firefighter. Authorities are still torn over whether this was an accident or arson. We'll return to the Tenderloin later, but for now, the weather. Tomorrow is the first day of August, and as expected, it's going to be a scorcher..."

"None of this concerns us. Let's find some music." I fiddled with the radio dials. I imagined the Harvester striding into those flames as if he belonged there, unnoticed by the terrified civilians as he reached the burning corpses.

I'd planned to mention our Harvester sighting to Retz when he said, "Don't suppose you have your phone on you."

"Lamia swiped it. Why?"

"We were gone longer than I thought. Wanted to call Mom and tell her we're okay, wish her a happy Lammas in case we don't make it home in time to celebrate. Hey, think when we reach a rest stop, it might have a payphone?" I couldn't remember the last time I'd celebrated one of Mom's pagan holidays, and I didn't want to promise Retz that we'd make it in case our assault on Lady Delight failed.

The van finally reached a bridge, and I was able to look across the city. The buildings were aglow in a prelude to the sunset. "Even if they were still common, we don't have any quarters. Unless you can also break into phone booths with your tricks."

"I dunno. Starting to think I might have a career in breaking and entering, instead of, well, just breaking. It'd be more exciting than hairdressing, at least." Retz shrugged and fiddled with the fans; he probably didn't want to roll the windows down, for fear of others glimpsing the bones in the back. "Tell you the truth, I don't want more exciting. Not all the time, at least. But I don't think that's going to be an option anymore, now is it?"

I wanted to tell him that it still could be, for him. He only had to help us defeat Lady Delight, after all, and then he'd be home free. But the life Alexander and I led never gave us a chance for breaks. Whether or not he meant to, Retz had been dragged into our world of fighting, investigating, saving. He was cursed by Alexander, and the supernatural world now knew he was Nalem's vessel. There was no way for him to go back to a life where the voice in his head was his only worry.

I held my tongue and searched the van on the off chance that a phone had been left behind.

"There's a metal dragon around here, somewhere on the right. Should be a bull too. Nothing supernatural or anything, just neat landmarks." I waved off at the fields outside of Yreka, still a couple of hours away from the California-Oregon border. While we hadn't found a phone for Retz at the last rest stop, we had hotwired the car and changed seats. I drove with Farris at shotgun, where he was plastered to the window in search of the aforementioned sculptures.

"Sure we can see them with just headlights?" Aimi asked, leaning over her brother to look. "And aren't you going a little slow?"

"These flatlands are a notorious speed trap. I don't think anyone here wants to explain our cargo to the highway patrol." We'd come close enough at the last rest stop, where someone's dog smelled the bones and tried to get into the car. And while I was trying to keep Nalem, who'd regained enough energy to take over Retz again, from breaking the dog's legs out of grumpy spite, the furaribi had made a distraction to clear the area of trouble-causing witnesses. Said distraction was setting fire to the restrooms.

Needless to say, the three offenders were seated together in the back and ignored. Their complaints were drowned out with the loudest rock stations I could find.

I told Farris, "After this, I'm never complaining about your driving antics again."

"Somehow, I doubt that." He pressed his forehead against the glass and shut his eyes. He'd been quiet most of the trip.

"You all right? Or can you not talk my ear off when we have company?"

Farris took a moment to respond. "Remember how back in Arcadia, I said my head felt busy and fit to burst?"

I nodded.

"Well, it doesn't anymore, but once we left, I swore I'd stepped in some invisible iron maiden without looking. It's faded since we reached San-Fran, but it comes and goes."

"Even though you can't die outside of Arcadia. perhaps you're feeling some residual pain. That would explain things."

"Great." He drummed his claws on the window. "Think they make morphine that works on dead people?" After a moment, he said, "Don't look at me that way, it's not that bad. I was joking. Just..." The humor didn't reach his voice. I wanted to ask what was wrong, when he said in a more alert tone, "There's something up ahead."

"This is a highway, after all. There are bound to be cars—"

"No. Something else, in the field. Don't you see it?"

I reminded him that even if my vision wasn't worse than his, I was busy driving and trying not to get pulled over.

Farris turned to the trio in the back. "You guys, d'you see anything over there?"

"Is it that stupid metal dragon? I still don't..." Aimi trailed off and tilted her head. She and Isamu exchanged a look. Retz tilted his head, as he often did when sensing things. He swore three seconds later as Aimi said, "You should get in the fast lane. Or better yet, get on a different road."

"Anyone mind filling me in?" I switched lanes and brought the van up to eighty.

"Would you believe me if I told you that more unicorns found us?"

I decided that unicorns were far more of a threat than traffic laws and slammed my foot down on the gas. "This is starting to get ridiculous. Retz, when did Nalem piss these things off?"

Retz's face contorted into a grimace. "I only removed the head of one, and Retz was too much of a coward to kill it! I doubt that was enough to upset two whole herds, so I refuse to take blame for this." He raised a hand and flexed his fingers, two of them stiff as the skin knit closed over returned bones. "There are ten behind us, and another ten up the road, both closing in fast."

"Pincer attack, huh? Smart. But not foolproof." Having already experienced their speed, I knew escape wasn't an option. I came up with a brief plan and dealt orders.

The heat rose as the furaribi braced against the doors, and Retz closed his eyes as he warped the bones behind him. Farris cracked his knuckles and rolled his shoulders as if that might shake his pain.

I asked him, "Will you be all right?"

"I think these claws will be more effective than that sword, don't you?" He winked; he knew what I meant. "You can count on me, hon. That'll never change."

I caught a glimpse of white in the distance as the unicorns charged. Behind us, a cop car on the side of the road blared to life and joined the chase. I checked the speedometer to realize it clocked out at one hundred twenty. Before I could worry about the cop's influence on the fight, the rear guard arrived. Most of them ran around the car, but three decided to charge right over. Hooves slammed the roof and crunched the lights, and the last unicorn took time to kick in the windshield before leaping off the hood. The car spiraled off the road and almost to the south side of the highway.

These unicorns matched the ones we had faced in Oregon, with thick red manes and deep scars mutilating their white flanks. But one was larger than the rest, its opalescent horn cracked and bloodstained at the tip. Their elder or herd leader? I steeled myself. Its identity didn't matter. I had to protect the others, and if that meant the death of the whole herd and a guilty conscience on my part, so be it.

I saw their black eyes, their jagged teeth.

The furaribi's hands burned as they clutched the door handles. Farris crouched on all fours on his seat, ready to bolt. Retz remained in his trance, accompanied by the chorus of bones snapping and rearranging.

I saw the tissue of their crisscrossed scars.

I cranked the wheel.

The van careened off the path and into the fields, ramming through the barbed-wire fence and up the sloping hills. The furaribi and Farris all jumped out of the car. Out of the corner of my eye, I caught Aimi pause as her flames illuminated the silhouette of a rusted dragon sculpture. I resisted the urge to shout that I told her so as I evacuated the driver's seat. I rolled as I hit the cool, dry grass of the field. I rose with my shotgun in hand.

A few unicorns crashed into each other, but those behind were smart enough to take the hint and speed into a turn. The head unicorn bellowed before any could reach the fence. They all came to a standstill as their leader stepped forward.

"We are only here for the Corpse King, the one you call Nalem." It pawed the ground and lowered its horn, aimed right at my chest. "Turn him over. It is time we end this evil, for the good of all."

19 - RETZ

Some would say turning a unicorn's head and spine into a flail is fucked up. Especially when used to hit other unicorns. I agree with them, but no one else seemed to realize how funny it was to fling a head through the air and hit its companions teeth-first. I laughed, Nalem laughed, and everyone else kept their distance.

The unicorns offered to keep everyone else safe if I gave myself up. Let them spear me in the chest until I fell down dead. They didn't seem to realize Nalem would find another body if I died, and even if I was the sort to play the martyr, Jarrod wouldn't let me. So since it was them or me, and me dying clearly wasn't an option, I decided to start the carnage myself.

The fields caught fire as the furaribi and unicorns chased each other. Farris tore through foes, cackling that manic hyena howl. Horns, teeth, and hooves struck his shadowed form, but he shrugged the blows off and dressed himself in the gore of his foes. Jarrod, not being the most fireproof of allies, shot his foes from atop the metal dragon statue; I was scared he'd fall off of his precarious perch every time his shotgun fired. And me, I flung my bones and my happy unicorn flail as Nalem clambered into the van, driving it out of the flame's path and onto the other side of the road.

He directed as he drove, *"Aim the flail for the unicorn on the left. If put off-balance, it'll crash at an angle and spear its companion."* The curse only kept Nalem from killing, not me. While he kept my body safe by moving us out of danger, I was the one in charge of controlling the bones in our fight, floating them through the air to strike the unicorns. Nalem's advice came with flashes of how the results should look and calculations too quick for me to catch. And hidden in view from everyone else, we constructed our own monstrosity out of the bones in the trunk. When the time was right, all Nalem had to do was open the door, and I'd make it charge.

I followed his orders. As predicted, a flail to the legs sent one unicorn careening into its mate, horn digging into the neck. While caught, I used the flail to catch their horns and snap them, bringing the bodies down.

"Think the lamia will be this easy?"

"I wish, but they will be in greater numbers. Exponentially so in heads."

"I can always rely on you to squash my hopes, can't I?" I didn't even get a response, so I focused on fighting. I

swore the brawl had gone on for ages, but even though the air filled with the stink of burning fields and flesh, I counted seven corpses. Most of those remaining, including the leader, swarmed the statue. Jarrod fired faster than an action moviestar, but guns still need to reload.

I stuck my head out the window and shouted, "Jarrod! Just kick 'em in the head or something!" I aimed my bone-borne weapons his way, but it wasn't possible for me to focus on all the remaining unicorns at once. Neither could Farris, though the Faerie tried to take on three by himself, claws tearing through necks and old scars.

Jarrod's body was tense, as if his fear and frustration had burrowed deep into his bones. He struck a unicorn with the butt of the shotgun as he got a pistol out,and shots rang through the air. But the statue's legs buckled from the repeated unicorn charges, and was about to collapse into the burning grass. Resigned, Jarrod holstered his pistol again. The tension bled out when he jumped, fluid as he landed on a unicorn's back. One hand gripped the mane for support as he pivoted and lunged for the head. He snapped the horn off and jumped again, landing on the next unicorn and plunging his new weapon into an eye.

"Loath as I am to admit it, your brother is competent. He will survive without your worries." I lashed my flail, the skull's

face frozen midscreech, at a unicorn trying in vain to spear Aimi's foot as she flew. The beast whinnied as gnashing teeth tore into its neck and the spine tightened around its legs to restrain it.

Aimi flitted over and pried off the horn with a burning hand, then zipped over to me. The waves of heat rolling off her matched the beating of her wings.

She told me, "Y'know, you're pretty helpful for a psychopath. That creep just wouldn't stand still. Thanks for that."

"Anytime. How're you holding up?" I directed the flail to a unicorn poised to spear Jarrod from behind. It hit at the same time Jarrod spun and struck, bringing the failed sneak attacker down. Jarrod nodded at me, a flash of appreciation, and went for the next target.

Flames coalesced in Aimi's open palm. "Alive, somehow. Before the lamia happened, we were always too busy running to stick around for a fight." She reared back and lobbed the fireball in a side-arm pitch, striking the legs of a unicorn Farris was fighting and setting the grass ablaze. Farris took advantage of the distraction to tackle the unicorn into the flames. I was reminded of the first unicorn fight, where he'd quipped and swung a graceful sword; a stark contrast to the shredding and cackling Fae I watched.

"I've never fought much either, if you can believe that. Or killed."

"You've got a knack for it either way. That worry you?"

"Should it?"

The heat wavered and blurred the expression on Aimi's face. Behind her, our brothers fought back-to-back, fists and flames flying to drive back their attackers. "Isamu once said that there're two kinds of warriors. Those too good at living, and those too good with death."

"And you're wondering which kind I am?"

Our brothers switched sides, Jarrod striking a unicorn where the furaribi had burned it and using the distraction to make a grab for the horn, while Isamu breathed a stream of fire down a unicorn's throat.

"I don't kill for killing's sake, if that's what you're asking."

"You just don't care for the lives of those who get in your way." Aimi lobbed another fireball but didn't watch the results. Her attention was glued to me, and the carnage I wrought with my bones.

The unicorn elder, torn and burned but still kicking, locked eyes with me. I blocked the view by pulling unicorn heads and spines to me, flail tips meeting at a fixed point in my own mockery of a lamia. Now there was an idea...

"Let's put it this way: My life, unlife, whatever I've got—it's not perfect. Far from it, even." I made the unicorn flails move as if laughing, taunting their leader from beyond the grave.

The leader fell for it and charged.

"But I'm too attached to living to let anyone stop me."

Nalem pulled the trunk release lever, and the back of the van opened to release the bone chimera I'd crafted. The head unicorn was so distracted by my blasphemies that it didn't notice until the claws tore into its flank. Both of them fell, grappling as they hit the gravel between the field and road.

Aimi sighed, slipping back into human form and landing on the hood of the car. She smoothed her dress and said, "I need to start thinking the way you two do, at least long enough to stop Lady Delight for good. But I have to wonder if helping you and Nalem technically makes us all the bad guys."

"Well, the enemy of your enemy is your friend, right?" I stepped out of the van as the unicorn elder's movements slowed, worn down by my creations and the despair of its dead comrades. I sauntered up to it weakened the skull until I could snap the horn off with my measly strength. It put up no resistance. "So let's get all buddy-buddy and take out Lady Delight together. The warm-up's done anyway."

I pulled the unicorn corpses to me, then ripped off the flesh and shook free the bones from their burning confines. Nalem counted the corpses and said there were two unicorns that escaped. He wanted to chase them down and finish the job, but I decided against it. Maybe they'd warn the others to stay away.

Farris and Jarrod were the first to return to the van. Their clothes were singed, but neither seemed burned; Jarrod clung to Farris's shoulders, but the latter's limbs were all smoke anyway. If anything, they just reeked of brimstone.

Jarrod slid off his boyfriend and asked, "You two all right?"

Aimi nodded, and I said, "I've got a plan and some new ammo. And hopefully, killing the leader of these unicorns will get them to stop chasing me. So it's a win-win all around, yeah?"

Jarrod stepped away from the corpses behind him, lips curling. "I...wouldn't call it a win all around. But I'm interested in this plan of yours."

"Is a unicorn barbecue part of the plan?" Farris asked. His eyes were feral, but he was trying to stand like a normal human instead of a rabid wolverine, shaking off his berserker high. "Though, seriously, think it's edible?"

Jarrod didn't get to voice his obvious disgust before Isamu rejoined us in his human form. He gestured to the wrecked cop car and said, "I found a cell and called in the fire department. We should get gone before they arrive."

"Was the cop still alive?" Jarrod asked.

Isamu shook his head.

"Poor guy," I said.

The others looked at me as if I'd suggested taking his bones too.

"What? Being crushed in your own car by a unicorn is a shit way to go."

"Every time you open your mouth, you confuse me even more." Aimi hopped off the hood and into the driver's seat. "C'mon, let's get out of here. Can I drive?"

I let the others argue over seating arrangements while I finished with the corpses. I opened up the trunk and walked all my reanimated weapons back in, collapsing them into a pile that threatened to spill into the front seats.

"They don't trust you." Nalem stretched and his popping joints echoed in my skull. *"Such is the life of a vessel. But you fought well. You might even be competent at it someday."*

"I'm not sure if I want to be." It had been easy. Exhilarating, even. But once the adrenaline faded, the others had still been jumpy until I'd disassembled my creations and returned them to the van. They hadn't said anything, but I'd seen the looks, felt the tension in their bones that took ages to bleed out.

"It's because you're an unpredictable freak. A heartless monster." Nalem hummed, and pressure moved along my head as if it was being stroked. *"You just need to accept that. It's not something you can change, after all."*

The fields crackled with flames and cooking flesh as I slammed the van door shut. Even with its buckled legs, the metal dragon statue loomed over the corpses as if in testament to their failures. I pressed my forehead against the glass of the door and tried to focus on being cold.

"It's August. How can it be raining?"

"Because it's Oregon. Seattle was the same, remember?"

I didn't remember falling asleep, only waking up and hearing the furaribi in the front. It was dark outside, and rain pelted the windows. The windshield wipers swiped faster and louder than a heartbeat, a sharp contrast to the snores to my left. Jarrod was still asleep, face pressed into my arm. Farris had his eyes shut, but made no noise.

"Think we'll go back there when it's all done?" Aimi asked. She was in the passenger seat, feet propped up on the dashboard. "I mean, it might be where we were caught, but if Lady Delight's gone..."

Isamu shook his head, grip tight on the steering wheel. "I think it'd be better if we stayed scarce for a while."

"Can we at least tell our friends we're alive? I mean, maybe they were looking for us."

"And drag them down with us?" Isamu exhaled a thin trail of smoke. "Aimi, I miss them too. I really do. But if something goes wrong, how can we defend them if we can't even protect ourselves?" He opened the window a crack to let the smoke out. The air whined in protest.

Jarrod shifted against me. I tried to remember the last time either of us had slept; I had briefly in Dad's realm of Arcadia, but that was over a day ago. Jarrod fell asleep on the train, but it hadn't been for long, so no wonder he was passed out on me. Out of the corner of my vision, Farris opened one eye, watching Jarrod before flickering to me. Did he even need to sleep anymore?

"But Isamu—"

"Later, Aimi. Later." Isamu leaned over the steering wheel and peered into the darkness. He exhaled another breath of smoke. "I hate this goddamned rain."

I looked out the window to figure out how close we were. I didn't recognize the area, but Nalem stirred in my head. *We're close to where you woke up. And here we are, ready to finish the real job. Didn't I promise that we'd betray her?*

"Yeah, but I should've figured that you'd fuck with everyone else too. Fool me once..." Still, it meant we were close. I shook one of Jarrod's shoulders, figuring he might want a minute to wake up before we stormed the castle.

"That's not gonna work, kiddo." Farris reached over and pulled Jarrod into an upright position. "When he hasn't slept for ages, it takes a miracle to wake him up. Fortunately, I think after all that's happened, I might just count as one. Or a disaster." Farris leaned in with a mischievous grin.

I didn't hear what he said, but Jarrod responded by punching him in the face. He blinked himself awake a second later. "Where are we?"

Isamu grumbled, "Bumblefuck Nowhere, US of A. Don't bother looking out the window, 'cause there's nothing to see."

"We're close to Delight's place," I added. "Have a nice nap?"

"I didn't..." Jarrod's eyebrows knit together. "I only meant to contact Alexander, to inform him of our plans and make sure he would join us. I must've fallen asleep afterward. Sorry."

Farris's words were muffled from the hand covering his face. "Don't be. In fact, maybe we should just toss you into battle while you're conked out. The lamia investigate, you punch their lights out. Instant victory."

Jarrod pulled Farris's hands away to check the damage. One cheek turned dark, as if the shadows pooled under his flesh. "Only a bruise. If I used my full strength, I'm not sure even Nalem could fix your skull."

I kept Nalem's retort to myself.

"As I was saying, I did get in touch with Alexander. I believe he'll fight alongside us. He wants to see justice done, after all."

"Yeah, but how's he helping?" Farris asked, wincing as Jarrod checked his bruise. "I mean, didn't the Harvester say most Faeries can't exist outside of Arcadia for more than a couple of hours?"

The furaribi flinched at the very mention of their boogeyman. I was rocked by a wave of numbness as Nalem rushed into control. He snarled, "And when, exactly, did you speak with him?"

Farris's eyes widened as he realized what he'd blabbed, and his hands clapped over his mouth like a child.

Jarrod just grimaced. "San Francisco. He arrived to discuss our deal. Helping Farris isn't something he can do just yet. And before you ask, I planned to tell you earlier, but I hadn't found the right moment for it."

"Sure you did." Nalem dug the heels of his palms into his eyes. "That bastard really needs to stop interfering with my work. He's little more than a leech. A patronizing, badly dressed leech."

"A leech that looks out for your well-being, despite how little you deserve it." I think Farris wanted to tear into him more, but a warning look from Jarrod silenced him. "I mean really, as far as fathers go—"

"The Harvester is not my father." Even through the numbness, the words tore through my throat. "He hasn't been for a long, long time."

Jarrod started to say, "But he—"

"Is a facsimile. A shadow of what once was, twisted and shattered like those carnival mirrors. Now, speak no further of it, little one. Or would you prefer I fuse your teeth together again and make you mute as your precious daddy?" Nalem's threat was empty; I was already regaining my senses, though my skin felt too tight over my bones. He wanted to save his energy for the fight ahead. But something heavy and painful hung in my chest, a maw of memories I was forbidden from but still waiting to suck me in.

Jarrod's scarf wrapped around his face as if that would prevent Nalem's threat. "You have my word. Or my lack of them, in this case."

"Good." As swiftly as he'd taken over, Nalem returned to his hidey-hole in my skull. The rest of my senses rushed back to me.

I had to regain my bearings before I told them, "All clear. It's me again."

"Thank goodness." Aimi turned in her seat to watch us and said, "Hey, maybe we can just stick the Harvester and Nalem in the same room and let them kill the lamia with all their personal issues. And hey, we can bring Vairi in and make it an immortal drama free-for-all!"

We soon agreed that such a plan could only result in the destruction of the world itself.

The next few miles were spent prepping. Nalem and I considered how best to arrange our hoard of bones. He'd actually accepted the idea I'd had when fighting unicorns; I shouldn't have felt as proud as I did. Beside me, Jarrod checked and rechecked his weapons, while informing his boyfriend of where best to strike a lamia with those claws of his. Up front, Aimi explained the whole Harvester-Nalem connection to her brother, who responded with disgusted groans. I had to keep Nalem from scaring the poor guy out of his wits with reminders that Isamu was driving and could easily blow up the van if he so much as sneezed.

"Did Dad explain how he was going to help us?" I asked Jarrod once our mutual plans were sorted out. "Or is he just doing his own thing?"

"The latter. He was busy when I spoke to him, so I didn't get much." Jarrod loaded the last pistol, eyes narrowed with concentration. "The most I got was a sea of vines. Same way he carried us to his lair, but less controlled. More chaotic. I was scared they'd drag me under."

The curse in my torso writhed as if it wanted to climb up my ribs and into my chest. "Think we can trust him?"

"Just because he's a Fae, doesn't mean he's changed on the inside. He's still Alexander."

"You better be right." The side road up the mountain was in sight. On my cue, the van stopped, lights powered down. It'd stay there until we were ready to make our getaway. We crept out, wishing each other enough luck for us all to stay alive.

Farris charged in first. Dying wasn't a problem for him anymore, after all. He flashed a grin before escaping into the shadows. Once we heard the first scream, the furaribi flew off, fireballs prepped to pick off the snakes distracted by Farris. This was my cue to build my weapon for the night.

I slipped myself into the numbness this time, leaving the body for Nalem to deal with as we pulled our creation together. Skulls and spines fused for size and stability. Jagged teeth grew long. I counted the femurs and humeruses—or was it humeri?—permutated into limbs of my own design. My creation was born of mammal and reptile, avian and legend, into something never meant to walk the earth. Nalem or myself, I still don't know which, keened a wordless tune as we built. I opened my eyes. The first of my creation's many heads bent down to greet me.

I rested my forehead against its snout for a brief moment of pride. "Look. It worked. Isn't it…isn't it breathtaking?"

"If its teeth crushed my throat, yes, it would be." Jarrod didn't share my enthusiasm, but there was awe in his words nonetheless. "What the hell is this?"

"I call it a skelepede. A multiheaded one, at that. I made it up." It was modeled after a lamia and was as close to Lady Delight's size as I could guess, but with a mockery of a centipede's legs and shell. It had pincers and unicorn fangs, and some of its legs were tipped with tiny hooves. I would argue that it was the most adorable creature I'd ever seen, but my bias is no surprise.

I lowered a second head, and Jarrod hopped on. He crouched, one hand on the skull, the other already reaching for a weapon. "It's…different, I'll give you that. But different is unexpected, and that's just what we need."

"I knew you'd approve." I hopped onto the middle of the five heads, but I didn't need to hold on. I raised my arms, and the skelepede lifted its heads. I pointed to the castle, and it lumbered forward on its skittering legs.

"I fear you were inspired by Vairi's train."

"Yeah, but this is even better. Can't make trains with multiple heads, can you? And no gross blood or organs to contend with, either."

"Thank goodness." Nalem took full control of my body and fixed my stance. *"Your move from here, little one. Do attempt to survive."*

"I plan on it." We reached the top of the hill to find the entrance already cleared, the drawbridge over the moat decorated in blood and burns. Shouts came from the entryway, so I squeezed my creation in one head at a time. The screams grew louder, then grew muffled as Nalem stole some of my hearing to help me focus. Below us were hordes of lamia, with Farris and the furaribi darting amongst their ranks in flashes of blacks and brights.

"Nalem, you were right. They really do look more like fleas than ants from up here."

20 - JARROD

I lost count of how many lives I've taken long ago. It's not that I enjoy murder. Far from it. But death is comparable to any other drug; the horrible consequences are clear, but you're so addicted to keeping yourself alive you just can't stop killing.

I started the count right after I jumped off the head of my brother's creation and pulled myself onto the balcony of the second floor. The combined efforts of Retz and his possessor gave him an aura of serenity, even as his "skelepede" tore through lamia and the few humans who assisted them. If I kept a count for him too, I feared I'd reach the triple digits by the time we were done.

A lamia in snake form, two heads, rushed me down the hallway. I tore my shotgun from its holster and fired into one open mouth. The loss of one head made the other flinch, and I took that one out as it hesitated.

One.

I ran. My job was to find Lady Delight and lure her out. Retz was to grapple her snake form with his own multiheaded creation so I could sneak in and deal the finishing blow. Farris, Aimi, and Isamu would assist however possible, but this wasn't their job. It was ours, and we had to finish it. Alexander said so.

There was a group of lamia up ahead: two in snake form and three others armed with weapons. I closed the gap and fired, hitting one square in the chest and damaging a the rest. I whirled out of the way of a snapping jaw and pivoted to tackle it's owner. Snap. I grabbed the second head of that lamia in its confusion and choked it with one arm while my other fired the shotgun again.

Two and three. No, that one stopped moving too; four.

I made short work of the remains and continued my trek. The repetitive red-and-blue pattern of the floor gave me the impression of a wild chessboard, and I was a pawn slaughtering others in hopes of reaching the queen. Hisses came from behind me. I grabbed a pistol and shot a chandelier; as expected, its crash was followed by the flare of flames jumping from candle to carpet. Less candles and more smoke turned the glittering hallway into a dark, macabre dungeon.

Agonized screams echoed down the hall. Because of me or casualties courtesy of my comrades? I wasn't sure. I didn't add the unconfirmed kills to my count. Six and counting. I bolted down stairs and hallways, sticking to Nalem's directions as best I could.

By the time my count reached twenty, I'd reached the golden doors of the menagerie. If Lady Delight wasn't there yet, she would be as soon as her prizes were in danger. Not that I planned to harm any of the captives, but freeing them was just as bad in a slaver's books. That plan turned sour as the doors swung open and it wasn't just lamia who faced me. Along with them were a griffon with clipped wings, two red-skinned oni with six arms each, and another gods-be-damned unicorn. Any fear these creatures felt must've been clouded with wrath. My mental count fluctuated and folded.

Not all the creatures fought me as I charged into that glittering hellhole. But all the cages were either opened or broken, occupants hiding and fighting in equal turn. Lady Delight was not there. I turned to leave and found all exits blocked.

I tried to hold Alexander's authority in my voice. "Move. I'm going to save you."

I never figured out who answered, "We're already safe here," but whoever it was, they didn't last long. Bullets sang, fists and fangs and talons responded. My count already lost, the numbers became a haze. I lost track of who or how I fought. I switched tactics on the fly for each beast. Cripple legs. Rip wings. Faces, meet bullets. I tried not to kill the creatures who'd been captive, but I didn't always have a choice. Part of the floor was glass, a giant aquarium for a small but ancient sea serpent. It took work, but I got the glass to break and escaped onto another cage while my pursuers fell in. The sea serpent scooped them up with a lazy gait.

I took three seconds to catch my breathand shoot a harpy with its claws aimed for my face. I clipped a wing and it spiraled into the lair of the sea serpent, who seemed pleasantly surprised by its impromptu and exotic feeding. The sea serpent opened its maw, when something shot out of the water, wrapped around the injured harpy, and pulled it under. My first thought was: which idiot decided keeping a sea serpent and a kraken in the same tank was a good idea?

Second thought: No, not tentacles. Vines. Vines breaking through the ground, grabbing both attackers and those trying to hide in their cages. Alexander was at work, but I had no guesses as to where he was dragging the menagerie. And my three seconds were up, so I had no time to ask. I leapt off the cage and made a break for the door.

The one guarding said door was a familiar lamia with violet hair and black scales. The side of her head was bandaged from the wound I'd patched up. She backed away when she saw me.

All she managed to shout was "You! Why did you save me when—" before the vines wrapped around her tail and pulled her down. I hazarded a glance down the hole left in her wake; the darkness went on deeper than my imagination could reach.

As I ran again, I wondered if Alexander ever kept his own kill count.

I ran into Farris as I tore through the medical wing. Literally. The wall caved in and I tackled him out of the way. Despite his Faerie form, I was still stronger.

"Thanks, hon. South side of this wing's cleared." He slunk to his feet and brushed the rubble off his shoulders. "Find anything?"

"She wasn't in the menagerie. Most of the inhabitants are dead or captured by Alexander—which might mean they're all dead."

Farris pursed his lips. The shadows around his face went flat like canine ears. "You think she'd be front and center to kill us, right? I mean, we just walked into her home and started wrecking it."

"That's what worries me." Once I was sure Farris was all right, I ran, certain he'd keep up. The lamia might be cleared, but Alexander didn't seem concerned by the damage his vines caused. He'd bring the whole castle down around Lady Delight without a second thought. Hell, maybe that was his plan, and he pulled the menagerie's inhabitants out to save them. If I told myself that enough, it might even be true.

Past the medical wing, its false serenity finally in ruins, were barracks. The floor was pockmarked with holes. Vines obscured windows as roots searched the ransacked rooms for any living unclaimed. One wrapped around my foot until it reached the curse on my leg, at which point it and the rest of the vegetation shrank away from my approach. I made sure Farris stayed close.

We reached the ballroom. It was also claimed by Alexander's power, vines reaching up the pillar supports to a balcony, thorns littering the ground. The stained-glass ceiling cast mesmeric lights on the white floor, save for where plants had torn through in an attempt to reach the lights. Those lights were alive and kept in their own gilt cages; collections of will-o'-the-wisps here, vampiric balls of fire from the Pacific islands over there—I think I even saw a phoenix in one cage. Their flames kept the vines at bay.

I did a quick scan from the middle of the dance floor. "Other than those in the lights, it's empty here. We should move." I made for the door, but Farris didn't follow. "Did you hear me?"

"Hold on. Give me two seconds."

"We don't have—"

"Two. Seconds." Farris paced around the middle of the dance floor, staring at the stained glass even as its broken shards crunched under his steps. He walked as if slowly stepping through a half-remembered dance. "I've been here before. No, somewhere real similar to here. Two places. One was bright, and the other…"

"Save it for later." I ran back to grab him. His memories were important, but first, we had to make sure we didn't get eaten or squished by castle debris. As I ran, the chains of the light cages rattled overhead, but I assumed it was part of the fight above and ignored it. I reached the center of the dance floor.

Another section of the glass ceiling shattered. I looked up just in time to see Lady Delight sliding down the chains—she'd used the cages as cover. There wasn't enough time for Farris to snap out of his reverie. She shifted into her true form as she fell, a creature so large that the fall from the ceiling was barely a hop. The floor shook when she crashed. Two of her heads lashed out, knocked us down, wrapped their long necks around our bodies.

Farris shouted my name, but I couldn't answer. The constriction threatened to crush my ribs, and with my cursed scarf already tight around my neck, I could barely breathe. I kicked to no avail as Lady Delight lifted me in the air. She shook me and my head spun and my glasses fell off. The world became a blur.

"Just who I was waiting for." Lady Delight spoke with the remaining three heads, voices blending into a breathy hiss. "Hulderkind, I finally found your true value. As bait."

"Let him go!" Farris shouted, then after a moment, "And me too. But him first."

Lady Delight's response was to dig another head's fangs into my shoulders. I bit back a yelp, but the pain on my face must've been evident. The poison burned through my veins.

"Careful, love," said my captor. "Wouldn't want your beloved to break, now would you?"

There was no answer.

To her credit, Lady Delight didn't taunt us further or claim her success was assured. She moved with silence, grace, and a fair share of sadism; she knocked me into more than a few walls as she slithered through her halls in search of her remaining prey. The vines, sensing my presence, shied away without realizing I was a captive. I did my best to stay calm, even as the poison raced from my wounds up to my brain, stinging worse than alcohol in a fresh wound. No wonder it had been enough to drive Isamu mad.

After a time, I heard something other than the cacophony in my head; we were nearing the main fight. I smelled smoke, rancid with melting metal and flesh. I didn't recognize the terrified screams, but I did hear the skittering thumps made by Retz and Nalem's morbid creation. But when the doors swung open, all noises stopped. Only the smell remained.

"There, was that so hard? I am here on the matters of a truce." She raised the head holding me, twisted so I was hanging upside down. "It's such a simple deal. I return this hulderkind to you, and you leave me, my people, and my castle alone. You leave and never look back. I'll even let you keep the furaribi and throw this prince-turned-mongrel in for free."

On the other side of the room, Retz's eyes flickered to mine first, but it was Nalem who spoke. "You always did love your low blows. Let me guess—if we refuse, you snap Jarrod in two as soon as we strike, and your followers retaliate in our moment of shock. Or hell, maybe you'll kill him anyway. I would."

"I know. I learned it from you, after all. All of it."

She shook me again.

I caught glimpses of vines overhead gathering into a human form, a mockery of Alexander with no skin and no soul. He watched with white rose eyes, but said nothing.

"You learned this from me? I'm not sure if I should be flattered or calling bullshit." Nalem stepped to the end of the skelepede skull, balancing on the tip of the snout. "I enlighten and inspire others toward a better cause. My cause. You would rather put warriors in cages to play the part of jesters."

Lady Delight's grip loosened just enough for me to get a good breath in. "I give them a haven. I give them security and happiness, something no one ever cared enough to give me. You only bring death."

was on my mind. I hurt. So the source of the pain, it had to go. And it had to hurt just as much as I did.

My brother offered to negotiate. Retz? Nalem pretending? It didn't matter. Her scales were thick, but that just meant she'd have a harder time feeling my movements, and she was too focused on Nalem to see that breaking my leg didn't stop me. Fueled by wrath alone, I pulled myself across the scales, toward her head. Someone called my name. Lady Delight's voice rumbled at the edges of my senses. I kept the extra static of my senses at bay by focusing on the pain in my leg. I'd return that pain tenfold with my fists.

You see, huldra obey two main forces: justice and passion. The worthy are rewarded, and the wicked are returned the pain they've caused. Yet how can a person be judged without their emotions running at a full high to reveal their true natures? The blood quickens from combat, sex, running too close to death. Huldras bring themselves to that point with their victims, and the climax is continued life or death. Erika had explained it to me as a child, but it didn't make sense back then. I was too stuck in my own head.

I'd already made my decision on justice, but the desire to completely destroy someone, well, those were urges I'd always ignored. But when it comes to it, passion can't be controlled, only contained. My blood boiled at the thought of hers running cold.

I judged as I'd told myself I never deserved to do. I reached the base of the neck, right where it met the head. Pressed a palm to the skull. Felt for a weak point. Another vine came down from the ceiling and wrapped around one arm. I tore it off. Someone shouted my name again. Another snake head twisted to see what I was up to.

Perfect, I thought as I raised my fist. *Watch as I wreck you.*

I threw my whole body into the blow. The punch broke through bone. The head under me shuddered and writhed, then fell as it went limp. I held tight. Overhead, the other heads shuddered, frozen in a moment as they lost contact with one of their own.

That was the moment everyone had been waiting for. The skelepede charged forward, jaws clamping onto the remaining necks. Farris escaped his coils with a manic howl, following my lead and making for a head. Instead of breaking the skull, he went straight for the eyes. I looked up to see Alexander grappling with the head next to mine, pulling it backward with vines until the neck was on the verge of snapping, while the furaribi tag-teamed to toss fireballs into an open mouth.

I tried to climb up the limp neck to join them, though I struggled with my broken leg. I cried out as a new pain shot through it, strong enough to bring tears to my eyes. But when I turned to face my new foe, the hurt dissipated and, with it, the flames fueling me.

I knew that voice. Beside me, Retz flinched. Nalem knew that voice too. The lamia backed away, and Aimi shrieked mid-cheer and flew back, pulling her brother with her. I turned and saw the voice's owner walking from Lady Delight's corpse, juggling two orbs, white with rings of brown.

The Harvester smiled with his shark teeth. His current Hawaiian shirt was red and violet, the same color as Lady Delight's corset. "We guess he didn't want to stay for the after-party, huh? Not that he'd come to any harm; the real Fae wasn't here, after all. But we give him points for exercising caution." He tossed Lady Delight's eyes into the air, catching and spinning them on two fingers. "Hello there, Nalem. You're looking well."

"What do you think you're doing here?" Nalem took a step back, waving his father away. "The fight's done, and I handled it well on my own. Your interference isn't needed."

"Oh little one, we're not here for you today. Though we guess this makes another notch on the dead in-law list, yes? We should really find a nice immortal to set you up with. Might calm your delusions of grandeur." The Harvester reached up and rustled his son's hair.

Nalem grimaced as if burning. "Well, if you aren't here for me, then you can go. Go on, get back to your little secret lair with your sick little eye fetish. That's a good father."

"We believe the modern retort for that is 'talk shit, get hit.' Don't test us." The Harvester finished embarrassing his son by tapping him on the nose and spinning on his heels to look at the furaribi. His gaze settled on Aimi. The amusement in his face shifted into something sadder. "Ah. So this was what became of you? It seems we must apologize for not reaching you in time."

"In time for what?" Aimi cried as she clung to her brother, her eyes still bright with fire and fear. "You mean when we were kidnapped by the lamia?"

"No. Earlier than that." The Harvester shook his head, as if chiding himself for saying that much. "We hope you'll never understand what we mean by that, but we had to say it anyway. We always do with your kind, but especially to you."

No one got to ask what he meant because, to my curiosity and terror, he turned to face me. "And you, young Gallows. We must again show our appreciation for your guardianship of our son in Arcadia. Our eldest daughter told us of your escapades. We met for tea in the Tenderloin, you see."

"That's...lovely." Gods, this man unnerved me, even in his human guise. And Lady Delight's eyes kept staring at me, no matter how much they spun. "I hate to be forward, but earlier, I believe you said you had a method for regaining Farris's memories?"

break life and the world as it now turns. Since you have already succeeded once in this regard, we are appointing you, Jarrod Gallows, as the official Watcher of Nalem and potential savior of the world. Keep an eye on him!" The Harvester made to reach for one of my eyes, which I shut on reflex. "Ha-ha, just kidding. Taking an eye while one is still alive gets…messy. Very, very messy. But do make sure he doesn't get into too much trouble, yes? We're counting on you!"

Before I managed a word, the Harvester, terror of the supernatural world, tapped the air in front of my nose with a *boop!* before he vanished. The only sign he'd been around at all was a silver ripple in the air that lasted for all of three seconds.

My scarf tightened around my neck again, though loose enough to breathe. My life now depended on keeping a psychopathic necromancer out of trouble. It had happened so fast, my head reeled.

"What…what just happened?"

Nalem was too busy shouting after his already-disappeared father to answer, and everyone else was preoccupied with getting as far away from the tirade as possible.

It was Farris, finally no longer screaming, who answered in slow disbelief, "The grim reaper just ate my eye and demoted you to babysitting duty. Sucks to be us, huh?"

21 - RETZ

"**D**o you feel bad that she's dead? Even a little?" The question nagged at me as soon as Lady Delight's body collapsed under my touch. I asked once Nalem and I were alone, stumbling through the rubble of the fallen castle. He was in control of the body, claiming there was something he had to check. The others were busy making plans and questions.

Nalem eased us down a staircase missing half its steps. *"You seem to forget I am thousands of years old. The novelty of death wore off long ago."*

"But didn't you love her once? Or at least like her enough to save her life and marry her?"

Nalem swore as he took a wrong step and tumbled the rest of the way down. The new bruises were dulled by how banged up I already was; my body was so battered, I'd figured out how baseballs felt.

"You are the most annoying distraction, little one."

"I try, and I think both of us deserve all the naps ever after we're done here. Gonna answer me?"

My other half sighed but made no move to get up. The lights overhead were snuffed out, darkness obscuring the damage up above. *"Old emotions make no difference. She got in my way, thus she became an obstacle to overcome. End of story."*

"So why are we going to her room?"

Nalem kept quiet under the guise of pulling himself back to his feet and continuing his trek.

I'd told the others where we were going, just in case one of the few survivors decided to jump me. So far, while the remaining lamia had been loyal to Lady Delight, they were more loyal to surviving. They'd hightailed it as soon as the Harvester disappeared. Last I saw Jarrod, he was trying to administer antivenom to anyone who'd been bitten by lamia, with the furaribi's help, while doing his best to keep Farris from freaking out over his lost eye.

"It should be here." Nalem pushed open a door to reveal a dark room of reds and violets. It reeked of rotten flesh and lavender perfume but, compared to the rest of the castle, was oddly intact. The bedsheets weren't even wrinkled.

"There was no one to attack here," Nalem explained as he wandered inside. I searched his passing thoughts for remorse or nostalgia, but felt nothing.

"Are we looking for something?"

"Yes indeed, Captain Obvious." Our powers pulled at my chest as Nalem searched the room, eventually leading him to the far end of a walk-in closet, where a table held a collection of mementos. Most were shiny baubles and jewelry, with some paintings on the wall. One had the Lady Delight I'd seen in memories with her arms wrapped around a noble with a hollow face and brown hair going prematurely white. His hands, which I knew to be skeletal, were out of the frame.

"That was a fun vessel. Rich with resources, though all the servants were so nosy." Nalem crouched to investigate the table and found a drawer. He slid it out, and inside was a violin. No, he corrected, it was a viola. An important distinction, apparently. Whatever it was, the wood was black and the strings silver. It was inlaid with bone, and the neck was topped with a bird skull. Nalem blew off the dust and pulled out the matching bow.

"She stole this from me—thought it would force me to stay with her. It didn't work, of course, which just further antagonized her." Nalem drew the bow across the strings, cringing from the out-of-tune shriek. The noise reverberated in my bones, and their aches faded. *"It was built to help me focus my powers, little one."*

"By the Harvester?"

Nalem growled at the mention of his father, though he'd refused to discuss the surprise visit once it was done. Yet he was seething, which dropped his guard just enough for memories to slip through. It was Loresha, that woman from the memories and mirrors, but this time there was a glint in her eyes. She held the viola around the neck as if choking a cat. A skeletal hand met with hers to grab it, touch lingering. I almost mistook her skin for polished stone, smooth and just as cold.

"It came from my true sister. She who is the skin to my bones."

The memory slipped away as something rough coiled around my present-time throat. I reached out with my powers to freeze the intruder, only for static to rock my brain. No, this wasn't a last lamia out for revenge. Sharp points pierced my skin. Brambles, I realized. The cursed vines inside me pressed against my skin and climbed up my throat, as if trying to meet their maker.

Dad turned me around to face him. It wasn't the purely vegetative puppet that had fought alongside us—this was the real deal, with a mask of skin to hide his warped insides. He clicked his root-claws together while waiting for our struggle to stop.

"Most parents knock before entering a bedroom," I choked out.

Dad's answer was to lift me a few feet off the ground. I kicked in reflex, and more thorns found their way around my ankles. He examined me, but I wouldn't look at his face. I instead contemplated why anyone would have a chandelier hanging right over their bed.

"You survived," Dad croaked. "Unexpected, I admit." His voice was rough as snapping branches, with none of the authority or power Arcadia had granted him. At least he wasn't going to sign at me and make me guess what he was saying.

"That's what I do. Living is one of my favorite activities, after all." The pain scrambled my thoughts; was this how Jarrod's scarf felt on him? No wonder he was so moody. "No offense, but you sound out of practice when it comes to congratulating people."

"I never said I was pleased."

"Oh. Well, I assumed—"

Dad smacked me against a far-too-ornate bedpost to shut me up. "Even disregarding Nalem, you are a nuisance. You have compromised Jarrod to the point of making him useless to me, and even limiting Nalem does not stop your carnage. I did not raise you this way."

"Mom raised me more than you did. And Nalem, at least in terms of warping my brain from a young age." Ouch, there was that post again. "Okay, I get it, you hate smartasses. Going to curse me to shut me up forever now? If so, I'd really appreciate it if you shut Nalem up too. It'd be the first time I'd have my thoughts to myself since...well, ever."

I thought it was a reasonable request, but Dad's response was to drop me. "I should take you too. Kill you in Arcadia. That is the most efficient solution.

But...you're my son." The bark on the root-claws cracked as Dad clenched his fists. "There has to be a way. But I'm running out of time, and they're getting so loud."

"They?" As much as my body protested, I sat up. "Dad, what did you get yourself into now?"

"Alexander. My name is Alexander." Dad's voice trembled in a way I'd never heard it, not even the night he pulled his gun on me and left. "I will do this my way. No matter how many bodies it takes, I will get it right. They will see."

I pulled myself up with the bedpost. I finally looked at Dad's face; the skin shifted to accommodate the vegetation underneath. He was so pale, so unstable.

My voice cracked; "Dad...?"

"I was. Am. Am Alexander." His fingertips scraped against my face. "Even in your face, I see him. Not me. Will have to fix that." The skin slipped from his face, revealing the vines under his forehead. No, there was no skull there anymore, not even a human one. "Everything is going to be okay."

The ground opened up, a hole mirroring all the others littering the castle. Dad's form broke apart into a writhing mass of vines sliding away. I tried to see the bottom as he went, but there were only shadows down there. My chest hurt, but the curse had returned to the pit of my stomach. Where did that pain come from?

"*So. Yours too.*" Nalem pulled me away from the hole, and I stumbled through the doorway. He told me he was tired and I should go find the others. I walked with the viola in one hand and the bow in the other, and found myself looking down every hole I passed.

"I miss my dad," I decided. *"The real one. The one he used to be."*

"Me too," Nalem agreed, but I knew we were talking about different people.

Jarrod had a new mark on the back of his left hand. To my surprise, it didn't bear any resemblance to eyes, but a tree with branches and leaves splayed out to resemble a sunrise cresting the horizon . He scratched the new mark as he paced, discussing where to go next and what supplies were needed. Farris followed and nodded, a bandage wrapped around his head and covering the missing eye.

"Our best bet would probably be to go job hunting down in So-Cal. The high population means more potential cases, and there's a good chance of being hired by someone rich enough to actually pay. Especially near Hollywood. Last time I was there, we..." Jarrod slowed to a stop when I joined him outside. Farris didn't and walked right into my brother.

"Hey, Jarrod. How're you holding up?" I took a deep breath of the night air; it was so much clearer than Lady Delight's room, even with the lingering iron scent.

Someone had moved Lady Delight's body, and all that remained of her was a puddle of blood.

Jarrod shrugged and said, "Well enough. Just planning. I figured our first stop should be Eri...Mom's house. So you can grab your stuff. We're stuck with each other now, after all." He lifted his hand to show me the mark the Harvester had left him. It was already scraped red. "And, well, I did promise I'd speak with her."

"You did." I noticed him eyeing the viola, so I raised it. "Nalem had to get an old memento, but we're ready now. I'll make sure he doesn't try to tune it on the drive up."

Farris quipped, "Yeah, I'm already half blind, so I don't really need to go deaf too." His mouth had flecks of blood around it, but it seemed he'd let Jarrod clean most of it up, judging by the stains on my brother's sleeve.

I tried to laugh, but all that came out was a strained chuckle. All the incidents since I'd first arrived at that castle were catching up to me; I wanted nothing more than to go home and collapse on my bed. But I had a few loose ends to tie up first.

"Jarrod, I saw Dad. The real him, not the one who fought with us."

"Really? He was here? Then why didn't he..." My brother crossed his arms so he didn't scrape his hand raw. "Is he still here?"

"No, went back to Arcadia. And I think he took most of the castle with him. He said something about 'no matter how many bodies it takes,' though I'm not sure what that meant." Judging by how lost Jarrod looked, he didn't get it either. "But he said he wasn't going to kill me, so that's good."

"Did he say anything else?"

I could've told him that Dad was losing his mind or that he apparently wanted us to fail at stopping Lady Delight. I lied instead. "That he was busy and had to go, but he wanted to tell you that he's proud of you. You did a good job."

I thought that would've made Jarrod happy, but he looked more confused instead.

Farris clapped him on the back and said, "C'mon, babe, buck up. You saved our hides and tore up a lamia with your bare hands. Even your old man can't deny how awesome that is."

"I guess." Jarrod sounded unconvinced but too drained to argue. He tried to keep his usual braced posture but was slumping, and his eyes had settled into a murky gray. "Thanks for the message. Can you do me one more favor? The furaribi were trying to decide if they wanted a lift from us. Can you find them and tell them we're ready to go?"

I agreed and went to search. Even though they weren't in fire-form, their skeletons were warm to my senses. I found them where the road met the top of the hill, just far enough for the castle to become a silhouette within trees cast blue from the night. I tried not to interrupt them, but they noticed me anyway. Despite the fight being over, they were still tense and ready to bolt. I understood; I would've run from me too.

"Relax," I said, "I'm just checking up on you guys. Jarrod was just wondering if you had your travel plans figured out yet."

Isamu nodded. "We pilfered a few valuables from the castle—it owed us that much. So we just need to find a pawn shop, and we'll have enough to last us awhile. We'll take a bus from there."

"To Seattle," Aimi added, loud and sharp compared to her brother's conspiring tone. "It's the closest place we've ever had to a home. We need time to figure things out and tell a few folks that we're still alive. And if anyone tries to fight us this time, we'll kick the crap out of them. We know we can do it now."

"Aimi—"

"Just a month, Sam. A week, even. We can afford that much."

Judging by the way his teeth clenched and her heels dug into the dirt, they'd been at this argument awhile. It wasn't my place to decide, but I offered them a ride either way. They both shook their heads.

"No," was all Isamu said.

Aimi at least bothered to give an excuse. "We really appreciate it, but if we went with you guys, chances are we'd end up fighting more unicorns or caught in another scheme of yours, or...or something." She twirled her hair around her fingers and stared past me at the castle that held them captive for so long. "I mean, you've done a lot for us, don't get me wrong. We owe you, and trust me, we'll pay you back somehow."

"But we're also dangerous and not quite right in the head. Don't worry, I get it. I wouldn't want to travel with me either." I rustled through my pockets before remembering that I didn't have any paper on hand. "At least let me give you my number. Well, it's my mom's. I don't have a cell anymore, but...well, so you can call us, if you need to."

"That's sweet. I...I'd appreciate that, yeah." Aimi grabbed her brother's arm. "Come on, we should at least say goodbye. You'd be dead without 'em."

"Almost died anyway with them," Isamu reminded her. Took about a minute before he sighed and admitted, "But being free and traumatized is better than being captive or dead. I guess we should thank them, huh?"

Aimi elbowed her brother in the ribs as we reached Jarrod and Farris. Numbers and wishes of good luck were exchanged. No one was sure where to go from there; it seemed none of us were used to saying goodbye. And after all we'd been through, how could it be finished with just a farewell?

"Sure you don't want a ride?" Jarrod asked instead. "At least out of the woods. No reason why you should have to walk the whole way."

"Who said we'd be walking?" Aimi pointed up at the sky, the tip of her finger catching fire. "We get mistaken for shooting stars if we go high enough. Been awhile since we got to stretch our wings anyhow."

The three of us stepped back to give the furaribi room. They held hands as they burned up, skin crackling, eyes glowing. Watching them made me forget the cold of the night.

"I get that trouble's your business," Isamu said, "But try to keep out of it when you can, all right?" I thought there was a hint of a smile, but it was hard to tell through all the smoke.

"And when the going gets tough, remember you guys are the heroes here. Even you." If I had a heart, it would've tied itself in knots—or is that what the stomach does?—when Aimi looked at me with those last words. She winked. I winked back, but she just giggled and held her brother's hand tighter.

Hot air gusted past us as sister and brother bolted into the sky, arcing over the mountains and off to the north. And it was true: once they were high enough, they looked just like stars falling through the darkness. I waved, even though I knew they couldn't see me anymore.

"I wonder how fast they're going?" Farris muttered, resting his chin on Jarrod's head as he watched the sky. "Hey, maybe if we hightail it back to the van now, we can race them up to Washington."

"See, that's why I don't let you drive." Even Jarrod took a moment to tear himself from the view overhead. "But you have a point. We should get moving."

I agreed. "There's nothing else for us to break here, after all."

We dragged our battered bodies away from the castle as the sun hit the sky.

By the time we stumbled into Kelso, the small Washington town Mom and I called home, the sun bore down on us with the full force of the midday August heat. Our last refuge before trekking through town was a gas station pit stop, remarkable only for its air-conditioning and its variety of jerky flavors. The van was left at the edge of town, free of bones or any other evidence of my presence.

It was a town where everyone knew everyone, and I, as the "local Jekyll and Hyde," was no exception, so all the eyes in the store were glued to me when I reached the register. I'd scrounged spare change out of the van before ditching it, so I had enough for a soda. When I set it down, Jarrod joined me and calmly set down a bottle of beer. Jarrod ignored the stares now directed at him and fished his wallet from his coat.

"Seems you have a reputation around here," he said as he flashed a driver's license I'm pretty sure was fake. "Are they going to leave me alone or bombard me with questions?"

"Between me being a freak and you having the social skills of a porcupine, I'm sure you'll be fine." I glanced at the customers behind us; the way they shied away from my gaze confirmed my answer. "Also, pretty sure happy hour's an evening thing, not a morning one. Sure you want to be sloshed when you meet Mom again?"

"Sloshed, no. Sober, also no. My courage doesn't go that far." Jarrod slid his wallet back into his coat, then popped open the beer. "And I promised Farris to stop by the liquor store later for some bourbon. To celebrate making it out mostly alive."

"That's a party to me. Cheers, then." We tapped our drinks together as we left the store. Farris was already waiting for us, fixing an eye patch over his face. "Wait, weren't you behind us in line?"

"Lines are for schmucks. Everyone was so busy watching you, I just grabbed what I needed without bothering anyone." He tugged the patch to make sure it was in place, then slid a stick of jerky out of his sleeve and tore into it. "Ask me what happened in Vegas later. I've worked some wonders down there."

We started walking before Farris flaunted any more of his shoplifting skills in front of the store. I led the way, pointing out our few local landmarks and waving to the handful of people who didn't think I was a complete freak. Those would be my coworkers at the salon, an old lady I often ran into at the post office, and two dogs.

"It's a nice town, though. Don't get me wrong." I reached in vain for the last dregs of soda as we stepped into my neighborhood. "I bet you could stay here if you really wanted. The Harvester only said you had to keep Nalem safe, and it's easier to stay in one place, right? Might be a nice break from all the travel."

"Yeah, but roaming the earth to kick the crap out of bad guys is what we're good at," Farris pointed out as he juggled the beer bottle, which Jarrod had emptied in under a minute. "I mean, imagine either of us at a desk job without breaking someone's face in. Or, Fate forbid, socializing with normal people."

Jarrod grimaced at the thought. "We can stay for a little, if you want. But I hope you understand that it won't last forever. You have Nalem." He reached over and grabbed the beer bottle as it flew out of Farris's control. "And I have this clown that really should be returned to the circus."

"Rude. You love me and you know it."

I smiled as the two bickered. I didn't want to disturb the balance they had or become a burden they'd have to save. But despite my worries, I was somehow excited to join them on their travels. As harrowing as the furaribi and lamia fiasco—my first case, in a way—had been, it was the most exciting thing I'd ever done. I figured that was the closest I'd ever felt to belonging somewhere and really living.

"Don't get ahead of yourself, little one." Nalem lay back in my skull, propping up his feet and digging his heels in right behind my eyes. *"Remember who's calling the shots here. I have plenty of work to do out in the world, and you're going to make sure it gets done. Treasure your time here while you can."*

I nodded and tossed my soda bottle behind me. Farris scrambled to catch it and Jarrod almost looked happy. Up ahead, I saw the silhouette of Mom striding toward us, ready to welcome both of her sons home. She looked older than I remembered, but her eyes glistened in the light like the summer sky overhead. And when she called my name, I grabbed my brother's hand and we ran back to her, together.

ACKNOWLEDGMENTS

First off, a thousand thanks to my beta readers, Charlotte and Rose. *Deadly Drinks* would still be a bundle of words in a .docx file if not for all your feedback. For this edition of the novel, thanks as well to Bill Tracy for his edits, making this book an even smoother read than before, and to M. Brackett for the amazing cover art.

My family has provided endless love and support, even as I wrestled with writer's block on their couches, and they even inspired some of the directions the plot wandered in. Thank you Mom, Chris, Unka Don, and my dearest darling Tris. Dad, you may have passed long before this journey started, but thank you too for helping set me on this path.

Finally, to all the friends, fans, and fellow authors who helped me, from the first drafts to the latest release. I wouldn't be here without all of you.

EXTRA FEATURES

Concept Art
and
A Preview of Deadly Drinks #2

RETZ GALLOWS AND NALEM

JARROD GALLOWS

FARRIS O'REILLY

ISAMU & AIMI KURUSAKI

THE HARVESTER, VAIRI, ALEXANDER GALLOWS & THE LAMIA

ABOUT THE AUTHOR

Hailing from the mountains of Oregon and the lecture halls of Mills College, Dorian Graves is an artistic cryptid found in the Pacific Northwest. When not writing or drawing, Dorian can be found adventuring in the woods with a romantic partner and a mischievous cat.

Website: www.doriangraves.com

Email: pictureofdoriangraves@gmail.com

Twitter or Facebook: @DorianGravesFTW

1 - JARROD

I hadn't planned to be run over by a minotaur's motorcycle that day.

For paranormal investigators like me, precautions must be made for certain inevitabilities. What to do if a case goes wrong. How to misdirect humans if they get involved without getting them or yourself killed in the process. How not to panic if a dragon, god, or other legendary being decides to make your case their business. I'd trained for years to predict the potential outcomes to all those scenarios and more. Yet, the idea of what to do if a bull-headed monstrosity charged me at full speed on a Harley somehow never crossed my mind.

If I'd stood in the middle of the road, being ambushed by a motorcycle would make some sense. This instead happened deep in the woods, perhaps a mile off a dirt road now only frequented by logging trucks, in the last dregs of summer when the falling leaves are fragile and flammable in equal measure. I had beasts in these woods on my hit list, but the minotaur hadn't numbered among them. I reeked of blood from my own wounds, and also of cheap whiskey, because I'd upended half a bottle over my head to deter my intended mark from attacking me.

My name is Jarrod Gallows, and while my human instinct was to bolt and pray I got out of the way in time, that's not the course of action I took. One might ask what kind of idiot has an instinct that screams "grab the motorcycle and throw it into a goddamn tree." The answer is me.

"What," the minotaur croaked in the brief seconds that he and his bike were airborne, "the ever-loving shi—" The crash of his impact shook the forest.

The hidebehind I'd just finished fighting twitched at my feet, scraping foot-long claws against the forest floor. I'm sure it would've used the surprise attack to try for the upper hand in our fight, but I'd already won by clasping silver manacles around its wrists moments before I'd heard roaring engines. I debated grabbing the beast by the scruff of its neck and dragging it back to my car. It would've been the safer plan.

Curiosity won out instead. I grabbed one of my pistols and kept it aimed on the minotaur as I approached. I waited to speak until the bull-headed man sat up and stared at me, terror in his eyes and splinters of bark sticking out of his skull.

"You've got two seconds to explain."

The minotaur patted the ground at his side for a weapon. He found only crumpled metal. "Forgive me, Lord Nalem. I was, well you see..." he cleared his throat. "I mistook your attacker for, well, for you until it was too late. Appearances can be deceiving, right?" His laugh was closer to a pitiful bray.

I wanted to pretend I'd heard him wrong, but I wasn't drunk enough for that. I'd been saving the other half of the whiskey bottle for later.

"Right. Which is why you'll be more surprised if you actually find him."

"Yeah, I guess I...wait. You're not him?" The minotaur bolted back to his feet—excuse me, hooves—and looked at our surroundings with rapid, wild eyes. "But you're a hulderkind! I was told to look for a hulderkind, one with a, what did she call it, a malicious aura..." The minotaur looked to me, my captured target, me again. "...I accidentally thought you and that hidebehind had the same aura, didn't I?"

I nodded. In all honesty, I had no idea. Other supernatural beings, such as the super-strong and hollow-bodied huldras that made up my mother's side of the family, were taught to sense each other through some sixth sense from a young age. I'd never had the knack for it. Otherwise, the minotaur wouldn't have been able to ambush me in the first place.

The minotaur buried his face in his hands with a mournful moo. "The rest of the herd will never let me live this down. But if you're not Nalem..."

I considered leaving him there. Nothing good ever came of dealing with Nalem, and I should've spared him of learning the pain that had plagued my family for years.

I offered him a hand instead. "Then you're lucky he's not the one you tried to run over. Come on, I'll show you where he is." The minotaur took the offering, so I pulled him to his feet even though he was almost twice my size. "Jarrod Gallows. Paranormal investigator. Grab what's left of your bike and follow me."

He scooped the pieces together as if cradling a child instead of splintered metal. "My name's Bolton," he said by way of introduction, "and I really appreciate this. I've got a special message for Nalem, see. An old friend needs his help."

I scoffed at that. "Better hope he's in a good mood." I hoped he wasn't. Nalem in a good mood often meant my mission had taken a turn for the disastrous.

I dragged the hidebehind behind me as I led Bolton toward where we'd parked the car. My job was to capture a pair of hidebehinds before they could mate and produce more spawn. Problem was, hidebehinds were fast and prone to backstabbing, so much that almost no one ever saw their faces and lived. It was rare for them to even drop their guard around their own kind. Me and my fellow investigators—that being my boyfriend and my brother—had been forced to split up, with the car being our designated meeting spot. If they hadn't arrived yet, it would only be a matter of time before they came back with the second hidebehind in tow. And if they had somehow bungled that job and killed it instead...well, I had my ways of knowing that too.

"Tell me, what do you know about Nalem?"

Bolton hummed as he thought, almost loud enough to drown out the sound of his hooves crunching leaves. "He has power over bones, that's the big thing. Living and dead. I was told to never shake hands with him, heh. He's ancient, too. Made a lot of enemies. But he's loyal deep down, to his friends and his dreams."

That last part struck an anger in me I worked hard to keep buried. "I helped him kill his own wife. After he'd helped her capture me and my partner and almost sell us, of course."

"They must not've been friends," Bolton answered with a shrug. "I guess all I really know is, my entire town's in trouble if we can't get his help. And if that happens, things'll be bad enough that even the humans will notice."

I swore under my breath. Human minds can't comprehend the supernatural—their minds twist and warp to explain away anything monstrous or magical that they see. There were rare exceptions. My father was one, my boyfriend had been another. But if a situation were bad enough that multiple humans would notice, would be forced to comprehend something their minds shouldn't be exposed to...

No, I couldn't think about that now. I had to find Nalem first of all, and then the second hidebehind to finish the job. They'd be in the same spot if I was lucky.

When Nalem is out and fighting, he's easy to find. All one has to do is follow where the bones should be, but aren't. Layers of decaying skin and muscle lying flat on the ground, torn so the skeletons could be freed. Holes in the earth where long-buried remains have been unearthed through sheer force of will. A dull ache in the jaw as he reached out with his powers from afar and tried to pull, only to remember that he hadn't killed me yet. The last days of summer were warm enough that the corpses stank as they rotted in the heat, nestled by decaying leaves and flies gorging themselves before the Autumn chill arrived.

I heard a crack up ahead. Couldn't tell if branch or bone. Undergrowth rustled behind us. Bolton stumbled to a stop, pieces of metal tumbling out of his grasp. "I think there's another one of those things behind us," he whispered. He tried to hold all of his motorcycle pieces in one arm while grabbing a bent wheel as a weapon.

"Are you actually sensing it this time, or is this just wishful thinking?" Either way, I tightened my hold on the hidebehind I'd already captured. I wasn't sure if they were strong enough to break the manacles or dexterous enough to pick the lock—and I didn't plan on finding out.

Bolton sniffed the air. "This time, I'd bet my—"

Whatever it was, he would've won that bet; a lanky, bristled form darted out of the trees behind us and pounced onto the minotaur's back, digging its claws deep into his hide. Motorcycle parts scattered across the ground as Bolton bellowed in pain. He tried to hit his assailant with the bent wheel, but the hidebehind's body twitched as the weapon drew near, and Bolton ended up smacking himself with his makeshift cudgel.

Would the hidebehind be able to dodge something as fast as a bullet? Was it worth the risk to finish the job?

My thoughts were interrupted as two more figures burst out of the foliage. The first was tall and skinny enough that his bones jutted through his near-white skin, stumbling toward us like a newborn foal taking its first wobbling steps. The other was a bear—not all of it, just the skeleton and a couple stubborn scraps of rotting flesh that wouldn't fall off its bones. It also, for some reason, had six legs and a set of horns.

"Hey! Perfect timing! I've almost got this hidebehind, but it just occurred to me, how am I supposed to handcuff the darn thing? Am I supposed to cuff it to me, or can I like...cuff it to this elkbear I made?" The only person who would even think to ask that was Retz Gallows, my lanky little brother with a fascination for magical, skeletal taxidermy. In fact, he was so proud of his creation that it took another scream from the minotaur for him to actually notice the fight. "Oh, shit. Who's our new friend there?"

"That's Bolton. He's looking for Nalem."

Retz bit his lip. "Think we can just...leave him?"

"If we didn't need to subdue that hidebehind, I'd be all for it. Watch this and cover me." I dropped hidebehind I'd already captured at Retz's feet and snatched the silver manacles out of his grasp.

There hadn't been much reliable research on hidebehinds, but I'd already learned about the two things they abhorred most: silver and alcohol. I'd had plans for the remaining half of my cheap whiskey, mainly to drink it, but I instead uncorked the bottle and ran toward Bolton and his assailant. The hidebehind turned to me and hissed at my booze-drenched approach. Its teeth were almost as long as its claws.

As planned, my stench distracted it enough that it forgot to dodge as Bolton smashed his bent wheel into its back. The creature fell off like a dislodged tick. Before it could regain its bearings, a swarm of bones surrounded it, pressing together and pushing it into the ground. Behind me, Retz cheered about teamwork as the horned bear skull floated just over his head.

I approached the skeletal trap. The hidebehind reached through the gaps in the bones and tried to tear at me. I dumped the rest of my bottle over its fur, and as it tore at itself to get the smell out, I grabbed hold of its wrists and clasped the manacles on. The hidebehind hissed and screeched and writhed. Its cry was like a child throwing a tantrum.

"Sorry. Don't feel like bleeding any more today." I shoved the empty bottle back into my coat. Since I had to wait for the hidebehind to calm down before I could carry it, I pulled out a small tin of salve and offered it to Bolton. "Here. It's got some yarrow and other herbs to help those wounds."

The tin was tiny in the minotaur's hands. One finger was enough to scrape out most of the salve. "Thanks. Whoever named those things was pretty spot-on, huh?" He reached to apply the salve to his wounds, and his finger came back red. "Ah, how bad does it look...?"

"Like a butcher hacked at your back," Retz said as he sauntered over. "Makes me glad I don't bleed. Or have skin on my back to tear up, now that I think about it."

As expected, Bolton cast a confused look, until I assume his supernatural sense kicked in. "Another hulderkind? That means…"

"Means you're pretty lucky to find two of us in one day, huh?" Retz's easygoing smile was all too human, but his body was even stranger than mine. He didn't have enhanced strength or a tail like I did, but he also didn't have muscles, blood, or any other internal organs. Just his skeleton—something not even other huldra had—and a hole in his back he had to hide from humans. Retz never mourned his lack of humanity, however. He was far more content to gloat about his ability to avoid bandages and bathrooms.

Bolton did seem impressed with himself for a moment, but then shook his head. "I guess. I was actually going to say, that means you're the one who's Nalem, aren't you?"

If not for the hidebehinds, our neck of the woods would've been shrouded in silence.

"Nalem's not available at the moment," Retz said after a time. "Please leave a message after the beep." He waved one hand; the bones surrounding the hidebehind floated away and back behind him, hovering over his body like haunted armor. "Beeeeeep."

Bolton shuddered and looked away, busying himself with applying the salve and picking up the scattered motorcycle pieces. "Uhmm, okay? Uh, Lord Nalem, I have been sent to find you for help. Without you, us and the humans are both in trouble, and a few other friends of yours beside. They need you. So, uh, you can call me back at five four...wait, do you need a phone number?"

"What we need is to get these hidebehinds transported," I interrupted, "So if either of you two would mind giving me a hand, I'd appreciate it."

The others busied themselves, even if it took the two of them to carry one hidebehind— Bolton because he had only one hand to offer, and Retz because he was, to be kind, an utter wimp. We trudged through the woods on the way back to our car. I kept my eyes peeled in case anything else, foe or supposed friend, tried to jump us. Nothing caught us off guard except for how chill the wind had already grown.

"So. You been Nalem's vessel long?" Bolton asked near the end of our trek.

"Almost all my life. Nineteen years now, or thereabouts? Turns out, the terrible two's are a lot more terrifying when you've got an ancient evil in your skull." His eyes glazed over, a sign that his end of the conversation had shifted into his thoughts. Nalem must've woken up.

"And you're...one of his followers?" Bolton was looking at me this time. Genuine curiosity in his eyes.

I balled my fist so tight, the chain of the handcuffs crushed together. "I'm just here to help out my brother. Nalem and I...don't agree most of the time."

"Nice of you to be supportive, at least. There's nothing more important than family, right? That's why I'm here, you see, on behalf of my herd more than anything else."

Without warning, Bolton's ears twitched. He looked off into the distance, staring past the trees and fallen leaves. "Oh no. Not here." He glanced around before noticing the motorcycle pieces in his grasp. "Aha! Let's see, where is that...there!" He reached into the remnants of the engine and yanked out a cylindrical hunk of metal. "Turns out, thanks for breaking my bike. Got the piece I needed real quick—hold onto the rest for me. Be right back."

He dumped the remaining pile of parts into Retz's arms with such strength, my brother and the hidebehind in his grasp both fell over. The minotaur was too busy running off into the distance to notice.

"What the hell are you doing?" I shouted after him.

"Saving your lives!" He lowered his head and charged out of sight. The crack of another struck tree soon followed.

Retz groaned and tried to sit up. He flailed until I had enough pity on him to pull the engine tank off his chest. The hidebehind had fallen next to him and tried to snap at his fingers; he retorted by dropping the handlebars on its head. "Can we leave him now?"

"Wish we could, but he ran off in the direction of our car."

Retz groaned. The bones following him swarmed and scooped up the hidebehind, transforming around it into a cage with long legs and taloned feet. After a moment's pause, one of the feet scooped up the motorcycle pieces and tossed them into the cage as well.

"Taking some inspiration from Baba Yaga, I see."

"Yaba who? I just wanted to make the rib cage a little easier to carry. Floating something that heavy's hard work."

I wasn't sure what was worse: the pun, or my brother's complete lack of knowledge about even basic supernatural lore. I did my best to ignore both and follow the minotaur's path, waving for Retz to follow me. "Do you sense him fighting anything yet?"

Retz tilted his head. "Still charging. Also, he's got some broken ribs and a fracture in one arm. Think I should bother fixing that?"

"Depends on what he's 'saving' us from." I couldn't think of anything that might warrant such concern. According to what little information I'd been given about this case, the hidebehinds had scared away all other sentient beings in the area, human and supernatural alike. Yet I doubted he was fighting something as mundane as a bear.

Retz seemed to have reached the same conclusion. Then his eyes grew wide. "Well, he found it. Ah, don't suppose your boyfriend has his phone on him?"

"Farris? What does he have to do with..."

My train of thought ground to a halt. I ran.

When it came to monsters and magic, humans kept themselves in the dark. Their brains couldn't handle even seeing something paranormal, engaging in some impressive mental gymnastics to explain away all they stumbled upon. They didn't know what kind of horrors lurked among them, or that they had their own guardian that kept them safe by fighting off the monsters and shepherding their souls. There were exceptions to this mass ignorance. Most of the time, they ended up either dead, or turned into a supernatural entity themselves. In the case of Farris O'Reilly, my boyfriend and business partner, he'd been unfortunate enough for both and became an undead force known as a Faerie.

Hence my initial confusion: in the back of my mind, the love of my life was still human, still protected from the worst of what our world had to offer. But no, the only thing keeping him safe now was me. Some help I was.

I might not have been able to sense where the combatants were, but I didn't need to. Bellows met manic, frenzied laughter. The snap and the following crash of a large branch echoed through the forest. The hidebehind in my grasp licked its lips with a jeering coo, excited for the prospect of blood. I considered drawing one of my guns, but settled for a less lethal option by grabbing the empty whiskey bottle instead.

I caught up with Bolton first. He had someone in a headlock, a figure half man and half shadow. With worry spiking my temper, I didn't hesitate slamming the bottle against the minotaur's back, the force of my blow shattering the glass and embedding the shards in the wounds he'd already endured from the hidebehind. As anticipated, he released his hostage and reared around to fight me.

"Bolton, stand down. This man's our ally."

"B-but he's corrupted! Aberrant! Can't you sense it? They're the entire reason I had to come find you!"

Before I could ask what he meant, Bolton was struck from above. The hostage who'd escaped had climbed up one of the trees and jumped back off of it to attack, landing a kick with metal-shard claws. The minotaur collapsed from the force of the strike. His attacker reared back, one golden eye glowing as smoke billowed out of the other empty socket.

With nothing else on hand to distract Farris, I threw the hidebehind into his chest, which knocked him over. "You stop it too. Bolton here came to us for help. No attacking him until we've heard him out."

"Babe, what the fuck," was all Farris could manage as he pried the hidebehind off. It had already tried to chew his shoulder, then spat the darkness out in distaste. Farris had been a daredevil as a human, though charming and handsome enough to get away with it. Still was, even though his skin was a few shades off from cadaver gray, his limbs were made of billowing shadows that reeked of brimstone with glass-metal claws, and his reckless streak now bordered on berserk fury once blood spilled. Even if throwing the hidebehind at him seemed cruel, the shock of it pulled him out of the fight before he could lose himself in it.

I explained, "We've got what we came here for, and I'm sure this fight stemmed from a misunderstanding. Right?" I cast a pointed look at Bolton.

He sighed and lowered his arms. "Yeah. Sure did."

I made the mistake of lowering my guard.

"Once you understand what's going on, you'll thank me."

With a flick of the wrist, Bolton flung something at me; I couldn't see what it was, but my skin burned in pain when it struck. I heard the minotaur bellow again as he charged, and the screeching of the hidebehind as Farris threw it back and prepared his own attack. I was busy trying to figure out what I'd been struck with. Whatever it was, it hadn't pierced my skin, so it wasn't an arrow or a…wait, what was that glint of metal on the ground? I couldn't pick it up without my fingers burning, but it seemed to be the motorcycle piece Bolton had grabbed earlier. My head spun in confusion.

A pair of terrified yelps stole my attention. I looked over to see Farris and Bolton, still trying to grapple each other, scurrying away from another assailant. I didn't see what it was—but the busted pair of silver manacles on the ground didn't escape my notice. I grabbed my shotgun.

A twitch in the shadows above. I turned and fired. Branches fell as a blurred figure darted across the branches. Bolton grabbed a log as Farris shifted back into a fighting stance, claws at ready. If they'd had any sense, they would've declared a brief truce and stood back to back. Since they didn't, the hidebehind ambushed Farris and bit him, decided it didn't like the taste of undead flesh, and clambered onto his shoulders to use him as a springboard. Bolton was distracted by his search for the lost motorcycle piece until he felt his wounds reopen from the hidebehind landing on him claws-first.

Then the bastard creature pivoted and flung itself toward me. I fired my shotgun and hit it straight in the chest, but this didn't halt its trajectory. We both crashed into the ground. The hidebehind clamped its teeth onto my arm, even as it bled all over my sweat-and-whiskey soaked clothes. My free hand let go of the shotgun so I could try to punch the damn thing off.

Bolton hollered, "Hold still, I'll get it!"

"You idiot, we need it alive!" I heard the accompanying growls of Farris trying to hold back Bolton from whatever his plan of attack was. "If we don't bring both of those hidebehinds in alive, we're in deep shit."

"And how're we s'posed to..."

I wasn't sure what got Bolton to stop talking, and I was too busy punching to care. There's a fine line between enough hurt to make a point and accidental lethality. It's the same line as not wanting to kill another, but also not wanting to die yourself. I walked both every time I clenched my fist or slid a bullet into its chamber. As if I didn't end up making the same choice every time. I had too much to do before I could allow myself to die. The hidebehind tore its teeth from my arm and bared them at my face. I reared a fist back.

My attacker froze. Its eyes grew wide as it pulled away with aching slowness. It got to its feet, forced to stand upright like a human, and pressed its wrists together. Bone broke out of skin and fused together. The hidebehind screamed until its teeth melded the same way.

"That makes it twice today that I have saved your worthless lives from these slobbering beasts. You're welcome." My brother's lips moved, but those were not his words. Nalem loomed over me, one hand on the hidebehind's neck. Behind him, the second hidebehind cried in its cage in sympathy for its mate.

"Took you long enough. You've got a fan here, you know." I got back up and tried not to look at the fused bones of the hidebehind. Reminded me too much of growing up with Nalem around.

"So I've heard. Haven't I told you that Lord Nalem has a nice ring to it?" He sneered, though he wavered where he stood seconds afterward. "But that can wait. My powers are not unlimited, and your incompetence is taxing. I shall lead this one if the rest of you can carry the remaining burden." He gestured over at the caged hidebehind and its nest of motorcycle pieces. "That is the point of hiring yourself as dumb muscle, correct?"

First rule of surviving Nalem: don't argue with his insults. "I'll carry the cuffed hidebehind. Bolton, get your motorcycle parts. Farris...here's my coat, find the first aid kit, don't pull out the poison oak too this time. We'll decide who's riding in the trunk when we reach the car."

"You know, normal people don't put poison oak in their pockets, right?" Farris caught my leather duster and took his time rifling through the contents, even though I was sure he'd memorized the contents for when he wanted to "borrow" something to juggle. "And if we're voting, I nominate Nalem to be the trunk goblin. He doesn't need to breathe."

"But I do require copious leg room," Nalem countered. He snapped his fingers, and the bone cage behind him collapsed to the ground, spilling motorcycle parts across the dead leaves. "Put the minotaur and his scrap metal in the trunk. I'm sure I can make him fit."

Bolton chuckled nervously under his breath. "You guys are such kidders. It's kinda' nice, you know? Thought you'd be all uptight and scary."

Nalem's resulting laughter proved him wrong.

Our client was beyond grateful for the delivery of the hidebehinds, both to study them and to keep the area safe. I even managed to patch up the one I'd injured and kept it from bleeding to death. That would've cost me more than just a paycheck. And Bolton was glad to have some fresh air once we made it to an empty rest area and popped the trunk open again.

"It smells like a sewer in there," the minotaur said mid-gag as he pulled himself out. "What kind of monsters have you kept in there?"

I started listing them off. Farris answered instead, "Jarrod's laundry." He only got away with it because I was fond of him and his dashing smirk, even if his teeth were more metal than bone now.

Bolton took his careful time clambering out of our Mercury Grand Marquis, which was just large enough to hold all of us. He had to stop once he got out to admire the paint job, which consisted of black spray paint over an originally red body and the name "CRUSHER oo" painted in white along the doors.

"Did you guys do the, ah, custom work on your ride here?" He had the same tone of a teacher trying to find something nice in a student's stick figures.

I shook my head. "Last owners did. This was a demolition derby car, and the only one still running once the night we found it was over. Figured it could handle anything else supernatural we threw at it too, so I bought it." It was one of the smarter purchases I'd made. It wasn't pretty, but being a tank of a car that was large enough to sleep in when funds were low, it didn't need to be.

"Frugal of ya', I guess." Bolton stomped around to stretch his legs after being cramped up in the trunk. He kept close to the car and made a point to steer clear of Farris. He still hadn't explained what he'd found so abhorrent about the love of my life. "Now that your job's all done, can I talk to Lord Nalem? I don't know how much time we've got left."

Nalem took this as his cue to make his entrance. "And here I thought minotaurs were known for their patience. Or has your lot truly changed so much since your days in Greece?" He strode toward us like a king gracing the peasants with his presence, when in reality he'd just stepped aside to put on a fresh suit and grab a soda from the vending machine.

"I mean, my family hasn't lived in Greece for a few generations now, but uh...er, what I mean to say is, that's beside the point. I really need your help, Lord Nalem. My whole town does." Under Nalem's stare, he knelt with fumbling awkwardness, head bowed and one arm over his chest. "Arcata is under attack. Folks around town have been disappearing for the past few years. Strange creatures, not supernaturals like us but definitely not human, have been cropping up in their place, but they're…if they were the people we knew once, they aren't anymore. And things just took a turn for the worse, so…Ginny said I had to come find you. You remember Ginny, don't you?"

For once, Nalem didn't make a smartass comeback. He even seemed intrigued, nodding in silent approval to continue. I whipped out my notebook and a pencil; if I wanted to get Nalem out of my brother's body, I needed every last drop of information I could get.

"Yeah, Ginny's still running Levi's Tomb, been looking out for all of us. 'Cept she's just one boggan, and there's a lot of people, you know?"

"She has lasted far longer without my presence. What do you dare demand of me in her place?" There was that familiar Nalem arrogance, dripping from his voice with every passing inconvenience. "If Ginny requested you find me, it surely must be more important than a few measly disappearances."

Bolton's head jerked up. "My lord, it's not just a few! A-and some of my herd's been attacked too, including the herd-caller's own daughter! At least half of the regulars at Levi's Tomb are just gone, and those few who've made it back…they aren't right anymore, like your, ah, friend here. They've been changed. Aberrant, we call 'em."

"Such is life. Souls are lost, change, and are found again. I may be a god, but I cannot keep track of every life that faces trouble." A chill breeze, a hint of incoming Autumn, blew past us. Nalem popped the tab on his soda with slow gravitas. "You said things took a turn for the worse. If it's important enough to summon me, you best tell me why, lest I send you back with the parts of your infernal machine melded into your very bones."

Bolton tried to scurry away before remembering that he was kneeling on the sidewalk, causing him to fall backwards on his ass. "The skull! The skull was stolen out of Levi's Tomb! We don't know how or why, we just came in one day and—"

A shockwave ran through our bodies. Since we were alive—or a Fae, in Farris's case—Nalem couldn't affect our bones without touching us, but on rare occasion, I'd felt his attempts. This was the first one strong enough to make me drop my notebook and pen. His face warped through shock and rage. Skin split from sharpened bones along his body. His teeth briefly lengthened to resemble a monster's maw.

"One doesn't just take a leviathan's skull," Nalem hissed.

"W-w-well my lord, someone did. We think it's those aberrant, though how and why, we were hoping you could find out." Bolton scuttled away across the sidewalk. "All I know is, the leviathan's ghost woke up right afterwards, and it's calm for now, but Ginny says that's not gonna' last for long. It's already affecting things on the surface, and the humans are starting to ask questions."

"Has it turned into a poltergeist yet?" I cut in, scrambling to pick up the notebook I'd dropped. Ghosts were just souls that hadn't moved on. Left without the reprieve of an afterlife, those souls took their rage and despair and turned them into power. I'd dealt with such poltergeists, but only of human souls. Something as ancient and alien as a leviathan...

Bolton shook his head. "No, thank the gods. But again, we think it's close. It was looking for its head, but it's...starting to give up, I think."

"She," Nalem corrected. We directed our confused stares at him. "She is...that leviathan is a being of utmost importance. We cannot abide her corruption." He stormed past us and threw the driver's door of the Marquis open. "Bolton, you've been upgraded to shotgun. The rest of you, get your worthless asses into the car and keep quiet. We've got a skull to track."